CALUMET

by

Duane Schwartz

A-Argus Better Book Publishers, LLC
North Carolina***New Jersey

CALUMET
All rights reserved © 2009
by Duane Schwartz

No part of this book may be reproduced or transmitted in any form or by any means, graphic, electronic, or mechanical, including photocopying, recording, taping, or by any informational storage retrieval system without prior permission in writing from the publisher.

A-Argus Better Book Publishers, LLC

For information:
A-Argus Better Book Publishers, LLC
Post Office Box 914
Kernersville, North Carolina 27285
www.a-argusbooks.com

ISBN: 978-0-9841342-9-8
ISBN: 0-9841342-9-8

Book Cover designed by Dubya

Printed in the United States of America

Dedication

This book is dedicated to the extraordinary breed of people who tamed the Mesabi Iron Range of northern Minnesota, my ancestors among them. They took from this earth, iron ore. They gave it back, the majestic red mountains and brilliant blue-green lakes that inspired this work of fiction.

But I would be negligent if I did not give my lady, my wife, Betty, her just credit. She reads. She suggests. And if that doesn't work, she demands changes, and the end result is a work far superior to that which I would create without her input.

Chapter One

Calumet, Minnesota, 1909

Carl Tilden had drunk his fill. He stepped out of Henry Holland's Red Rose Saloon into a dark street — no moon lit the sky, no stars shined through the clouds, only the light from saloon doors and the occasional flash of lightning on the western horizon would guide him home to Libby and their little girl. He stopped to let his eyes adjust after he passed through the glow of the last of the saloon doors into total blackness. Perhaps he would wait for another flash of lightning. That would help him set a course. Then, like magic, from behind came the light of an automobile. Constable Profit, no doubt. Few cars traveled the muddy streets of Calumet, less this time of night — it had to be Profit. No matter, whomever it was their headlights would show the way, and even as it passed Carl would make out the one tiny red taillight for a time.

He suddenly wished he hadn't stayed so late or drank so much. It had been a long grueling day in the ore mine and he wanted, maybe even needed one whisky before going home — just to calm the nerves. But one turned into too many as it too often does. Emil Crowe and his bunch, there were six of them altogether, had been riding roughshod on the miners for several weeks now, trying their best to head off the inevitable, the growing resentment of the Company among miners and their growing favor of the union. Tempers flared, it seemed like always these days when it used to be seldom.

Carl rounded the last corner and stepped into the alley that would take him to the back door of his house. He stopped for a moment, waited for his eyes to adjust to the deeper darkness. He heard sounds from a nearby patch of brush, a shuffling. The idle of a far-off engine vibrated in the night air, probably the truck that had passed him earlier. Then he felt the blow.

Hot blood filled his eyes and his head spun out of control. Muffled voices echoed in his ears, one seemingly asking, "Where do we take him?" — then ringing — then silence. When he came around, he found himself in a barn, curled into a ball on its dirt floor. He looked around, his vision — blurred. He spotted six men standing near a large kettle hanging over an open fire. A gunnysack lay near them, open at the top, feathers spewing from it. "My God," he whispered. "Dear Lord, help me." And he felt behind himself at the back of his trousers where he kept a hideout gun. Still there.

Carl pulled the gun out, took aim, and blasted away. Three men scattered, three men fell to the ground. He fired three more times... then... click. His luck, along with his bullets, had run out.

~*~

The freshness of a sunlit morning after the terror of the season's worst thunderstorm brought Mrs. Libby Tilden and her daughter Clara out unusually early. Neither of them had slept well. Crashes of thunder, flashes of lightning, and the grisly sound of snapping tree limbs falling on the eaves of houses and on barn roofs, all of these bringing a panic which would not let eyes shut or sleep come. And there was Carl. Where was he? Had he been injured in a mining accident—or killed? Had he drank so much at the saloon after work that he now lay sleeping in someone's shed or doorway, or had he fallen into a water-filled ditch and drowned? Libby longed to know what had been bothering him of late. This was his third no-show at home in the evening in as many weeks. Carl had never been one to pull such things on his family, not in the seven years of their marriage. Why now? She wished she understood. But how could she. Carl would not talk about it.

Clara ran to her favorite tree, the swing her father had hung from the largest of its limbs beckoning her, '*Come play with me.*' She brushed water from the seat, an old piece of rubber conveyor belt brought home from the mine, and then sat. She placed her tiny feet into the soft sand and pushed off into the air. She pumped, pulling back on the ropes, then stretching her legs out as far as they would go, swinging higher and higher. Suddenly… she planted her feet on the ground, stood, and ran at full speed to her mother, her arms outstretch, panic on her tiny face.

"What is it?" Libby asked.

The girl pointed to the tree. There through the branches and the leaves, Libby saw a shape that should not be—in colors that did not belong.

"Go in the house, child." she spoke softly to not alarm her.

Clara obeyed.

Libby moved closer. She bowed her head and shook it from side to side. She turned away and walked toward the house. She found Carl's hunting knife in a drawer in the kitchen and returned to the tree to cut her husband's tarred and feathered body down, then sat with it for a time. Then she watched a truck drive off and turn the corner at the end of her street, a star on its door.

~*~

The open prairie near St. Louis, Missouri

Newton Blake stopped his horse in the shade of a giant elm. He pulled the wrinkled telegram from his vest and read it once again. A rider had sought him out two days earlier and delivered the note. Newt had been on the trail of an escapee for almost a week, and the trail had gone cold, and, since it had been so easy for a delivery boy to find him, he felt maybe, just maybe, the desperado he had been pursuing might know exactly where he was as well.

He was almost pleased that this kind of life, this hunting of criminals on horseback, was giving way to the trains and automobiles of the new century. He was tired of the stink of leather and of sweaty horseflesh, and road dust so thick it had to be peeled off. He did like catching them though, the degenerates of society who felt themselves bound by no law, clever enough to keep out of the clutches of lawmen. And he loved witnessing the disconsolate look on their faces whenever they discovered they had been wrong.

He read the telegram again. *Calumet! Minnesota!*

Where the hell is Calumet, Minnesota? he asked himself. He looked around for tracks. None! It was time to find out where it was.

~*~

St. Paul, Minnesota

Ransom Feltus visited with pretty Dolly Marcus, Abraham Curran's receptionist at union headquarters while he waited for the union boss to finish with his meeting. Rans was an organizer. His expertise was needed somewhere. He thought he might have a break from work since he had just days ago returned from setting paper producers on track in a small boarder town at the north limit of the state, but he was mistaken. Union business was always the business of opportunity and opportunity was at hand, at a mine in the little town of Calumet, or so Dolly had been telling him. He had no wish for this. He was still thawing from his far-north experience, a situation that had taken several winter months to clean up.

His meeting — brief, his objective — clear, and Ransom Feltus would be on his way by passenger train to Duluth that afternoon. From there, he would catch a series of ore trains, the last of which he had been instructed to jump aboard like a hobo, would take him to Calumet, where it had been arranged for him to meet a man named Carl Tilden, a union partisan who would then introduce Rans to Curtiss Clay, the man to see for a job in the local mine. An interlude he had been working on with the lovely Miss Dolly Marcus would be postponed until his next stop at union headquarters.

His journey brought Ransom Feltus into Calumet at dawn the following day. He sought out the Tilden place aided by a pencil sketch map his boss had given him, and now he stood across the street from Carl Tilden's house staring at a creature, tarred and feathered, hanging by the neck from a sturdy oak.

Tilden himself, no doubt, Rans sunk into thought for a long moment, then he spat into the dirt of the street. "Goddamn Klan!" he uttered.

He watched for a moment while a pretty lady accompanied by a child, a little girl, came from the house and stared up at the creature. He turned away and walked off in what he thought to be the direction of the mine. This would be no easy job. More dangerous than most.

~*~

St. Louis, Missouri

Newton Blake kicked at the tires of the Packard automobile. He resolved on his way in from the range, that someone other than he was going to have his old buckskin, and he would drive himself to Calumet.

Jesse Blake, Newt's only cousin who had strayed from the long family tradition of being either a lawmen or a cowpoke, often times both, sold used cars from his filling station on the outskirts of town. He was not an easy man to deal with, not even for a relative. He held firm to his prices and even firmer when it came to throwing anything extra in on the deal, chiefly free gasoline.

Jesse had a Tin Lizzie, which he thought could make the trip without difficulty, a four-year-old black Packard that would do the same more comfortably, and a Reo six cylinder he felt could make the trip not only comfortably, but fast as well. The Lizzie did not impress Newt. The Reo was perfect, but at a cost he could not afford and Jesse would not stray from. He settled for the Packard despite the fact its price was greater than two good saddle horses, but only if his cousin would agree to teach him to drive. On the third day after that purchase he set out, white-knuckled, back seat full of gasoline containers, heading north toward Minneapolis and St. Paul.

A week later and he was storing the Packard at a livery stable a few miles from Calumet. He would make the remainder of his journey on horseback so locals would not think him wealthy. He needed to blend in, become one of them, or his mission would fail. He chose, when he stored his Packard, another buckskin.

Chapter Two

Calumet, Minnesota

Newton Blake drew back when he felt a sting from the tip of Emil Crowe's hunting knife as it drew a fine red line diagonally across his stomach. He should have cut and run like most other men in the mining camp would have done but he was new hereabouts, unaware of Crowe's ability with the knife. He stepped back in and took a stab to the fleshy part of the left shoulder. He clamped down hard on Emil Crowe's knife hand, squeezed until he heard bones cracking, then he looked Emil Crowe in the eye, smashed his own forehead into his nose, and jerked the knife out. He held his eyes on Emil's until Emil let the knife fall to the ground. This was one hell of an introduction to iron country. Newt wondered if everyone traveled this path when they showed up here. He sized up the onlookers to see if more trouble would be coming his way. Envy is what he found in their eyes. He had seen it before, in Missouri when he worked the cattle drives. A similar fight took place between him and a man named Buck Morgan, only Morgan wasn't nearly a tough as Crowe, and Morgan didn't come at him with a knife. The look of envy though — that was the same.

A medium height, slim, mustached man in his early forties wearing a suit and a derby hat stepped forward and pulled a bandanna out of a pocket. "Let me have a look," he said. "Ain't it always like this, some miserable bastard right handy when a peaceable man comes along, just there to show who's boss?"

"I recon you're right, stranger. At least it's always been that way for me," Newt said.

"My name is Waters," the man announced. "Most around here call me Doc."

"Newton Blake," Newt said. "I generally go by Newt."

"Well, Newt, I ain't no real doctor, but I'm all your gonna find, unless you're of a mind to go to the Company doctor, and owe your first month's wages for these scratches."

Scratches, hell! Newt thought. He looked at the blood on his shirt, and then glanced at his shoulder. *That one's a hole.* "I recon I don't care to give up a month's anything."

"Best you come with me then." Doc Waters placed an arm around Newt's waist to steady him and led him up the street toward the center of town.

Newt looked back at Crowe. Two hard cases were pulling him to his feet.

"Steer clear of them for a piece. They're Klan," Doc Waters said.

"What's Klan?"

"I don't rightly know. They're a tough breed though. They come from Duluth. The mining company brought them in to police the miners. They don't seem too fond of Catholics either."

Newt recalled an aunt who had raised him. She was Catholic as Catholic could get — kneeling and praying, crossing herself and whatnot. All the time. It struck him as silly mostly. No wonder there were folks who disliked them. "Many of them around here?" Newt asked.

"Many what? Catholics or Klan?"

"Klan." Newt said. "I recon they're a whole lot more dangerous than Catholics."

"Them three for sure. I've heard some of the local preachers favor them, but I don't know that much about it all myself," Waters admitted. "Just best you stay clear as you can."

"Sounds like good advice," Newt said, thinking again of the aunt who had raised him. Some of the comments made by her protestant neighbors were none too friendly, damn near threatening at times. "Sounds like real good advice."

~*~

The town of Calumet lay near the western edge of the Mesabi Iron Range of northern Minnesota. Although its main street was lined mostly with saloons, there were fourteen of them in 1909, which catered typically to single male miners of the red ore; there were a few women around. Most were wives, but not all. Molly Carpenter was no wife. Molly was a whore, and a good one at that. She had come up the last fall, from the south — Missouri country she claimed. Her arrival in the frozen north, most everyone came to know, started out as an escape. The law had been breathing down her neck, something about a cattle baron and a stabbing. She recognized the tall, handsome, dark-haired man despite the fact that he was slumped over and almost being dragged into the Red Rose by Doc Waters. The Red Rose was where she peddled her talents these days, and where Doc Waters lived.

She went to them, slid a soft hand under the stranger's chin and lifted so she could see into his eyes.

"Well… I'll be damned! Newton Blake. Ain't you a sight," she said.

"Molly?" Newt questioned, not at all sure if he was seeing right, or if pain and blood loss was giving him some kind of a distorted image.

"You bet your ass it's Molly," she boasted and kissed him on the cheek. "How the hell are you, I mean aside from bleedin' all over the goddamn place."

Newt's eyes rolled back. He wobbled and fell into Doc Waters. Waters braced himself and steadied both of them. "Easy there, partner. Come here, Molly. Help me get him to a room."

"Hold on a second there," Henry Holland, keeper of the Red Rose, called out. "Who's gonna pay for that room?"

"Put him in my room, Doc," Molly said.

"Ain't that gonna put you outta business then, Molly?" a single voice rang out. A barrage of boisterous laughter filled the place.

"Ignore them, honey," Waters told her.

"I should," Molly said, "but damned if they ain't right."

"We'll put him in my room," Doc offered and they started unsteadily up the steps.

From the head of the stairs, Doc Waters looked down to see Emil Crowe slither up to the bar, still being steadied by the two hard cases he always traveled with. "I'd need a drink too if it was me just got my ass kicked by Newton Blake here," Doc mumbled. Molly laughed. Emil Crowe looked up at them.

"Whiskey!" Crowe snapped at Henry Holland. Laughter from rest of the saloon's patrons dwindled to a whisper. It always did when these three showed themselves. They were a bad combination, forever on the lookout for trouble, too often finding it, and usually avoided by most others.

Holland slapped an amber bottle on the bar in front of him, then went for three glasses.

"I don't want this shit! Get me the good stuff," Crowe shouted as he pulled his still bloodied knife from its sheath and slapped it down hard on the bar in front of him.

Holland swapped the watered down liquor for a fresh bottle of pure, then moved to the other, safer end of the bar. *Fourteen places in this goddamn town, and these assholes gotta come into mine,* he silently complained.

~*~

The Calumet mine

Randal Parks, the mining company supervisor who chose to employ Emil Crowe, now paced back and forth in his tiny office, wondering where Crowe had disappeared to and when he was coming back. He was needed. There was trouble in the yard — a fight. It was Crowe's job to keep the peace, not his. If Parks himself had to go out there to try to break things up two things would likely happen. First, nobody would listen to him; and second, somebody would probably kick his ass. Things had gotten that way recently. Damn few of the miners cared all that much about their jobs anymore, at least not enough to let the bosses boss. Nowadays it took a thug like Crowe to settle them down. The change had come with this spring's reopening of the mine. Two men, new to the area, had been hired on and then tried to organize the workers.

That's when Crowe, along with a few of his cronies from the Klan, was called in, his purpose — to put an end to the would-be organizers, a task they had been successful at accomplishing. But attitudes had already been altered. Now the mining company had a full crew of independent thinkers to deal with, far too many to replace at a moment's notice, a luxury officials had previously enjoyed, and the need for such deviants as Crowe became unavoidable if they were to keep things running smoothly.

A little weasel of a man, spectacles hanging from the tip of his nose, entered the office. "Mr. Crowe is nowhere to be found," he told Parks.

"Then go to town. Find him. Tell him to get back here before they tear the place apart."

"Yes, sir." And the weasel scurried out of the room.

~*~

In Doc Waters' rented room above the Red Rose, the place where he and Molly Carpenter had taken Newton Blake to tend his wounds, Molly Carpenter wrung cool water from a cloth and handed it to Doc. "He looks dead. Is he dead?"

"No! At least not yet. He probably won't be either, that is if I can get the bleeding to quit." Waters soaked up more blood with the cloth Molly had handed him. "Rinse it out again." He handed it back. "How do you know this fellow, Molly?"

"Ah… he hung around the saloon I worked in back in Missouri. Not a lot, but some. All the girls liked him — a real gentleman. Kinda looked after us now and then, too. One time he come in just after a feller named Buck Morgan blackened one of my eyes. Why… Newt there, he lit into Morgan and fur flew. That was the last time anybody around those parts tried that with me."

"What'd this man do in Missouri?"

"He was a cattleman. A bit of a lawman at times, too. Never imagined he would show up in mining country, but… I suppose, what with the automobile, even cattle drivin' is gonna change. The guy gotta do something for a livin', don't he, Doc?"

"You suppose whorein' will change?" Doc Waters winked as he asked. "I mean… what with automobiles and all."

"Well…now there are back seats and rumble seats, ain't there now, Doc?"

Newton Blake began to stir. His eyes opened just a slit. "Well, would you look at that? The boy lives," Doc Waters said. "We were getting a might concerned about you, young fella."

"It'll take more than a knife in the shoulder to kill me, Doc. Molly there should be able to tell you that much about me," Newt said.

"That and a bunch more, Newton Blake. A whole bunch more."

"Well… just the same, you won't mind if I sew up that there hole in your shoulder, will ya?" Doc did not wait for Newt's approval. "Pour a bit of that chloroform on that cloth, Molly. That's it. A bit more. Good. Now hold it over his nose. Don't you go breathing any now."

While Doc and Molly looked after Newton Blake's wounds, the beady-eyed Lawrence Fish, Randal Parks' weasel of an assistant, had been peering into saloon after saloon until he spotted Emil Crowe sitting unsteadily on a barstool at the Red Rose. He entered cautiously. Crowe saw him coming. "What the hell do you want, Fish?" Crowe slurred.

"The boss sent me to get you. There's trouble… down at the mine."

"Ah! Shit! C'mon boys. Best get to it." He acted disappointed, but really, after the ass kicking the new guy gave him, he was itching for a scrap, one he could win, as a way of redeeming himself in the eyes of the others, mainly the two hard cases who traveled with him. "You got a company truck, Fish?"

"I do," Fish said.

"You two ride in the back," Crowe told his assistants. "I'll ride up front with old Fish here." He hung an arm over Lawrence Fish's shoulder, knocking him off balance in the process. Crowe laughed loudly so everyone in the place could hear. He bullied Fish all the way to the truck, and then stuffed him in on the driver's side. Moments later, they came to a stop at the crest of a hill overlooking mining company property. It was Fish's habit. He was a cautious little man. The road into the mine was treacherous, winding, steep, and whenever Fish had to drive it he held up at the top to make certain he had brakes adequate to stop him at the bottom. They sat for a moment. Crowe looked down at the group of unruly miners and watched them disperse. The sight Crowe and his two Klansmen always caused the miners to rethink their protest and usually headed them off to do their jobs. "Get her movin'. They're breaking up." Crowe ordered. He did not want to miss an opportunity to fight. Fish put the truck back in motion, and as it snaked slowly down the narrow road into the mine, intimidating blasts from the shotguns of Crowe's two henchmen rang out one after another. Men moved fast. No one cared to deal with Crowe — maybe Parks, definitely Fish, but never Crowe or his men. Would Emil Crowe be disappointed? Hell no! Not for long. Men had not made the winding tower in time. And Crowe's much needed altercation, by God he'd have. He jumped from the moving truck, his own shotgun blasting in the air, him yelling at the top of his lungs, demanding to know who the uprising's ringleader was. He would have his fight, one way or another.

A slight miner, already in the clutches of one of Crowe's stout assistants and fearing for his life, swung his head in the direction of another miner. Soon the slight miner lay in the dirt and the stout Klansman was storming toward the man he had just ratted out. The Klansman took immediate action and the bloodied body of the instigator of the day's outburst lay at his feet being kicked into unconsciousness by all three of the Klansmen, Emil Crowe included.

~*~

Back at Doc Waters' place above the Red Rose, Doc watched out the window of his second story room while his patient, Newton Blake, slept off the effects of the chloroform he had been given. An enormous man who he did not recognize was being carried by stretcher into the mining company's doctor's office across the street. Waters recalled watching Emil Crowe and his thugs drive off with Fish, and he reasoned that Crowe had something to do with it all. Some poor bastard from the mine got his. No doubt about it. Doc shook his head silently in dismay.

Newt Blake started to move. He let out a weak

moan. "Took a bit of sewing to close that hole Crowe left in you," Doc told him.

"How long have I been sleeping?"

"Most of the day," Waters told him.

"Where'd Molly get to?"

"She went back to the saloon — been about an hour ago now."

Doc went back to his quiet observation of the goings on across the street.

Emil Crowe had showed up and now stood proudly on the boardwalk in front of the doctor's office. He had won. The giant leader of the unruly miners had been slain and hauled off, though the slaying may not be absolute. The man may live. But at least the example had been set. He smiled broadly.

As Doc opened the window a crack, just to rid the room of the sweet smell of chloroform and its effect on him, he heard Crowe say, "Hope the son-of-a-bitch dies."

"Me too!" said one of his sidekicks.

"Me too!" said the other.

Doc Waters once again shook his head.

Chapter Three

At the end of a three-day sleep, Newton Blake found himself feeling downright strong, and grateful for Doc Waters' help and hospitality. He wondered if there was something — aside from giving him money, which of course he intended to do anyway — that he could do for Doc.

"No money, none at all." Doc said. "As far as doing something? You get the chance, you do old Crowe and his thugs in for me — for Molly and the girls — for the miners — for the whole damn town."

Newt was no fool. He knew full well the altercation he had with Emil Crowe would not be his last. After all, if he had read things right, Crowe was his job, and experience had already taught him it wasn't going to be an easy one. He had known men like Crowe before, men who would sink their teeth into a grudge like a rabid and angry hound and would never let up. "I'll do what I can."

As he stepped into the street, Newt was held up by a funeral procession. Doc had told him of the miner whom Crowe and his men had beaten at the mine not long after his fight with him. Doc also told him the miner died of his wounds, but the constable had no jurisdiction on company property, so Crowe had been charged with no crime. And now, as the end of the procession passed before him, he spotted Crowe watching from the other side of the street. Crowe's hand was bandaged. Newt knew it was he who had damaged it. And Crowe held in his good hand, a rather large and intimidating chunk of hardwood. *Was that what done in the dead miner? Was it the murder weapon,* Newt asked himself.

"He's still alive, that son-of-a-bitch," Emil Crowe said looking across the street at Newton Blake. He spat a nasty glob of tobacco on the boardwalk in front of the general store. A well-dressed handsome woman sidestepped the slime. The little girl holding tightly to the woman's hand scowled at Crowe. Crowe snarled at the girl and she ran.

A show of strength would do Newton Blake no harm. He walked across the dirt street of downtown Calumet, never taking his eyes off Emil Crowe. As he stepped onto the board sidewalk in front of the general store one of Crowe's henchmen started to block him. Crowe reached his bandaged hand out to stop his man, and winced. Blake smiled, slid by the henchman, and entered the general store.

"What'll it be, stranger?" the storekeeper asked Newt.

"Box of 45's, and a pack of tobacco. Papers too, cigarette papers." Newt watched as the storekeeper gathered the items, then reached into a pocked for cash. "You wouldn't be Otis Johnson, would you?"

"Nope!" he answered, then, "Otis," he shouted, "Somebody lookin' for ya."

Otis Johnson shocked Newt when he came through the curtain that separated the back office and storeroom from the business side of the store. He was a tiny man, thick spectacles, frail looking, not at all what Newt imagined when he got Johnson's telegram.

"You Blake?" he asked.

"Yep! I am. Newton Blake."

"Back here," Otis said, as he turned and walked back through the curtain. Newt followed. Johnson snaked his way around shelves of stored hardware, dry goods, implements, etc, until he came to the bottom of a crude staircase leading to a room above the store. He did not talk until he reached the top step. "I hear you already met Crowe."

"First thing," Newt said. "He the man you wired me about?"

"That's him."

"Got my money?" Newt asked.

Otis worked the dial on a small safe in the corner of the room. He dug around for a moment, and then came up with a leather pouch. He flung it in Newt's direction. "That there's half. You get the rest when the job's done."

"Provided I'm still alive."

"You ain't, you didn't earn it," Johnson said.

"Fair enough," Newt agreed.

On the boardwalk in front of the general store, Crowe and his men were getting anxious. "What you spose 'e's doin' in there so long, Boss?" one of them asked.

"Got no idea. Rivers, peak in there, see what he's up to," Crowe ordered.

The look on Rivers' face as he came back out of the store told Emil Crowe something was wrong. "He ain't in there," Rivers said. "Must-a slipped out the back."

"God damn it," Crowe said swinging the hardwood club at Rivers. He should have known better, not Rivers, Crowe. He should have sent one of his men to watch the back door. But he consoled himself — finally calming down — with the knowledge that this guy, this Newton Blake must be some sort of coward slipping out the back way like that.

Newt watched out Otis Johnson's window with moderate amusement as the threesome scrambled around in confusion below. Then he turned his attention back to Johnson. "I'm told Crowe and his men are Klan. Is that true, Mr. Johnson?" Newt asked as he counted the money in the leather pouch.

"True enough."

"Them three, they the only Klan hereabouts? Or are there more."

"Far as I know, they're it. For now at least?" Otis said.

"For now? What you mean for now?"

"Tell me, Mr. Blake, what do you know about the Klan?"

"Not much," Newt admitted. "Either there aren't any of them around Missouri, or I just ain't never run into any of them before."

"They're likely around, Mr. Blake. They're most places." He studied Newt for a moment. "The thing is, Klan is Klan. Where there are a few of them, there will soon be more — like bugs. So watch yourself. You will need to get them before they know you came here to do that. Otherwise, Crowe will have more of them around here, so many you won't be able to count them, let alone kill them all."

"Wait a minute," Newt said as he peeked back into the sack of cash Johnson had given him.

"Don't worry, Mr. Blake. You will be paid justly for what you have to do. You're not expected to kill them all for that amount. If more come, you'll get more for them. Now... what's your plan?"

"I thought I'd go to work in the mine to start with,

learn their habits, and then go from there."

"I thought you might," Otis Johnson said. "Curtiss Clay, he's the fellow who does all the hiring out at the mine, he's waiting for you to come and see him. Don't you go telling him you're working for the town and me. Clay is a true blue mining company man and if he suspects you are anything other than man hunting a job, why… you'll be out of there faster than a jackrabbit on fire. Now… you got any questions?"

"What brings you into the middle of this, Mr. Johnson?"

"Election time, Mr. Blake. I'm running for mayor. So is Crowe. He plans to win by scaring everyone into voting for him. And I am not in the middle of this alone. None of the town's elders wants the Klan in here. We're together on this. You got a six weeks, Mr. Blake. That's election time."

"If I get the job done, how about a real job for me… permanent?" Newt asked. He was tired of moving around, selling his gun. This was the twentieth century. Gun slingers would soon be a thing of the past. He needed a future. "Say… sheriff."

"We already got a constable."

"I don't want to be a constable. I want power in the whole area, the mine included. What do you say, Mr. Johnson? I clean up your mess. You get to be the mayor. I get to be the sheriff."

"I'll look into it," Johnson agreed.

"You do that." And Newton Blake left Otis Johnson's quarters over the general store, on his way to see Curtiss Clay at the mining company hiring office. As he stepped onto the boardwalk in front of the general store, Newt was relieved to see that Crowe and his men had already gone. He crossed the street, and as he came to the boardwalk in front of the Red Rose, he heard Molly Carpenter let out a screech. He looked in the saloon doors to see Emil Crowe pinning her to a wall, groping at her while his two cohorts held her in place. Newt stormed in. *No time like right now*, he thought. He recalled Otis Johnson's warning and wondered if fast action would bring on more Klan. His operation needed seclusion, just in case Johnson had been wrong, just in case there were more Klan around, or Klan sympathizers, anyone who could alert the Klan and bring numbers out against him. Newt would act though, if needed. This was, after all, Molly, and Molly was his friend. But it wasn't necessary. A couple of the other girls sauntered to the side of the two goons holding Molly and they lessened their grip on Molly's arms. Molly then easily fought off Emil Crowe's advances with no outside help required from Newt or any of the other men in the place, not that she would receive help from any of the other men in the place.

Deep scratches down the side of Emil Crowe's cheek and a crippling blow to the groin from Molly Carpenter's sharp knee brought out the worst in him. "You bitch!" he shouted. The barkeep laid his sawed-off shotgun over the bar, its mussel pointed menacingly in Crowe's direction. Crowe looked at the shotgun, then backed down.

Newt, the scene having quieted, left the saloon unnoticed and continued on his journey to the mine.

Chapter Four

The life of an iron miner had little in common with anything Newton Blake had done before. Tonnage was the key. Tonnage was how men made their wages. And tonnage was accomplished with a pick and shovel, a strong and limber back, and lungs capable of taking in more red dust than clean air. None of this was the calling of a cowboy and lawman from Missouri. One week in and Newton Blake's every muscle cried uncle, his palms produced blisters the size of dimes as did the bottoms of his feet, and his chest ached from a cough reminiscent of a tuberculosis victim. And Newt's mind told him, if acting the part of a miner was a necessary to all of this, completing his mission might just be an impossibility. He decided, after a grueling twelve-hour shift of manning that shovel and pick, it was time to see Doc Waters.

"Boy howdy! Them are some… blisters," Doc said as he peeled Newt's gloves from his hands. "That hand shovel's not near as gentle as saddle leather, now is it?"

"Got 'em on my feet too, Doc. Anything you can do for me?"

"Well… those boots you miners wear down in the hole aren't exactly made for comfort. They're made to hold up against the ore, that's all. And hold up they do, but the cost is blisters."

Doc Waters opened the door to a cabinet in the corner of his room. He retrieved a small tin. "I call this concoction Doc Waters Medicinal Cure Or Kill Salve. A glob of this and those sores will disappear before morning — like magic." He held the tin out so Newt could get a look.

"Jesus, Doc. That stuff smells like shit. What's in it anyway?"

"A whole bunch of stuff. Roots, berries, grasses, stuff like that. I don't recall what all is in there."

"Thought you said it was your concoction."

"It is," Doc insisted.

"Then why don't you know what's in it?" Newt asked.

"I don't need to remember. I wrote it down someplace around here. It isn't really all my concoction though. It's mostly an old Indian remedy… good for treating sores on cow teats and such. Works pretty fair on blisters too; I've used it on lots of miners," Doc assured him. Doc fell silent for a time, spreading generous amounts of the noxious smelling ointment on Newt's blisters. Then he began to speak. "Newt, mind if I ask you something?"

"Of course not, Doc. Ask me anything."

"What brought you here? I mean, why'd you end up around these parts, in iron country?"

It wasn't a question Newt was prepared to answered. "Ah… I… I really don't know, Doc?"

"Sure you do," Doc insisted as he spread more salve on Newt's blistered hands. "You don't strike me as the kind who does something on accident. You strike me as a fellow who knows exactly what he's doing — always."

Newt was taken aback. He liked Doc Waters, he liked him a lot. And he wanted above all to trust him. This was a strange place for Newton Blake and he was alone here. Someone he could share what he was up to his ears in would be a blessing. But was that someone Doc Waters? Should he trust Doc with all that was at stake here? Should he level with him? He could use an ally. *Oh, what the hell*, he thought. *I already gave Doc Waters the sense I'd kill Crowe for him if I got the chance.* He chose to risk it.

"I came here hunting Crowe."

"Haven't they got enough Crowes down there in Missouri for you?"

"None like Emil." Newt said. He slipped his jacket on and started toward the door. "Doc, ain't there a back way out of here? I don't feel like running into somebody who'll keep me away from my bedroll any longer."

"Just go left down the hallway. You'll find a door at the end on the right. Beyond will be a stairway that'll bring you into a walkway between buildings. Nobody will see you going out that way. Hell, nobody ever uses it."

The storm settling in from the west brought with it an early darkness and a brisk, stinging drizzle. Newt's eyes squinted against the weather the moment he stepped out of Doc Water's boarding house above the Red Rose. He found it difficult to focus on the blur of a person crossing the opening of the narrow walkway at the street just thirty feet away. The scuffle of feet behind him caught him off-guard, then there was nothing — blackness. When he came to, he found himself tied to the wooden gate of a pen in a barn he did not recognize, his head pounding, his eyes burning from the peculiar smelling smoke of a nearby fire, and his every muscle protested his bonds.

"He's comin' 'round," a gruff voice claimed.

"Hit him again. This stuff ain't ready yet."

And for Newt, things returned to black.

~*~

Twenty miles south of Calumet

Newton Blake did not know how long he had been out, or if he had even been out, or if all of this was dream or reality when he awoke, for he was no longer tied. He lay in a featherbed, warm and comfortable. "He's awake, Ma." It was a small voice he heard. He tried to sit up. Every inch of his skin seemed to tingle and burn and itch all at the same time.

"Why'd they do that to you, Mister?" a lady asked.

"Do what?" Newt asked.

"You don't know?"

"No, Ma-am."

"Then you're lucky. Me and my girl, we cleaned you up good as we could. Sorry for the smell — lamp oil," she said apologetically. "How'd you get way out here anyway?"

Newt sniffed the air and his stomach went weak. He looked at his arm, slightly black, looking frighteningly like one big bruise. "Out where? Where am I?"

"Nearest town's seventeen miles, Grand Rapids, due west." she told Newt.

"Where would Calumet be?"

"North! Maybe twenty miles. Mister, you don't remember what was done to you?"

"No! I'm afraid not. I recall waking up once tied to a gate or fence or something, then somebody hit me and I don't remember anything after that."

"Like I said, that's probably lucky," his hostess told him.

"Why?" Newt did not feel lucky, not by any measure.

"Because somebody tarred and feathered you. That's why."

Newt tried to move. His skin felt dry as parchment, like it would crack wide open if stretched.

"You're gonna be sore for a time. Best you lay there still. Clara here, Clara's my little one, she'll feed you. Clara, you go get some soup for this man. Now…," she said after the girl left the room. "I'm Libby Tilden. Who are you?"

"Newton Blake, Ma-am."

"You one of them miners from over in Calumet, Mr. Blake?"

"Call me Newt. Yes, I work the mines," he lied, but not entirely. "Your man about?"

"I haven't got a man. I had one once. He was a miner too, over in Calumet like you, Mr. Blake."

"Call me Newt — please," Blake said again.

"Nope! Don't think I will, at least not yet. Like I was starting to tell you, Carl — that was my husband — he was killed by those nice folks in that mining town. They hung him! Me and Clara, we lit out directly for my father's old homestead just after it happened. There's no place for a woman without a husband in a mining town. And I promised myself I'd never have anything to do with any miner ever again, and if you weren't so hurt, Mr. Blake, I'd have nothing to do with you either, you being one of them and all."

"I'm not the kind who hangs folks, Mrs. Tilden," Newt said.

"I'm not too sure of that. If you're truly a miner,

you haven't been one for long, not according to those blisters on your hands. And I found a badge in your things too. Somebody, probably whoever did this to you, rolled your clothes and left them lay by you, odd as it seems. After all, it doesn't quite add up, somebody capable of tarring and feathering a man having the kindness in them to leave his things with him. Your badge was in your vest pocket. Now… I cleaned your things, Mr. Blake, and Clara's gonna keep you fed, so you rest and heal so you can get out of here fast as possible, because folks with badges, Mr. Blake, hang people. It was a man with a badge who strung up my Carl, sir." And she left the room.

Libby Tilden knew it had been Constable Profit, or at least she suspected it had been him who hanged her husband. She saw a truck shortly after she found Carl hanging there in her front yard, and so far as she knew, his was the only truck around Calumet with a star on the door. It had to have been Profit. That's all there was to it.

~*~

Molly Carpenter awoke early with the sense that something was wrong. It had been several days since Newton Blake had stopped by The Red Rose to pay her a visit. That was out of character for Newt. They were friends, more than that, they were close, both of them coming from Missouri and being strangers in a new land and all. She left her room and knocked on Doc Waters' door. She would ask him if he had seen Newt.

"I don't know where he is, Molly," Doc Waters said. "The last time I saw him, was two days ago, late in the day. I dressed his blisters and he left. Just about dark, it was. You check the hall?" Newt lived in the miner's hall, a kind of dormitory operated by the company for men who worked the ore and needed a basic sleeping place. Doc thought about his question. Of course Molly hadn't checked. How could she? Women weren't allowed anywhere near the miner's hall. "I imagine not," he said.

"I had Rusty take a look." Rusty was one of Molly's regulars. Nobody knew his real name; he had been Rusty to all, named for his hair, because he had mined for so long, his hair had turned a permanent orange. "Nobody's seen him, Doc. Something's wrong. I know Newton Blake. He don't disappear — not like this. I'm real worried, Doc."

"You talk to Profit?" Doc asked.

"Profit! Shit, Doc. Profit's the bought and paid for kind. I hear a lot of bar talk, and nobody seems to know what side of this little game owns him right now, Blake's or Crowe's. Best we don't assume it's Blake's." Molly based her thinking on Newt and Emil Crowe's fight that first day Newt arrived in town, and the continued animosity they held for each other since. Profit backed Crowe then — likely still does.

"I know. I know," Doc insisted, "But, let's go see him just the same. A lot can be learned just watching a man's face when you ask the right question." And together, they set out to find Amos Profit, Calumet's constable, duly appointed under pressure from the mining company higher-ups. Doc and Molly found him in a saloon at the other end of Main Street, a shady disgusting place where the town's misfits, those who panned for drinks either because they never worked or had been fired from the mines, spent most of their waking hours. It was still early when they walked in the door, not yet ten in the morning, and Profit already had just enough watered-down whisky in him to loosen his tongue.

"Blake," he said. "Blake," he repeated like he was trying to place the guy. "He that feller come into town a week or so back, the man who got into that fight with Emil Crowe?"

"That's him," Molly said.

"He owe you fer a poke there, Molly?" He grinned. "Or, he owe you for patchin' blisters, Doc?"

"How'd you know about his blisters, Profit?"

Profit hid his expression in his whisky glass and Doc knew he had tripped him up. "Where is he?" Waters pressed.

Profit remained silent.

"Constable," Molly said. "Tell us what you know about Newton Blake's disappearance."

"It ain't town business. You'll have to ask out at the mine," Profit said.

Doc Waters and Molly left the dingy saloon after a bit more prodding which produced minimal results, with the sense they had obtained all the information they were likely to get from the inebriated constable. They headed back to Doc's. "I told you his look would tell us more than his words."

"Gotta admit, Doc, you sure made him dive back into his glass. We going to the mine?"

"No! That'll get us killed. We best just be quiet and listen for a spell. Somebody's bound, sooner or later, to spill the beans," Doc reasoned.

"How do you figure?" Molly asked him.

"Profit knows we're on to him. He'll gab it to whoever's in on it with him. Then somebody's going to come looking for us, wanting to find out just how much we know. So watch yourself. It's not going to be anybody who's on Newt's side, or ours either. But it will be somebody who's dangerous, so you look out, girl."

"How am I supposed to do that?" Molly asked, knowing where she worked along with what she did for a living pretty much kept her in harms way a good share of the time.

"Stay near folks. Don't go off alone with anyone," Doc suggested.

"I'll go broke."

"Well… better broke than dead," Doc insisted. "I got money if you need some."

~*~

At the Calumet mine, Emil Crowe had proven himself a poor driver. He had borrowed Fish's company truck, had gone out in search of a place where he and his goons could look down on the mine and its employees, and for his efforts, now had the vehicle buried to its axles. "Push! You goddamn morons," he was now shouting at four miners, reluctant volunteers who lined the rear of the truck. The narrow trail he had taken was knee deep in mud in several places. His two goons sat in the tall grass beside the narrow path, watching the miners sweat and toil with the immovable vehicle until Crowe got out, hickory stick in hand, and moved to the rear and clubbed one of the miners across the back. "Now push!" Then he looked over at his men. "And you two, you get in here and help," he yelled.

"But, Boss," one of them objected. "That there's

mud." But the look in Crowe's eyes told them both that the argument would get them what the miner had just gotten, the slap of hickory across the back, and their best option was to get in there and push. They did.

Thirty minutes of lifting and shoving gained the crew five feet of progress and a break. It was Rex Hartley, a good friend of Doc Waters, who made a comment about the missing Newton Blake, and received in return a smirk from one of Crowe's men that told him they knew something about it all, perhaps much. "Where'd he get off to?" Rex had asked.

"Someplace he ain't comin' back from," was what he received for an answer. Then the conversation was severed by Crowe's order to get back to the task of getting his buried truck, or more correctly, Fish's truck, out of the mud.

~*~

Meanwhile at the Libby Tilden farm twenty miles south of Calumet, Clara, Libby's young daughter, had to wake Newton Blake to feed him soup. "This'll fix ya right up, Mr. Newt," she said.

"Just Newt will do," he told her.

"Mama said I wasn't to call you anything other than Mr. Blake, or Mr. Newt." She spooned some soup into his mouth. "I like Mr. Newt," she insisted.

It was tasty. Newt wondered how long it had been since he last ate. There was plenty Newt wondered. For instance, he wondered how anyone got the jump on him so easily. Did they know his next move? He was not a creature of habit. He was not someone who would go to a doctor with blisters. Had he told someone at the mine that evening after work, and did that someone tell his attackers where he would be? And how did they tar and feather him without him knowing it? He recalled hearing someone issue the order to hit him again, but who? And just how hard did they hit him, and how many times? How many were in on the beating for that matter. It had to be more than one, for Newt had been in many fights during his life and never had one or two been able to push him past feeling or remembering, in this case both. But the big question was why, not how, not who, not even how many. Something was wrong. Information about his reason for coming to the north had obviously leaked, and he needed to get better, to get back to Calumet and find out who knows what and who told, and to whom information had been given. But for now, the soup was sure tasty. He opened his mouth for another spoonful. He would explore these mysteries after he healed.

"Clara," her mother called from the doorway. "Go out and pick some tomatoes and cucumbers for supper."

"But, Mama, I gotta feed Mr. Newt."

"I'll do that. You run now… get those vegetables." Clara placed the soup bowl on the table beside the bed and left for the garden. Libby took up the feeding detail.

It was on the first spoonful of hot soup served from the gentle hand of Libby Tilden that Newton Blake first realized the beauty of his hostess. Previously, he hadn't really given her a thought. Frankly, his mind had somehow seen her as older, more mature, but now, in this light, or possibly in this, his somewhat improved condition, he could clearly see his mind had lied to him. This Mrs. Tilden was a mere girl, not an older woman, and quite handsome in a country bride sort of way, and he was attracted to her. "You make a fine soup, Mrs. Tilden."

She considered him for a moment. It had been a long time since Carl's death. This Mr. Blake was a fine looking man beneath the stains of the tar — and she was young. "Thank you." She spooned him more of the soup. "Do you think you can do this for yourself?" She dared not stay.

"I recon I can."

She handed him the soup, spoon leaning to one side of the bowl. She repositioned a cloth her daughter had placed on his bare chest so hot soup could not accidentally spill onto his already tender skin, and rose from the edge of his bed. "I have much to do," she said.

"Mrs. Tilden."

"Yes?"

"How did you find me?"

"It was Clara. She heard the truck, just before dawn. When daylight came, she went out for a look."

"That must have been awful for her."

"She's accustomed to such things. We all seen a lot of that over in Calumet. She even saw her daddy hanging from the tree in our front yard. Course she didn't quite know what it was — he was tarred and feathered too — before they hung him."

Chapter Five

    The one and a half story house on the south end of town that just came open suited Doc Waters perfectly. He hadn't lived in other than boarding house quarters for a very long time, and now that he was getting a bit of a reputation of being more than some horse doctor among the miners who did not wish to give all of their earnings to the company doctor, he needed space for his practice — a clinic of sorts — and space for himself — living quarters. The story and a half would do nicely. Miss Molly helped him move.
    Neither he or Molly could drive an automobile so Doc borrowed a wagon and team from Mathew Gray at the livery stable and they had spent the morning loading his belongings in it. It surprised even Doc to see how much he had gathered over his time of boarding house living. He had clothing. He had a saddle although he had sold his horse a while back, he had a couple kerosene lamps and some cookware, a few tools and magazines of his trade, medical books — both human and animal, and a nightstand that might come in handy should there turn out to be a bed in his new house, left there when the previous family moved on. He had with him too, his mother's treasured wooden rocking chair, the only thing left for him to remember her by. He had taken it after her funeral when he lit out from his home, and it had traveled with him for nearly a decade. It too, Doc felt, deserved a home of its own.
    "What're you gonna use for furniture, Doc?" Molly

asked.

"Well... there's a few pieces that come with the place, and for the rest, I thought I might take some items for pay, just till I get the place nice and comfy. There ought to be lots of miners willing to give up a lamp, or a table — I mean instead of their hard-earned cash."

"I bet they will, Doc," Molly agreed, as she climbed the side of the wagon and slid into the seat. "Let's go get you settled."

As they traveled Molly thought about Doc's luck in finding a place. She wondered. Houses weren't abundant. Most were owned by the company and reserved for families of miners. "When did this place come vacant?" she asked.

"When they buried Henry Kyle," Doc answered. Henry Kyle was the man Crowe and his men clubbed and kicked to death, the miner who led the other miners in that nasty little uprising a couple of weeks back.

"Where'd the family go?"

"I don't rightly know." It had become habit. When a man went down, his widow and children seemed to disappear, go on to live off relatives, or just plain go. Nobody seemed to give it much thought, it happened so often and so easily around mining towns like Calumet. "I suppose they have family someplace or other."

"So why didn't the company put another family in the house?" Molly asked.

"It isn't a company house."

"How'd you get it?"

"The bank. It seems Henry was losing the place. That's probably what made him angry enough to do battle with the mining company in the first place. It seems I recall hearing one of his children took sick and the Company doc got too much of his wages for too long. It busted poor Henry Kyle. He couldn't recover." He pulled the first of his belongings, his mother's wooden rocker, from the wagon and set on the grassy lawn of his new home. As he turned to take another of his treasures from Molly, a man approached.

"You be Doc Waters?" the man asked.

"I am," Doc said.

"You a friend of that there Blake feller?"

"I am," Doc said. "And who are you?"

"I'm not gonna tell you that, case it gets back to the company I told you somethin'. I can say, though, what I got to say to you comes from Rex Hartley."

"Well... what is it you have to tell me?" Rex was a friend. Doc was interested in what the stranger had to say.

"It's 'bout Mr. Blake. The other day, while me and Rex was helpin' get a truck unstuck from the mud Rex got friendly with one of Crowe's mutts. It seems it was Crowe and his what did that to 'im."

"Did what?" Molly asked.

The stranger looked at Molly skeptically. "It's okay, stranger, Molly here, she's a real good friend of Newton Blake's."

"Tarred and feathered 'im. That's what they done. Then they drove 'im off twenty miles — south I think — and dumped 'im in the woods, that Crowe an his two ruffians. They said 'e's dead. They also said they'd do the same to us if any of us told. Now... that's all I'm gonna say. Good day to you both." And the stranger was gone as fast as he had appeared.

"My God, Doc," Molly said. "What's twenty miles south of here?"

"Woods," Doc said. "Desperation. Death, I recon.

Once in a while a farm, maybe somebody found him before it was too late," he added, his tone — discouraging.

"You trust the guy, Doc?" Molly asked. "Cause you said whoever told wouldn't be a friend."

"Guess I was wrong this time. Yeah, I trust him. He seems on the level sure enough."

Waters pondered all the possibilities of what might have happened to his friend, Newton Blake, while he and Molly unloaded the remainder of his belongings onto his front lawn, and then hauled them into his house. Newt could be hurt bad. He could be dead and his carcass eaten by coyotes. Maybe he had been lucky, maybe he had been rescued. Doc sure hoped so. But he doubted that. He knew of nothing, save the scattered and probably abandoned farm twenty miles south of Calumet. That was the land of desolation. Minnesota winters drove most farmers from that area years ago. He came to realize Newton Blake was most likely a goner. A man who's been tarred and feathered stands little chance; and none at all if he isn't awfully tough. And even being tough won't save him unless somebody finds him quick. Doc Waters bowed his head briefly in silent prayer for his friend Newton Blake.

"Think Newt's okay?" Molly asked.

"Yeah. Newt's not like most. He'll be fine, you wait and see," Doc assured her.

When all of Doc's possessions were safely tucked inside his new quarters he and Molly set out to return the wagon and team to the livery. He bought Molly her supper at the Red Rose, then excused himself. He had someplace he wanted to be, someplace he dared not take her.

The secret meeting being held in a clearing just north of the Calumet mine began near dusk while miners still labored. In attendance were most of the town's elders, Otis Johnson, the merchant aspiring to be the town's first mayor, and Constable Profit, hoping for a place on the ticket with Johnson as a reward for his years of public service. Johnson presided and Profit served as sergeant at arms. Something had to be done. The KKK, Crowe and his men being what they all recognized as just the beginning, thanks to the invitation of mining company officials, were beginning to acquire a following among the working class protestants — Catholics were unwelcome. The Company had no qualms about bringing in the Klan, so long as the end result for them was a stronger arm for use against miners who wanted more out of life than dusk to dawn sweat and toil for pauper's wages. They cared not about religious or race issues which might upset the delicate balance of society in those early days of mining, or for the Klan's inevitable influence in the politics of the area. And they were naïve enough, or maybe simply arrogant enough, to think it all would have no power of influence over them. So it was, that Johnson caught wind, through the unconstrained tongue of the town's telegrapher, of Emil Crowe's attempt to send a message to his superiors in Duluth, advising them that he thought it time to bring in more Klan, that his own ploy for the mayoral office needed fellow Klansmen votes to be successful. "Something's got to be done," Johnson told all in attendance.

"I thought you brought someone in to take care of this problem," Edgar Kruet, saloon operator, said.

"My man's gone missing," Otis Johnson admitted.

"He's been tarred and feathered," the voice of Doc

Watters rang out from a bluff overlooking the meeting. "Crowe and his did it."

"How do you know that?" someone asked.

Doc scurried down the bank, "A miner told me."

"What miner," Profit asked.

"He never gave his name. I never asked." Waters brushed ore dust from his suit.

Otis Johnson hadn't thought of Doc Watters when he called this meeting, Doc being rather invisible until he gained a residence to do his doctoring from. After all, who thought of a veterinarian who resided in a boarding house, especially one above a saloon and shared with whores, as a town elder, or as a town anything for that matter. "Care to join us, Doc?"

"I do care to, Otis," Doc said as he settled onto a log beside one of the saloon owners.

"Is Newton Blake alive?" Johnson asked. He had forgotten that most of those at his meeting did not know who he had contracted to take care of their Klan problem. "That's the man I hired," he quickly added.

Men looked at one another. The few who knew it had been Newt Blake that Otis Johnson had brought in kept it quiet. All of them knew Newt, most of them being storekeepers or barkeeps, and all of them liked him. But Newton Blake's easy way gave no reason to see him as a lawman — a gun for hire. Sure, he had shown courage on that first day in town, his sound thrashing of Emil Crowe and all, but to date, that had been his only show of strength. He was simply too mild-mannered. And now, with the report from Doc Waters that their hope, the hope that Johnson had spent their hard earned money on, had been tarred and feathered and was in all likelihood dead someplace in the woods, most eyes turned skeptically in Otis Johnson's direction.

"Now… let's don't be hasty," Johnson said. "We need to find out what's happened. For now, anyway, the telegram has been stopped, and Crowe has no knowledge of any of this. He's thinking his people are on the way. That'll buy us time."

"Time for what, Otis?" a voice rang from the Crowed.

"Time to find Newton Blake. To get him back here. I assure you, he can do the job."

"If he's sill alive," another voice came.

"Doc Watters," Otis said, "what more do you know? What'd this mystery miner of your's tell you, besides he's tarred and feathered and gone?"

"He said Newt had been dumped about twenty miles south," Doc said. "But he's been gone near to two weeks already."

"Well… I suggest we send out two or three men, have them check out farms in the area. Should take only a day, maybe two. I doubt Crowe's smart enough to catch on that quickly."

Two men, miners who could be counted on, Catholic miners who were hated by the Klan so wouldn't be able to switch their loyalties if they wanted to, were chosen to go out and look for Newton Blake. Amos Profit was placed in charge. He was to inform the two and then accompany them on their search.

"I ain't got no jurisdiction way out there," Profit objected.

"You won't need any. Nobody needs arresting," Otis told him looking over the top of his spectacles to show Amos he did what the rest of them wanted, or he could forget the thought of becoming his second in command should Otis win the election and become mayor. Not that Amos would get that spot, Otis did not like Amos in the first place, but Otis was smart enough to use Amos' desire as control over him.

"Now, all that having been settled, I suggest we adjourn. And I think next time we should meet in town like a real government, not out here in the cover of the wilderness like the Klan. We have a city hall. Time we use it," Otis said, and dismissed the meeting.

Amos Profit headed directly to the sleazy saloon on the edge of town, the Iron Man Saloon, the one where Crowe and his men usually hung out. He played both sides. He wanted political position in the worst way and he would align himself with demons to get what he was after. Now he was proving just that.

Emil Crowe was torn. What if Newt Blake had not been killed? Should he be afraid? After all, any man who could survive the treatment he and his boys dished out on Blake was a tough man indeed. Or should Crowe be simply grateful that he would now get a second shot at Blake. No matter, he guessed. The reality was, if Blake was still alive, he had to deal with it. Profit, however, Crowe considered a fool and someone he just needed to use for a time. Once he gained the mayor's office, he'd have Profit killed and be done with him. As for this Blake fellow, if he found him alive he would finish the job — his way. Simply shooting him would not do. They, meaning the town's hierarchy, would send for another and that wouldn't do. No, Newton Blake couldn't just show up dead, he had to show up as an example of what would happen to any replacement for him as well. He would be captured, taken back to Calumet, and he would be tarred and feathered once again, only this time he would have bullets in him as well — many bullets. And if he was already dead, well… Crowe would think of something. "You gather your two Catholic miners, Profit, just like Otis and the boys told you to, only you take them someplace where Blake isn't. Me and the boys will see to Newton Blake ourselves.

~*~

Unaware that trouble was heading her way, Libby Tilden stood quietly in her front yard admiring Newton Blake's muscular frame as he chopped firewood. Her daughter, Clara, had gone to the creek that afternoon, fishing, an activity she was poor at but enjoyed doing so much that when she went, she would stay the whole day, daylight till dark. Newt raised the axe high over his head and guided it effortlessly into an oak stump, the two halves toppling to the ground easily. The muscles of his back rippled and glistened in the heat of the afternoon sun. Libby sighed. It had been a long, long time it seemed, since Carl, since she had known a man, and this Newt, well… now there was a man. And over the time of his recovery, not so much from burns of the hot tar as from the extreme beating he had taken in order for him to not have felt the tar, they had become friends. Was it time for them to take things up a notch? She ached for him. Watching him work was not helping? "Newt?" She sought his attention.

"Yes, Libby?"

"Were you ever married?"

"Nope!"

"Why not?"

"Well… marriage and badges just don't seem to go together so good," he said. "As a matter of fact, neither does cowboyin' and marriage. So since that's all I ever done, those two things, well… no marriage."

"Ever think of it?"

Of course he had. He had thought of marrying a few times over the years, just never found the right girl. "Nope!" he told her. He wondered how she would take the truth. He liked her and he did not know if he should even hint that there might have been others. But what about her? Did he wish her to know he had an interest in her? Should he say anything at all? "Not yet, anyway."

"So it isn't out of the question?" she suggested.

Newt smiled, his back towards her so she could not see. Then he felt her come up close behind him. He felt her hot breath on the back of his neck, her firm breasts as they brushed lightly across his back, and then he felt the gentle kiss of her soft lips at his hairline. He turned. He put his arms around her. He looked deep into her eyes and kissed her hard on the mouth, lips parted, tongues probing. Then he pulled back and looked down at his boots. "I'm sorry," he said.

"I'm not," she said, and she led him into the house, and they made love until they heard the whinny of old Nell, the plow horse Clara had ridden to the creek.

Half dressed, Newt stormed out of the house. When he saw Nell, no Clara on her back, he began to call out.

"Right over here, Blake," a gruff voice echoed from the tree line. A shot followed missing widely, its lead puffing up sand and dust five feet away. Newt dove through Libby's still open front door and scurried out of sight just as Libby slammed the door behind him, the door catching lead form one of the intruders' handguns. Newt stood and grabbed for the rifle Libby held ready. He snatched his pistol, still in its holster, from a wooden peg on the front wall of the house and quickly swung it over his shoulder. "You got another rifle?" he asked.

"Yes," she said and grabbed it from where it always leaned for just such an emergency, right next to the door. She watched as Newt took a rapid and cautious glance out the window, then looked toward the back of the house. "There's no back door," she said.

"Is there a back window?" he asked. No door was good news. Whoever was out there would have scoped it out by now and a bullet would be waiting for him. But a dash out the front wouldn't do. That'd only make an easy target of him, too easy, and this whole thing would be over almost as fast as it had begun. And it wouldn't end in Newt's or Libby's or Clara's favor either.

"There's one small window. It's pretty much covered by brush though." She hadn't felt safe when she and Clara arrived here without Carl, and had blocked off all other windows but those in the front. The one remaining window, though, she hadn't seen as a danger. It had already been concealed by thick underbrush then. "Might be too blocked to get through."

Newt quickly his pulled boots over his bare feet, then pried at the latch of the small window. "I'll make it do," he said, then began to lowered himself into the brush.

"Newt," Libby said. He stopped and looked up at her but said nothing. "Be careful. I think I love you."

He smiled, finished lowering himself, and slipped silently into the trees behind the house and began making his way through the woods in the direction of the gruff voice he had heard earlier. He thought while he traveled. A five foot miss was not good. Nobody misses by that much. Something else is up. Somebody wants him alive, and Clara's bait for the trap. Only caution would save him, but, no matter what, he would save Clara, even if it meant trading himself for her. He heard voices as he crept closer.

"Time to spread out." It was Crowe. "Remember, don't go killin' 'im."

"Why not, Boss?"

"Cause I mean to do that back in Calumet, where the whole town can see it."

Newt heard twigs crackling under a heavy foot as someone, Crowe likely, moved off. Newt waited, gave him time to get far enough away. He hadn't heard the other man leave, but sensed that he had. It would be a risk, but a risk he would have to take. Logic and experience told him the girl would be with the one who didn't vacate his spot. It wouldn't be easy to move around, prisoner under one arm, even if that prisoner was just a little girl. He would sneak up to where he had heard the voices. That's where Clara would be held. He hoped she would be held by Emil Crowe but supposed it was one of his goons.

Newton Blake's dive from the brush caught Emil Crowe's partner by complete surprise, and Newt's momentum backed by his weight drove the hunting knife deep into his heart. Clara Tilden flew from his grasp as if spring loaded. A gag in her mouth prevented her from crying out in horror. She looked up at Newt. Fear slowly lifted from her young eyes. Tears replaced it. Newt pulled her close and held her there for a moment, released her from the bonds Crowe and his men and placed her in, cautioned her to remain silent, and remain where she sat until he returned for her.

Then he was gone, in search of another intruder.

Crowe's other man saw Newt coming. He was a bold man, not bright. He stood. He beckoned Newt — *Come*. He wished to take him with his bare hands, not with a gun or a knife. Newt pulled out his six-gun and shot the man in the forehead. He went down like a sack of wheat, dust flying high into the air like a smoke signal. Crowe saw the dust rise and lit out for his horse. He was gone in seconds.

Moments later Clara Tilden was in her mother's arms and Newton Blake was gathering the horses that had belonged to the two dead men in the woods. A few hours later the two dead men were in shallow unmarked graves a few miles from Libby Tilden's family homestead. Newt returned to Libby's house. He would set out to finish this fight at dawn.

Chapter Six

Amos Profit stepped into the Iron Man Saloon in Calumet and settled himself onto a stool beside Emil Crowe. "Get 'im?" he asked.

"No!" Crowe said. "He's good. Both my guys is dead. He'll come for me now. And you."

"Me? He don't know 'bout me," Amos Profit said.

"Don't be stupid, Profit. I told you! He's good, good enough to figure out you're in on it. Probably good enough to figure out anybody else that's with us too."

Profit mulled it over. There was no justification. The only way Blake could know about him is if Crowe told him. He examined Crowe with a discerning eye.

"What!" Crowe said. "What's the look for?"

"You say something to Newton Blake?"

"Nope!"

"One of your boys say something?"

"Now how in the hell would I know that? They were both killed. They couldn't tell nobody nothing, not after Blake got done with them."

Amos could not be sure Blake wasn't coming for him, but he was sure he did not trust Emil Crowe. But he was a reasoning man. He would keep Crowe close, close enough to keep a sharp eye out, but not so close that Crowe — or Blake for that matter — would suspect him. As for Blake, he would keep a close eye on him anyway. After all, wasn't it his job to do just that? Blake was a stranger, and one who had disappeared for a time, then showed up again. Mysterious. Suspicious. "You gonna get some more of your guys to replace your dead ones?"

"You bet your ass I am," Crowe said. "My people, the Klan wants in on this town. There'll be more of us alright, faster than you think."

"Well... see if you can get a couple a bit smarter than them two. Now I gotta get the hell out of here. I got me some business to attend to, Crowe." He downed his whisky and slid from his stool. He slapped his holster with his hand, a silent warning of sorts. "Damn thing gives me a sore hip sometimes," he explained, but Crowe got the real idea just the same. Then Profit left him sitting there.

~*~

Twenty miles south of Calumet, while Newton Blake packed his things behind his saddle, Libby Tilden wept openly. "I've had my fill, Newton Blake. This has all been too much. It brings to mind memories of Carl — tarred and feathered, hanging in that tree in our front yard, memories I don't need or want. It reminds Clara and me of finding you in the brush, looking like some poor abused animal. You need to stay here, Newt. You need to rid yourself of that other life, for me — for Clara." She threw her arms around him, tears streaming down her cheeks, and kissed him hard and long on the mouth. "Just in case you haven't gotten it yet, we both come to love you and need you, maybe too much. But that don't change anything, we still do anyway."

Newt was taken aback. Libby had said she loved him, she said it as he climbed out the window and lowered himself into the brush, but he thought it had been the urgency of the moment that caused her to say it. He had no idea that she might think the same way after all was said and done, after the fight was over and Clara was back in her arms. Where matters of the heart were concerned, he was nothing but a cowboy turned lawman — not accustomed to feelings — not accustomed to the workings of a woman. He didn't know what to say.

"Say something," Libby demanded.

"I got to see this through, Libby. A man has got to. It's how it is."

"Then… go!" she said. "Go and be a man. Just don't you come back here when you're done, Newton Blake. We ain't gonna have no use for you. No, sir! None!"

"Libby, they're not going to let up. They'll come back, and they'll keep coming back until I'm dead — probably you and Clara too." He knew no other way to put it. Those were the facts, harsh as they seemed. And as Libby looked at him disbelievingly, Newt shook his head from side to side, then set out to do what he had to do, what he had contracted to do, get the Calumet citizenry away from the clutches of Emil Crowe and his fellow Klansmen. He was two-thirds of the way there and he would not stop now, and it had little to do with the love of a woman. As for love, Libby Tilden wasn't the only one plagued by feelings of love. He too had them. Although… he hadn't given them a name until she defined them for him. And as for being needed, sure, where there's love there's need, but there was also prior need, the need for his talents he had already sold to the good people of Calumet. And what of Libby and Clara? Wasn't there a need to protect them as well? He would see to it all. Then he would return to Libby and Clara and see if anything was still there for him. He mounted one of the horses formerly belonging to one of Emil Crowe's henchmen and reined him in the direction of Calumet.

~*~

Amos Profit decided it was time for him to have it out with Otis Johnson. They were supposed to be together, he and Otis, partners on the ticket and hopefully partners in running the town after the election. So why was it that Otis had secretly brought in Profit's latest problem, Newton Blake. Amos was a bit past put out about it all.

He locked the brakes of his pickup truck in front of Otis Johnson's general store. A cloud of dust rose, swirling around a black pony tethered to a hitching rail not ten feet away, spooking the poor critter into a bucking dance that ended with a hoof in the radiator of Profit's truck. "Son-of-a-bitch!" Profit yelled and slammed the door of his truck prompting the horse into even more bucking and kicking. "Goddamn horse," he said as he let the wooden screen door of the store slam shut behind him. "Where's Johnson?" he demanded of a young woman at the counter. When she hesitated to answer, Profit said, "Jesus Christ," and flew through the curtain into the storeroom shouting, "Johnson! Otis Johnson," until Otis stood at the top of the stairs and acknowledged his unruly guests appearance. Profit climbed the stairs.

"What can I do for you, Constable?"

"Didn't see nobody but that skinny girl of yours down stairs. Who belongs to that black stud tied out front?"

"Why, he's mine."

"Then you owe some repairs to my automobile. The goddamn thing kicked in my front," Profit said.

Wish that it were true, Johnson was thinking, but said, "By kicking in your front, I take it you meant the front of your truck."

"That's right! Now what're ya gonna do 'bout it?"

"Is the horse hurt?" Johnson asked.

"I told ya! It's my truck that's hurt. Now... what are you gonna do about it?"

"First of all, Amos, it's the town's truck, not yours. Second, I plan to take it up with the council. Whatever they decide is what will get done, and you'll have no say in the matter. Now... just what is it that brings you to my office?"

"So now you're a council. Before you was just a bunch of citizens hopin' to be a council. Well... here's a proper question. That council of yours, they act together to get Blake here? Rumor is, you acted alone for your council."

"That would be council business," Otis Johnson insisted.

Amos Profit had been getting the sense lately that Otis Johnson did not like him, and he had surmised that Newton Blake was some sort of a lawman. He had witnessed the fight between Blake and Crowe when Blake first landed in Calumet — his performance said lawman, and there was the way Blake carried himself as well — like a lawman. "I know you don't like me much, Johnson, but some of the others 'round here, some of the other so-called council members do. Remember that!" His fear, that Blake had been brought in to replace him, maybe even as second in command to

Otis should he become Mayor Johnson, was growing by leaps and bounds these days. And then there was what Crowe had been telling him, that this Newton Blake was about to come gunning for him as well.

"Has Newton Blake got something against you, Profit?"

"Nothin' I know of."

"Then none of this has to do with you. Fact is, Constable, this is all town business and ain't none of it yours to decide on. You work for us, the council members, not the other way around. So whether I got Mr. Blake to come, or one of the others on the council got him to come, or all of us together got him to come, it just ain't none of your concern. Oh, and Amos, I wasn't alone in the decision to get someone in here. I just suggested Blake for the job, that's all. Now... if you don't mind, Constable Profit, I have work to do. Good day!"

A desperate attempt to make his truck run ended in failure for Amos Profit and sent him on his way afoot. He poked his head into the livery on his way back to his small combination office and jail-house — an overused desk and two make-shift cells — to see if there would be a horse available for his use while his truck was being repaired, and to get the livery operator, also the town's mechanic, to retrieve the broken vehicle and see what could be done for it. "Goddamn horse," Amos complained.

"I seen it all, Amos. What the hell were you thinking running up on an animal like that? Lucky ya didn't kill Otis' horse," Mathew Gray, the livery operator said and shook his head in disgust. He was a horse man, always had been, and he did not favor those who abused the animals. Amos Profit's treatment of Otis

Johnson's tethered horse he perceived as downright cruel. "I'll see what can be done. Meanwhile, you can ride my Appaloosa. He's out on loan but due back anytime," he added then went on about his business as if Amos no longer existed. But when Profit walked into the street, Gray shouted after him, "Want me to clean the tar out of the back for ya?"

Profit turned and looked at Gray, his eyes cold and hard. "Just you bring me that Appaloosa once you get 'im back — over to the jail."

~*~

Out at the Calumet Mine, Emil Crowe threw a fit when he learned the telephone was inoperable and even Lawrence Fish's assurance that the system would be up and running by the next morning did little to calm him. He was desperate. He was alone. He would lose his power without men to back him up. "Why the hell ain't it workin'?" He asked as he shot Fish a wild-eyed stare. He gave him no opportunity to reply. "What the hell happened to it? Who broke it?"

"One of the follows cut through the line with some digging equipment. We're not sure where, but, soon as they locate the damage, they'll fix it."

"Who?" Crowe asked. Sure, there were other telephones in town, but the mine's, that was the one he considered his. The kind of business he needed to conduct wasn't for outside ears. It was bad enough that the mining company employees for whom he worked could listen in. He needed this telephone — for privacy.

"Excuse me?"

"Who, Fish? Who cut the goddamn wire?"

"I believe it was Ransom Feltus. But I'm not absolutely positive."

Feltus! That figured! He had been, at least in Crowe's mind, a bit of a rebel-rouser since the first day he arrived in Calumet looking for a job. He claimed he had come from Ely, but Crowe thought not at the time. But since the union had their nose so deep in Ely mine business, and most rebel-rousers these days were union men, it might make sense that he had come from Ely.

Emil Crowe did not think it through. He took his newfound information, that it had been Ransom Feltus who had cut the wire, and stormed out of Fish's office. Soon he stood nose to nose with Feltus.

The miner didn't see it coming. Crowe snatched a shovel out of the hands of a passing workman and caught Feltus across the back of the head, sending him to his knees, then into the dirt face first, blood spurting from a gaping wound and pooling in the red ore dust beside him. Crowe kicked him several times to the midsection for good measure. Then he smashed the flat of the shovel into the small of his back. After that he tossed the shovel into a nearby pool of orange water and stormed off to the mining company office, shouting all the while at the men who had been working alongside Feltus, threatening each of their lives should the telephone not be working before the end of the day. He needed it and he needed it now. His men were dead. He had heard nothing back on his telegram to the Duluth office requesting more Klan. He needed to call Hibbing. He needed backers and he needed them fast.

~*~

In the Red Rose Saloon Doc Waters was drinking

and whooping it up in Molly's company when a couple of men from the mine came searching him out. "It's Ransom Feltus, Doc. He's been hurt. Out at the mine."

"Well… then why didn't you haul him to the Company doctor."

"We tried, but old Rans, why he woke up just long enough to say he didn't want no Company doc. He wants you. We got 'im over on your front porch, c'mon Doc, time's a-wastin' and Rans is a-bleedin'."

"On my front porch?" Doc sobered. The sobering wasn't because someone needed his medical expertise, it was all about his new house. Blood on the porch? Indeed! "Let's get moving!"

~*~

Newton Blake thought Calumet lay due north of Libby Tilden' family homestead. He was wrong and by the time he calculated his position, it turned out he had not only gone right past the town, a few miles to the west of it, he had lost a full day doing it as well. He landed half as far north of Calumet as Libby's place had been south of it. As he squatted in front of a campfire warming himself, he hoped his error hadn't given Emil Crowe the needed time to make contact with and bring in more of his KKK brothers to rally against him. Newt knew the chance of him getting anyone to fight on his side was slim, not unimaginable — seeing his side was the side of the town and its miners — but slim just the same. These men weren't warriors, they were miners.

Newt heard a small critter in the brush not ten feet away. Rabbit? Partridge? He waited. He watched. He quietly pulled his gun from its holster and hammered back. He waited until the critter ambled into a clearing, grazing on sweet grass, unconcerned with Newt or his fire. A quick pull of the trigger and Newt was soon filling his belly with rabbit cooked over a campfire. *Coffee sure would top this off,* he thought to himself. But there was none, so sleep would come early.

The first indication of company came as a feeling to Newton Blake. He awoke from a sound sleep, hair standing on the nape of his neck, ears tuning in on any relevant sound. A slight breeze rustled the leaves of the brush around him hampering his ability to hear out of the ordinary sounds, then, suddenly the wind stilled. The snap of a trampled twig rang like a cathedral bell in the night air. Newt drew a pistol and dove for the shadows. He plucked a pebble from the ground and tossed it across his dying campfire and wished for a flame to offer light. The breeze granted him his wish just as a dark figure slid from the brush in search of the sound the pebble had made. Newt fired his gun, bullet grazing the dark figure's hat. "Hold it right there," he called out.

"Don't shoot, Mister. I'm unarmed."

"Move to the fire," Newt ordered, and the intruder obeyed. "Now… kick at the coals. Get that flame going so I can have a look at you. Who are you anyway?"

"My name is Ira Shank."

"Well… Ira Shank, what is it you hoped to gain sneaking up on a lone man in the middle of his sleep?"

"Nothin', really. I was just travelin' by and smelled the fire," Ira said.

"Traveling? Traveling where?"

"Not rightly sure of that," Ira admitted. "I'm a might lost at the moment."

"Then... traveling from where?" Newt demanded.

The flames hopped into action. Ira Shank stood and opened his coat. Newt sized him up, an unobtrusive man, average in every way. "Really, Mister, I'm not armed. I'm not gonna harm anyone. Please come into the light, so as I can see who you might be."

Newt looked Ira over. He wasn't lying. Newt saw no pistol, no sheathed knife, nothing threatening. He stepped out from the shadows. "So where you comin' from, Mr. Shank?"

"Say... you're that Blake feller, ain't ya? The one who whooped Emil Crowe."

No need to ascertain where Ira had come from, not so long as he knew that much. He was from Calumet. "Are you a miner?" Newt asked him.

"Yes, sir. I am."

"What brings you out here in the dark of night?" Newt asked as he slid his gun back into its holster. He squatted near the fire, threw a couple loose branches on it, and stirred the ash with a twig. Bark caught and flames grew.

"I worked a time at a loggin' outfit north of here. When Crowe bashed in Ransom Feltus's head like that..."

"Hold up a minute there. Who's Ransom Feltus and when did Crowe do this head bashing?"

Ira took it from the beginning, explaining about the mishap rendering the mine telephone useless, the stormy mindset it threw Crowe into, the shovel to the back of the head of Ransom Feltus, etc. "Lord only knows how bad it could of got had Crowe had those two mules with him."

"Two mules? If you're talking about those two sidekicks of his, they're dead," Newt said.

"How would you know that?" Ira asked.

"I killed them. That's how. Now... what about this logging outfit?"

"That's where I'm headed."

"What is it you plan on doing at this logging outfit you're heading to?"

"Get help. There's some pretty stout men workin' out there. One of 'em even used ta be a gunslinger. I aim to get 'em to help rid the town of Crowe and his kind before they grow into an army of Klan."

"How many men?" Newt's interest was growing. This meant he was not alone in all of this. With a possibility of help, success looked a lot closer all of a sudden. "And how about Profit?"

"Profit! Damn, Mister. Profit's one of 'em. He's sidin' with Crowe — same as Crowe — bought and paid for by the company. He just pretends to be with the town on the chance he might get some office if Otis is elected mayor. He's playin' both sides."

"What of the men you're after? How many do you expect to gather?"

"Oh... half-dozen or so, I recon. There's more, but I doubt they can all be spared."

"And what of this Ransom Feltus? Is he dead?"

"Nope! We brung 'im to Doc Waters' place."

"Holland's saloon? The Red Rose?" Newt asked. He thought it odd anyone would bring an injured man to a veterinarian above a saloon, even though he himself was taken there once. He would have thought the man would be taken to the company doctor, having been injured at work.

"Doc's not there no more. He moved into the old Kyle place. Henry Kyle. He's the miner Crowe killed a while back — 'bout the time you come 'round I'd guess."

Newt rolled it over in his mind for a moment… Henry Kyle… sure… he remembered. It was just as he was healing from his fight with Crowe. The funeral passed by on the street in front of Doc's. "So… where's this Kyle place, Doc Watters' new place." Shank drew a crude map in the earth for Blake showing him where Doc's was, and a back-way for him to get there unnoticed by Crowe, or Profit, or anyone else.   "You're welcome to stay the night, Mr. Shank. Then tomorrow when you leave, gather what men you can and meet me at Doc's," Newt instructed. "We both got the same purpose in mind, I'd guess. Oh, and Ira, come in after dark."

Chapter Seven

As soon as daylight broke at Doc Waters' place, Molly Carpenter took it upon herself to begin scrubbing the bloodstain left on Doc's front porch floor by the injured Ransom Feltus the night before. The two of them, Doc and Molly, were headed down a path leading to a relationship. Molly had left the saloon, moved into a spare room at Doc's, and had given up her former career as a whore in favor of becoming Doc Waters' nursing assistant. She had designs on the other half of Doc's sleeping quarters in the near future as well. She thought Doc saw her design as winning out in the end. But for now, Ransom Feltus' blood needed scrubbed up. Time would see to the other.

Molly was far too involved in her work to hear anyone approach. She jumped when Newton Blake said, "Not that I mind the view (she was on hands and knees, backside poking into the air), but I never thought I'd see you in such a position, at least not on a porch."

"Jesus Christ, Newt! You scared the shit out of me." She stood. "We thought you were dead. Where the hell have you been? Wait till Doc gets a look at you."

"Calm down, Molly. Is Doc inside?" he asked.

"Yeah! He sure is."

Newt looked up the street toward town. "I need a place to hide this horse. Then Doc and me need to talk

— you too."

"There's an old shed out back. Bring your horse. He'll be comfy there, and he'll be hidden. Then we'll see Doc," Molly said.

Newt's horse having been unsaddled and unbridled, and put up in the shed out back, Molly took Newt to Doc Waters. "Look what I found," she told Waters.

Doc looked at Newt as though he was a ghost. "I thought you were dead. The whole town thinks you're dead."

"That might've been of some help," Newt suggested, "if Crowe didn't know I'm alive. He come looking for me, him and those two hard-cases. Found me, too. Bad for his two sidekicks."

"How's that?" Doc asked.

"I killed them," Newt explained and went on to describe his complete ordeal, beginning with the night Crowe and a couple others who he could not name attacked, beat, and tarred and feathered him, then dumped him near Libby Tilden's place, to when Crowe and his guys showed for an ambush. "Profit might have been there too."

"Did you say Profit?" Doc asked. "Our constable? That Profit?"

"That was him. But I gotta say, Doc, I didn't exactly see him at the tar and feathering. I just know what Libby Tilden told me. It seems her husband, a miner named Carl Tilden, got himself tarred and feathered, then hung in his front yard."

"I remember. That happened shortly after I came here," Doc said. "Tragic. Rumor is, their little girl found him hanging in the tree in their own front yard."

"That's pretty close to the truth, I recon. I think

the little girl and the woman were together when they found him."

"That's awful, but how does that implicate Profit?" Doc asked.

"The woman said she saw a truck out in front of her place that morning. Whoever drove it watched her and her daughter, and kept on watching after Libby sent the little girl inside and came back out alone to cut Carl down from the tree. Then she saw him drive off and as he turned the corner at the end of her street, she swears she saw a star on the truck's door. It had to be Constable Profit."

"Then he must have thrown in with the Klan. That tar and feather treatment, that's one of the Klan's. That explains a great deal," Doc said.

"Explains what?" Molly asked.

"Amos Profit's been acting mighty peculiar of late. He's been digging for information from Otis down at the general store, accusing the council of things, wrecked the town's truck, hanging out with Crowe down at the Red Rose, and I guess the Iron Man too — all sorts of things."

"Accusing the council? Of what, Doc," Newt asked.

"Of wanting to take his job away for one. Otis tells me Profit thinks you're after it."

Newt thought it through. Logic was telling him Profit found out he was a lawman. *Time to come clean,* he thought. "I'm going to tell the two of you something and I need your word you won't pass it along." He did not wait for a response. "I'm here at the request of the town council. Otis himself sent for me." He pulled a badge from a jacket pocket and slapped it on the table. "I'm a US Marshal. I came here to investigate the activities of the Klan and to put an end to them here in Calumet if I can. It's my guess Amos Profit found out I'm a lawman. I'll bet that's what's leading him to think I've been brought in to replace him."

"Why don't we just fill him in?" Molly suggested. "He'll back you then, won't he?"

"Profit's a whore," Doc said. "No offence, Molly, I just mean he'll throw in with anybody, but he won't ever be a man we can trust. A man who's crossed over, even for a good reason, will do it again, only the next time, he won't need a reason. Besides, didn't you hear? He was in on the tar and feathering."

"I said probably, Doc, not for sure. But Doc's right, Molly. We'll move without Profit. At least then I won't be tempted to kill him," Newt said. "Now... what about this Ransom Feltus? Is he still alive?"

"Yeah! I think he'll make it too," Doc said. "Gonna have a sore head for a time, but he'll pull out of it."

"What did Crowe have on him, I mean, why the beating."

"It seems Crowe needed the telephone — likely wanted to call in replacements for them two you done in — and Rans had broken the line, put the telephone out of commission. At least it was told to Crowe that way. Whether he did or not, who knows, but Crowe took it out on him anyway. He would have done a whole bunch worse if he knew who Rans really is." Doc suddenly looked to the side and clammed up.

"Better tell him, Doc," Molly said.

Doc looked at Molly, then at Newt, then back at Molly, "I recon your right. Newt, Ransom Feltus is a union leader sent here from St. Paul to help organize the workers out at the mine. That's what this whole thing is about, just in case you haven't guessed by now. The company knows there's union among them, but don't know who. They brought in Crowe... well the Klan... they sent Crowe, to put an end to the workers organizing." Doc shook his head in sudden sadness. "I'm guessing there'll be a bunch more blood before this is over."

"I recon you're right, Doc," Newt agreed. "The problem is though, blood is Crowe's business. And to make it worse, I have to say it's mine too. And to make it worse than that, I need to let you know what else is going on." Then Newt filled Doc and Molly in on his chance meeting with Ira Shank out in the woods and the plan they came up with to meet up at Doc's. "I'm afraid I've brought the two of you into this too."

"This is our town too," Molly said. "Ain't it, Doc?"

Waters looked out at the stain on his front porch. "Yes it is, Molly, and that makes it our fight too."

Amos Profit slept later than normal. He had taken one of the cell bunks the night before, not caring to go home, really, not wanting anyone to see him on horseback rather than behind the wheel of his truck, something he considered as much a badge of his high office as the tin star on his chest. When he strolled out sleepy eyed into his office he found his chair occupied by Emil Crowe. "You gotta do something 'bout Blake," Crowe told him.

"I did," Amos said. "I hauled his ass way out in the middle of nowhere, just like ya told me to." He swiped at the sleep in his eyes and tried to focus. "What're you doin' in my chair, Crowe?"

"You was also supposed to see to it he was dead, and as you know, Newton Blake ain't dead!" Crowe said sharply.

"I know that, but how the hell…"

"You didn't get the job done, that's how the hell," Crowe said as he stood. "You weren't just supposed to dump him, you were told to plug him too. You didn't finish him off and now my two guys are dead instead of him. And guess what, Profit."

"What?"

"Now you get to finish the job." Crowe said.

"I ain't seen Blake around here since the night we tarred and feathered him. You even sure it was him that jumped you and your guys?"

"It was him, alright. I seen 'im with my own eyes, and he was plenty healthy fer a dead man." Crowe shook his head back and forth. "Hard to believe, Profit. I send you to kill a man and instead of finding' 'im dead, I find 'im shackin' up with some sweet young widow."

"Nothin' I can do 'bout that, now is there?"

"You're probably right since nothin's what you do best! You'll just screw it up again and I'll lose more men. No, Profit, you stay out of it. I'll take care of Blake this time and it'll be done right. Now… I'll need your telephone, and I need you to get me past that nosey operator. Can you do that without too much trouble?" He slid the telephone across the desk. "There's some of my people in Hibbing. Get me through to the mayor over there."

Profit pulled the earpiece from its cradle. "Mary Belle?" Pause, then, "Mary Belle, connect me to the Hibbing operator — long distance. I need to talk to…" Crowe hit his hand with the butt of his gun to stop him from saying more. "Just get me the Hibbing operator," he said.

~*~

Ira Shank rode into the logging camp that was north of Calumet. The Jensen Farm, a two hundred-sixty acre dairy and timber spread which employed in excess of twenty men, was once his home. He had been a farmer by summer, logger by winter from when he was a boy until he decided to give mining a try and moved to Calumet. The twenty men he left behind, all strong, all good with a gun, having been seasoned by the now gone cowboy days, and most itching for the fight of that by-gone era, greeted him with cheerfulness. He had been a favorite among the men and was missed by all. So naturally, recruiting for his upcoming war with the authorities of the mining company and the KKK thugs they had employed, two groups these men held in low regard to begin with, Ira found easy. "Speak the word, Ira, and we'll be with you," was the common response from his old workmates. One day's rest, one night's sleep, and Ira Shank would leave the Jenson farm with old man Jenson's blessing and six of the toughest hands the Jenson operation had ever known.

~*~

Hibbing, Minnesota

Emil Crowe had set out on the trail to Hibbing as soon as his call from Amos Profit's phone was completed. It had been a formal request for permission to hand-pick as many Klansmen as he felt he needed to defeat the union agitators who were causing all the trouble there in Calumet. It had been suggested that, so long as he was able to convince his superiors that the end result would be a stronghold for the KKK on that end of the Mesabi Iron Range, it was possible he would get his wish.

Crowe was convincing. The Klan agreed the situation offered them opportunity. They had position in Hibbing, some holding public office, others merely influential, but the other end of the range had so far been unattainable. Grand Rapids, a paper town slightly beyond the west end of the Mesabi, forty-five miles away from Hibbing, was a prize they needed to win. Between it and Hibbing lay several mining communities, Calumet close to the middle. The taking of Calumet by preventing miner and union joining, the Klan considered the key to it all. That's why they sent Crowe, not one of their brightest but certainly one of their more ruthless, when the mining company first petitioned them for help. Other small communities would certainly follow Calumet's lead and Klan members would spread like locusts, and would be at the coveted paper town's border in no time at all.

That was the plan; Calumet was the key. When Emil Crowe rode into Hibbing behind the wheel of the mining company's truck, he would get the truckload of fellow Klansmen he needed.

~*~

The trail from Jenson's farm and logging camp

Virgil Dare, an aging gunslinger whose prime had come and gone with the turn of the century, led the hands from the Jenson outfit. His hope for a long time now had been to go out in a blaze of glory. He saw his old friend Ira Shank's issues with the Klan and the mining company as the dream come true opportunity which he was beginning to think would never present itself. He had even given thought recently to doing as Butch Cassidy had done, head out toward Bolivia, or Mexico, or any of a number of other places rumored to still live by the gun. He had been thinking along such lines since the doctor had given him a long face, that look, which told him his time was growing short. Virgil Dare had no desire to run out his life as a farmer or a logger. Where was the glory in that? The trouble Ira and the other miners had evolving at the moment was welcome news. Virgil packed everything he might need. He packed things he would not need. He packed as though his journey to Calumet would be one-way. "Woody," he told a crony who would not be joining the fight, "somethin' goes sour, send my gray suit to the undertaker down in Calumet." And he mounted his horse for the twenty-six mile ride to the mining town.

~*~

Ransom Feltus moaned in his bed at Doc Waters' place. He cocked his head to one side as Molly Carpenter placed a cool cloth on his forehead. "Doc," she shouted, "I think he's coming around."

Chapter Eight

Libby Tilden paced the floor of the tiny farmhouse her father had left to her. She wondered if Newton Blake was alright. She worried over how she had treated him three days before, the day after he killed two intruders on her property and buried them nearby, the day he packed his things and lit out for Calumet where he was undoubtedly headed to a war he might well end up a casualty of. She was ashamed. "That was no way to treat anyone, Libby," she scolded herself in a soft yet audible voice. "Especially someone you love."

"Who you talkin' to, Mama?" Clara had been playing quietly on the front porch. Libby had thought her to be further away, beyond earshot. She walked into the house, screen door slapping shut behind her.

"Clara, how many times have I told you? Don't let that door slam. Pity sakes, child. One of these times you'll frighten me right out of my skin."

"Sorry, Mama," Clara apologized. She wondered how her mother might look without her skin. She looked around the room — no one in sight. "Who was ya talkin' to?"

"Myself, child. Just myself."

"Why?" She studied her mother's face for a moment. She looked sad. It made Clara sad. It made her think. "Will Newt come back, Mama?"

"Maybe," she answered. Then she turned away. A

tear came to her eye and slid down her cheek. She did not wish for Clara to see it. "Now… go back out and play for a bit while I get supper ready."

Libby returned to her thoughts. She silently prayed for God to watch over Newton Blake. She saw in him a future for her and Clara and she did not want it to be anything like their past. She prayed all the while she cooked supper. And when she was done, she put on a bright smile and called Clara back in to eat. After supper they would play a game, the same game they had played before Newt left for Calumet.

~*~

Doc Waters' place

"Easy," Doc told Ransom Feltus. "Don't you go thrashing around and get yourself bleeding, Rans. You got quite a gash on your noggin, and you lost about all the blood you can afford to give up."

"How long have I been here?" Rans asked.

"Two days," Molly said.

"What's the whore doing here?" Ransom Feltus scowled.

"Saving you from the grave. Now… you'll treat her with respect, or I'll throw your sorry ass out of here and you can be back on your way to that grave."

"Respect's something you earn," Feltus obstinately insisted.

"Then there's the kind you teach. Want some of that?" Doc glared at his patient, then getting no response continued. "Help me here, Molly. Let's get him to his feet."

"What for?" Molly asked.

"I'm tossing him out of here," Doc said angrily. "That's for what!"

"Hold on there, Doc," you can't…"

"The hell I can't, and it's exactly what I intend, you don't do some fast apologizing." Doc gave a silent count of five, then reached for Ransom Feltus' shoulder to pull him up.

"Sorry, Ma-am. I'm just a bit out of sorts, that's all. Must be the pain."

Molly smiled. She knew it would be an uphill climb with no end, this getting the men of Calumet to respect her. She had bedded far too many of them to think otherwise, but she appreciated Doc's effort on her behalf just the same. "Thanks, Doc," she said.

"He starts in again, Molly, you come for me. We'll open that wound back up for him. That's what we'll do alright." Then he stomped out of the room and slammed the door behind himself, just for effect.

Molly rung out a cloth and laid it across Feltus' forehead. Ransom Feltus relaxed his neck muscles, let his eyelids close gently, and took in a deep breath. He was asleep before he was done exhaling.

~*~

Newt Blake angled back against his saddle in the lean-to behind Doc's house and closed his eyes. He chose the shed over the house as his resting place partly because he wanted privacy and partly because he wanted to protect the element of surprise he felt might be essential for success in his upcoming battle with the mining company and the Klan. Doc's house might be quiet, or it might get busy. He didn't know. But he reasoned at the very least, this Feltus fellow might receive a visitor — a wife perhaps, if he even had one, or a coworker — whatever. Anyone, friend or foe, shows up at Docs and they'll carry with them the ability of ruining the surprise, wanting to or not, if they saw Newt there. So he rested — in peace and quiet — out of site and away from the house. He fell asleep, and as he slept, he dreamed. His vision took him twenty miles south, to Libby Tilden's farmhouse. It was night and Libby's little one, Clara, was fast asleep. He and Libby had hauled in many loads of firewood that evening, enjoyed a tasty meal, played a board game with Clara, and were now sitting quietly in front of a stone fireplace enjoying the heat and each other equally. Their conversation, going from small talk to questions and answers about the Newton Blake of before Calumet, to talk of Libby's life before and after Carl, finally came to a still silence where the couple simply looked at one another. The next step, both of them knew, should they sit in front of the fire any longer, would be a kiss. Newt began to rise, gentleman that he was, to release Libby from any discomfort she might feel. She locked her hand on the tail of his shirt. She pulled him back down. She stared into his eyes and kissed him hard and long on the lips, her mouth slightly open, her tongue probing passionately.

A sudden noise woke him, his handgun appearing lightning-quick, hammer pulled back and ready to fire.

"You always were quick with that thing, Newt."

"Jesus, Molly! You trying to get yourself killed?"

"I just thought you might be hungry," Molly said as she placed a tin plate in front of him on the dirt floor. "You know, there's a house right there. No need to be out here in the sand, unless you're thinkin' that horse of yours will get lonely."

"I don't want to take the chance," Newt said.

"Chance of what?"

"Chance of somebody seeing me here, of word getting out that I'm in town."

"I doubt that'll happen. Ransom Feltus ain't got no kin. Chance of a friend visiting is slim. These miners are usually working or sleeping or at the saloon drinking. I outta know." She smiled cynically. "Just the same though, if you're scared of being spotted, there's a pantry off the back of the kitchen. Good sized room too — and empty. Doc hasn't been here long enough to fill it up. Why not let me fix you up in there. I'll see to it, me and Doc will, if someone shows, they won't get back there. How's that?"

Newt picked up his plate and followed Molly to the pantry. He didn't treasure the thought of spending the night with his horse anyway, despite the fact he had done so many times in his life. That last time, the night Ira Shank disturbed his sleep, the cool damp ground left him stiff and sore — scarcely able to ride the next day. He blamed age for that, or possibly the tar and feathering. Whatever it was that caused it, if he slept inside, he would not need to relive that experience. His tired bones and muscles would surely thank him for his wise choice.

~*~

Hibbing, Minnesota

"How's your bid for town mayor coming, Crowe?" Isaac Burris, leader of the KKK faction in Hibbing asked.

"Otis Johnson has a lot of support but most votes

come from miners. You give me what I need and I'll see to it those votes is cancelled."

"Big words!" Burris said. "But... can we trust them?"

"I swear, Mr. Burris, it's true. He ain't got no other voters but a few of the town elders. The miners I got scared enough they won't dare vote for Johnson. All I need is men to back me, so I can keep it that way, and Otis Johnson don't stand no chance."

Isaac Burris wished he had time. Crowe was uneducated and unintelligent to boot. Had the KKK thought there might be a way to get one of theirs in the Calumet Mayor's Office this election, they might have sent Crowe in for muscle, but they would not have sent him in alone. But it was late in the game. Elections were weeks away now and closing fast, too fast to make changes. It worried Burris that this Crowe had become his only chance, the Klan's only chance, of getting into power in Calumet. "I hope you're right, Crowe. We need that office."

"We'll get it. You just give me the men. We'll get it."

Burris knew Crowe had been told he would be able to hand-pick his crew to take back to Calumet with him, but Burris had never met Crowe before, and now that he had, he didn't trust his judgment. "I'll help you find the right men for the job."

"But I was told I could pick 'em myself," Crowe objected.

"That's changed," Isaac Burris insisted. "You wait outside, Mr. Crowe. We," he hand gestured toward a small gathering of men in his office, "will hash this over for a moment or two. Someone will come for you shortly."

"But I see no reason for this," Crowe began to protest. But Burris motioned with his eyes to one of his people, and Emil Crowe was promptly escorted out of the room.

"Send him with half a dozen good men. Then we'll send along another dozen he don't know about to raise a little hell with the miners, keep things stirred up so he stands a chance of victory."

"What'll we do if he does win?" someone asked.

"Who has Crowe chosen to be his deputy mayor?" Burris asked.

"Rumor has it it'll be the town constable, a man named Profit."

Burris looked around the room curiously. He had been keeping an eye and an ear on things in Calumet, or at least he thought he had. "I thought that fellow was going to be Otis Johnson's second."

"What can I say?" one of his guys, the man primarily responsible for keeping Burris abreast of any political developments in Calumet, commented. "It's Calumet. They've never had an election before. This Profit, he plans to be Deputy Mayor of Calumet no matter who wins, I guess."

Burris looked around in disbelief. Then he smiled broadly. "It does simplify things. I'll have to admit that. Now here's what we'll do. Send Tully Backus over there. He's personable. Have him get close to Otis Johnson in case he wins. If Otis Johnson wins, he puts Profit in place, we kill Profit and help Otis pick Tully to succeed Profit. Then we kill Otis. And we own the town. Now, let's say our man Crowe gets in. He chooses Profit, we kill Profit, and Crowe appoints Tully. Anybody else got a better plan? No? Then bring Crowe back in here. And somebody find Tully Backus for me."

"Mr. Crowe," Burris started, "I'm sending you back to Calumet with six of our best men. See to it you make good use of them, understand?"

"Yes, sir."

"Good day then, Crowe. These men will assist you." He pointed out two of the men in his company and went back to a pile of papers on his desk.

Crowe followed Burris's two guys from the building and into a saloon down the street where Burris's men, not Crowe, picked out six good men.

Chapter Nine

Calumet, Doc Waters' place

"I heard some voices," Ransom Feltus started. "Who you got out back?"

"Nobody of interest to you," Doc told him. He had just come into the room to change the dressing on Rans' head-wound, and to see if it was healing. "Looking pretty fair," Doc commented.

"How long do I need to stay here?" Feltus asked.

Doc was still upset with Feltus over his comments about Molly. He didn't want the man in his house a minute longer than needed. "Until you're rested and healed a bit. I wouldn't want you to go out too soon and get yourself to bleeding again."

"I find that Crowe, and there's gonna be plenty of blood. You'll see."

"Nice to see you're temper flaring again, Rans. That can only mean one thing. You're on your way to mend," Doc said. He wound the bandage back in place. "Molly will see to it you get something to fill that stomach. That might help to improve your temper as well." He fastened the bandage in place and left the room in search of Molly. He found her in the pantry talking with Newt.

"Might have to hand feed 'im, Molly, but I think once he's ate, we'll hear no more from him tonight," Doc said. Then, after Molly left the room, Doc struck up a conversation with Newt. "How well do you know her?" he asked.

"Molly? Pretty good I recon," Newt answered. "Why?" He studied Doc's expression for a moment. "Why, Doc Waters, you sly old fox. You're getting a feeling for that gal." Doc looked down at the floor. "C'mon. Admit it."

"What if I am?"

Newt smiled. "She's a fine woman, Doc. You won't do better. I mean, sure, she's had her ups and downs, led a sorted life — due to no fault of her own I assure you — but she's always held her head high and done the best she could. She's a strong woman and I can tell she likes you."

"You know, Newt," Doc Waters changed the subject. "You never did tell me how you let somebody get the jump on you like that."

Newt felt almost embarrassed at his only answer. It was like something some fool lets happen, not him. "I left your place," Newt started, "that smelly salve of yours smeared all over me and stinking to high heaven, anyway, when I came out of the door it was dark and drizzling. I couldn't see a thing. I suppose I was trying so hard to focus on the street I didn't pay no attention to the fellow creeping up behind me. I got clubbed good and hard, then two of them drug me out behind the building. I was still awake when I got there but hurting something awful. I couldn't fight. Hell... I couldn't move."

"You hear who was doing the dragging?"

"There was two of them. One was your constable. Didn't think so till recently, but now? Yeah, I'm pretty sure it was him. The other one I didn't know."

"Profit? Amos Profit clubbed you?" Doc sounded

surprised. Profit was the kind, or so Doc saw him, who let someone else do the dirty work. "I don't get it. He's a bully, but he ain't a brave one." Doc thought it over a bit, then let it go. "So… where did you get hauled off to?"

"Ain't rightly sure, Doc. Some broke-down old barn a good distance from town, at least it took a bit of time to get there."

"What did they want from you, Newt?" Waters asked.

"I'm not sure. None of them ever said."

"What'd they do then, I mean once they got you to the barn?"

"Well… first they tied me to a fence gate and beat the shit out of me." Newt explained.

"You see who any of them were then?"

"Nah! By then they all had hoods on."

"Then what happened?" Doc asked.

"I really don't recall much after that. I guess that's when they tarred and feathered me. I woke up, don't rightly know how much later, in a featherbed twenty miles from Calumet. It was a woman who lived on the farm and her little girl who found me in a stand of bushes and nursed me back."

"Jesus," Molly said appearing in the doorway. "That must have been awful."

"Likely not as bad as it could have been," Newt said.

"How's that?" Molly asked.

"I hear tell that tar hurts like hell. I was past hurting when they did that."

"I don't know as I would have had courage to come back to Calumet had I been in your shoes," Doc admitted. "You got guts, Newt. I'll give you that."

"Or he's stupid as hell," Molly said.
"Oh, I almost moved on once I started to heal up," Newt said.
"What stopped you?" Doc said.
"I told you, Doc. I got rescued by a woman and her little one, a widow, that Libby Tilden, a mighty handsome widow, too."
"I see," Doc said.

~*~

On the trail from the Jenson farm

Ira Shank's spine sounded like the shuffle of a deck of cards when he dismounted his horse. "Jesus, Ira, you okay?" Virgil Dare asked him.
"Ain't done this much ridin' since I logged with you fellers. My back's just objectin' a bit, that's all."
"From the sound of it, that's enough," Virgil said. "Seems mining's made you soft."
"For ridin' maybe," Ira admitted, "but not for fightin'. You'll soon see." He pulled the reigns from the horse's neck and tied him to a bush. Virgil Dare followed suit.
The other Jenson hands lagged a bit behind, one of them having to stop with a busted cinch strap, the rest choosing to rest their horses while he made the repair. Virgil and Ira rode ahead in search of a good campsite. They would enter Calumet in the morning, early, before daybreak. And they would meet up with Newton Blake at Doc Waters' place then, under cover of darkness, so no one could spot them and report their numbers to Crowe and his bunch. It made good sense. At last count, they would not be outnumbered, but things

might well have changed.

"How many we got on our side, Ira," Virgil asked.

"Now's a good time to ask," Ira said. "Seems to me, that might be something a feller might need to know before he signs on."

"And some years back I would have asked. Back then it would have been useful to know. These days I'm just curious."

"Well then, it really won't bother you much if I tell you I don't know," Ira said and tossed an armload of firewood he had gathered on the ground. "Got a match?" he asked. "You get the fire going and I'll get some beans and coffee out of my bag." Provisions had been gathered for the trip, courtesy of Jenson's farm.

Virgil fumbled with the fire for a spell, then Ira approached. "What's the matter, Virg? Forget how to light a fire?"

"Arthritis, the doc says. Hits me some times and I can't seem to grip hard enough to light a match."

"Well how the hell you gonna shoot?"

"Oh, now, don't you go worryin' about that. When shootin' time comes 'round, I'll be shootin'. You just watch and see," Virgil Dare insisted. He cocked his head suddenly, gun drawn lightning quick and aimed toward the brush. "Hear that?"

"Didn't hear nothin'," Ira Shank said. He looked with amazement at the gun in Virgil Dare's hand. *Arthritis my ass,* he thought.

"Comin' in," someone shouted from the brush. Dare relaxed and holstered his gun.

Dexter Connors popped out of the bushes grinning. Dex was a youngster compared to Virgil Dare, and serious about little. He was undisciplined, so much so that Virgil felt as though he needed to watch out for him at all times. He liked Dex, enjoyed his lighthearted sense of humor, his madcap way of dealing with the serious issues, his admiration of the ladies and theirs toward him, and he didn't mind at all looking after the kid, but sometimes the relationship could leave Virgil a bit on the vulnerable side. Often he paid too much attention to what Dexter Connors was up to and too little to what a potential enemy was up to. Men who did such a thing when Virgil Dare was Dexter Connors' age, generally didn't live long. Virgil was almost sorry he had allowed Dex along on this ride. "Best lose that boyish grin of yours before we reach Calumet, Boy, or you'll get yourself killed, likely me along with you."

Connors drew his gun. He was quick as Virgil. "They won't be getting me, Virg. Ain't none of those Klan fellers can outdraw my gun-hand."

"You're likely right, but you best grow some eyes on the back of your head as well. You'll be needing them before this is over."

Dexter Connors slapped his gun back in its holster nearly as quick as he had removed it and settled into the dirt beside the fire, Indian style. "Rest of them will be along shortly, that is, if they don't get lost. Say, where are we anyway?"

"About a mile from Calumet," Ira Shank offered. "We'll head in before dawn."

A noise a few yards into the surrounding woods caught everyone's attention. Certain it was the remainder of their men finally catching up with them, no one gave it much thought at first, then, as time passed, Virgil Dare became nervous. He shot Ira Shank a quick glance that said sit tight, be silent, then he motioned to Dexter Connors. Dex knew what Vergil wanted. He wanted Dex to look into the disruption — without detection. Dex drew a finger silently across his throat, his way of asking Virgil if he should kill any intruder he might find. Virgil shook his head and pointed at the ground in front of him. He wanted to question him if it did indeed turn out to be someone listening to their conversation.

As Dexter Connors shifted casually and slid back away from the fire, he became invisible, blending into the dark of the trees at his back. Then he rose and made his way silently to the position where the noise had come from, cautious to approach from behind. If someone was spying on them, all attention would be aimed toward the campfire.

Riders approached from the north, no one taking care to hide their advance. Dex knew it was the rest of his gang. He stood still, watching the man in front of him redirect his attention to the newcomers. The stranger parted the branches of a sapling and appeared to be counting the men on horseback. Then he turned to face the barrel of Dex's six-gun and to hear the sound of its hammer being pulled back. "Let's go!" Dex ordered. "Over to the fire." And as the stranger turned, Dex slid a hand around and disarmed him.

"Who's your new friend?" One of the Jenson cowboys asked as he watched Dex march his captive into the open.

"Mister!" Virgil started, ignoring the cowboy's question. "You got one hell of a lot of explaining to do, that is if you plan to walk out of here alive."

Chapter Ten

"What'll we do with 'im, Virg?" Dexter Connors asked. He pushed the intruder, a slight man, not much of a build for a mining community like Calumet Dex thought, into the dirt across the campfire from Virgil Dare.

"That's a good place for him, Dex," Virgil said. "Now, just who are you, Mister, and what're you doin' spyin' on us?"

The man remained silent. Virgil nodded at Dexter. Dex tapped him on the back of the head with the butt of his six-shooter just hard enough to let him know his silence was not a wise choice. "Okay! My name is Lawrence Fish. I'm the assistant to Randal Parks, mining company supervisor, and I came out here because I saw your fire. You fellows are on mining company land you know."

"Well…apologies, Mr. Fish. I did not know this was mining company land," Virgil said then nodded again to Dex who promptly butted Fish with his gun one more time. Fish glared in amazement at Virgil. Virgil's eyes took on a hard cold look. "Now… I'll ask it again. What the hell are you spyin' on us for?"

Fish stared. Virgil nodded again. Dex lifted his gun arm. "Okay! Enough. I'll tell you whatever you want to know."

"Then start!" Virgil ordered. "I'm getting tired of waitin' on you."

"It was Mr. Parks. He's the one who saw the fire

and sent me out here. He told me to find out who you are and what you're up to," Fish confessed.

"Well, Mr. Fish, we're hands from the Jenson dairy farm, about twenty five miles north of here," Virgil explained, "and we're just passing through on our way south to pick up a hundred head of milk cows and drive them back. That suit your Mr. Parks, you recon?"

"I imagine it will," Fish got to his feet. Then he turned and came face to face with Ira Shank. He paused.

"Mr. Fish," Ira said.

"Ira. What are you doing out here with these drovers?"

"Visitin'," Ira said. "I was one of 'em before I started mine work."

"One of them, or a cowpoke?" Fish asked for clarification. His manner more imperious now that he discovered a subordinate in the group.

"One of them," Ira said. "I come from the Jenson spread to Calumet. These fellers are my old bunkmates." Ira, along with Virgil Dare who had been watching things cautiously, could clearly tell from Fish's expression that he had bought the story. Ira added, "I should have told these fellers they was on company land. I'm sorry. I didn't give it no thought, I was so pleased to see 'em again."

"Well… no harm done. You fellows will be gone in the morning, I take it."

"Yes, sir. We surely will," Virgil Dare agreed.

"Then," Fish rubbed his head for a moment, "No harm. I'll just be on my way. Good evening, gentlemen."

"Dex," Virgil whispered a few moments after Fish

disappeared into the woods, "follow him. See where he goes and who he talks to. See if you can get close enough to hear."

~*~

In the town of Calumet

Late in the evening, Otis Johnson splashed cold water over his face, cautious that the excess would fall into the basin and not on his floor. He was a neat freak. Never mind that his floor was made of cheap pine shiplap boards, he did not want anything staining it just the same.

Owen Pruitt, Calumet's undertaker stood at the top of Otis's stairs, waiting for him to finish getting the soap out of his eyes. The time had come for that talk Owen had been putting off far too long, since the day Crowe and his men first showed their faces in town. He watched Otis fold his towel with meticulous precision. He had enough. "Christ sakes, Otis. Just lay the towel down and talk."

"What do you want me to talk about? What do you want me to say?"

"You can start by answering my question."

"You mean, do I think there's a war coming?" Otis said. "Yeah. I think there'll be a war, one hell of a war, too. I don't see how there can't be one. We have the first election in Calumet history. Until now, the mining company has run most things, and soon, elected officials will. That puts all of us, especially those of us running for office, against the mines. And to add to it all, I'm told that fellow Doc Watters has down at his place, the man Crowe shovel-whipped and left for dead, he's a union organizer of sorts. Now Crowe doing that to a union man, why that'll put the union and the miners in an uproar against the Klan, and the mines, having brought the Klan in, will be joining that fight, and, of course, there are the mines and the Klan. What do suppose will happen when the mining company figures out that the Klan's only interested in helping them so long as there's something in it for the Klan, and the mines hold out on the Klan? What happens then? Why, this is all one big goddamn mess, Owen. That's what this is."

"I figured."

"Well then, if you already figured, why are you here?"

"I'm here to see if there's something we need to be doing," Owen said.

"Like what?"

"Like, maybe moving some of the folks out of town for a time: innocents, school children and their teacher, the women."

"I recon we should, Owen," Otis Johnson agreed.

"Want me to tell Profit to see to it?"

"I don't trust Profit. You best see to it."

"But I thought, I mean, everyone thinks Profit will be Deputy Mayor if you win."

"Everyone including Profit," Johnson admitted, "everyone but me. No! No Amos Profit. You see to it. And while you're at it, Owen, see to it you have plenty of coffins on hand. You'll be needing them. Now, if you're done, I'd like to go to bed."

~*~

Back at the trail camp cowboys slept. Dexter

Connors did not return until nearly midnight, but when he did return he felt his report for Virgil Dare urgent enough to wake Virgil from his sound sleep. It had been a long stretch since old instincts had been needed, so Dex was more than surprised when one touch on the shoulder brought the barrel of Virgil's Colt to within six inches of his face in the blink of an eye. "Jesus, Virg! Don't shoot me," Dex shouted, and everyone in the camp was awake, guns in hands, pointing at Dexter Connors. "Jesus Christ!" he said excitedly.

Pistols slid back into leather. "You been gone long enough," Virgil Dare said. "What'd you learn?"

"There's a feller name of Emil Crowe. You know who that is, Ira?"

"I sure do. Crowe's the Klan leader at the Calumet mine. Real mean son-of-a-bitch, too."

"Well… this Crowe, he went to Hibbing and according to that skinny weasel that was spyin' on us and his boss over at the mine, I heard the boss man on the phone, then talkin' to the weasel later, anyway, according to what I heard this Crowe feller, he's bringin' six Klansmen back with him. That's not much. We can handle six Klansmen and get back to the farm by nightfall," Dex said with a grin.

"You ain't got a clue, Kid," Ira Shank broke in. "Six Klan's bad. Crowe only had two at the last and 'e still road roughshod over the miners. You got no idear what these Klansmen have in 'em. They're mean. They're cruel. They're able to do the unthinkable to another man without blinkin'. And they're tough, tough enough to get away with it, specially out at the mine where the only law is them. Now if Crowe's bringin' six more, if they're anything mean as Crowe, it'll be like a dozen. Then there's Profit. Rumor says he's lookin' to join with the winning side. You watch. Amos Profit will surely be right in there with Crowe and his six before we know it."

"Wow! Now there's a mouthful of fear," Dex said. "Is there more, Ira?"

"You bet your young ass there's more. The preachers of the whole area, the protestant ones, Baptists and such, they may not be Klan, but they sure think like 'em, specially toward Catholics, and we got a ton of Catholics hereabouts. Wouldn't surprise me none to see some of the religions throwin' in with the Klan."

"So we got a half-dozen tough guys and a handful of preachers," Dex said.

"Seven. You're forgettin' Crowe. Eight if Profit joins 'em. And it ain't the preachers. Not likely to see any of them armed and dangerous. It'll be those they preach to, and we won't know who they are. They'll be miners like me."

"Okay!" Virgil Dare threw in. "That's enough. Dexter here, he's just trying to get your goat, Ira, that's all. Now Dex, you be a good lad, shut your mouth for a while, and shut your eyes too. You'll need to be fresh as you can come morning." Virgil laid his head against his saddle and closed his eyes. " Dex?" he said.

"Yeah, Boss."

"Them mining company fellows, they say anything about us?"

"Oh, they said plenty. We ain't got 'em fooled none. Called us a vigilante bunch. Even told whoever the boss-man was talkin' to on the phone we was out here."

"Great!" Virgil said. "The KKK sympathizers calling us vigilantes. Let's get some sleep, men. We got an early morning ahead."

~*~

Two hours before daybreak in Hibbing, six men, strong and loyal, climbed aboard the Calumet mining company's flatbed truck. This was a mistake and Emil Crowe knew it. These men, Klan that they were, tough that they were, were not of his choosing. There wasn't one among them he actually knew. How, then, was he to lead. Why, then, should they follow.

Crowe settled into the driver's seat and fired up the engine. He leaned out the window and begged Isaac Burris' two men, whose names he had never been told, to think this through and ask their boss to reconsider before it was too late. He argued that he would not have the control needed, that strangers could not be trusted to follow his orders.

"You fellers gonna do as Crowe here says?" one of them yelled out. Boisterous laughter form the back of the truck followed. "Didn't hear any no's, Crowe, so there you are then." He grinned and patted Crowe on the head. "Now get the hell out of here. Go get the job done." And he slammed a palm against the steel of the door. Crowe shifted the truck into gear and started down the dusty trail toward Calumet. He would make only five miles before trouble came.

Emil Crowe pulled into a field just off the roadway. The best he could hope for was a friendly passerby. His tire was flat, not one of the rears, naturally, where they were duals and a truck could limp a fair distance with one of them flat. It just had to be a front. The best the crew could do was get the thing off. Then it would be a waiting game. Crowe knew there was a town ahead, one behind for that matter, Hibbing, but a walk with one of the truck's tires hung from his shoulder seemed undue punishment. God, how he longed for just one of the two men Newton Blake had killed. And the more time that passed, the more angry the thought of Blake getting the jump on him and his men made him. Soon he reached his boiling point. "Somebody got to walk this tire to town," he told the six men who joined him in Hibbing. "Which one of ya's goin'?"

"Why not you, Crowe?" asked a rather large man as he let himself slip from the bed of the truck to the ground where he lit just arms-length in front of Emil Crowe.

Crowe backed off a foot, pulled his knife from its sheath, and lashed out at the man, slicing his shirt open across the midsection without breaking skin. "I guess… that's why not me." The battle was over as quickly as it had begun and the large man was well on his way, tire hanging over one of his massive shoulders, to seek out a repair shop. Crowe sat in the grass on a hillside where he had a good view of the truck and his other five men. He returned to his hatred of and desire for revenge toward Newton Blake. He vowed, once this business in Calumet was settled and he was the new mayor and the Klan was in stronger control of the mine and the town, that he would take the time to travel the twenty miles to where he found Blake before, and he would finish the job once and for all. That is, if Newton Blake wasn't already back in Calumet gunning for him.

Dark began to settle on the Klansmen. No tire had arrived. One of the Hibbing group, a man named Oscar Barlow who, it appeared to Emil Crowe, led the others to some degree, approached Crowe. "We need to set up camp, Crowe. He ain't gonna get back here with that tire before dark. Best we sleep here and set out again at daybreak."

"I'll do the decidin'," Crowe insisted and jumped to his feet ready to defend his position.

"Ain't nobody arguin' that, Crowe. We got our orders. We know you'll be the one in charge of this operation. We've all been told that much." Barlow said.

"Well, then, Oscar Barlow, you and your pals there, you get some firewood and get us a fire goin' so that other feller don't go gettin' himself lost with our tire." It felt right for Crowe to be giving the orders. He sat back in the grass, then he leaned back and shut his eyes. "Barlow," he shouted, his eyes still shut.

"What?"

"Any of you pack food?"

"Nope!"

"Send somebody hunting," Crowe ordered.

"Jackson's a good hunter. I'll sent him."

"Send the rest of them for firewood and get that campfire goin'."

The Klansman named Johnson turned out to be a fine hunter. Partridge would be the main course, and wild yams he dug from the earth between efforts to flush out more of the birds filled out the meal. The large man Crowe had sent off in search of somewhere the tire could be repaired finally returned, hungry and tired, about the time everyone else had settled in for the night and the fire had died to ashes. He would sleep on an empty stomach for his efforts. And he would hold a grudge that would later cost Emil Crowe a great deal.

~*~

At Doc Waters place in Calumet, Waters laid still in his bed — silent. He had no gun. He would have reached for it as soon as he heard the creak of the dry door hinge if he had one. So he lay quiet, waiting in the dark for the intruder to come closer, his plan — to jump from the bed at the last moment and, hopefully, overpower whoever it was before harm could come to him. Surprise would be his only weapon. He waited. The figure drew closer — just a shadow. It stopped at the edge of his bed, then as he began his leap to safety,

"Doc? Are you awake?"

"Molly?"

"Yeah, Doc. It's me."

"What… what do you want?" Doc asked.

"Nothin' really. I just couldn't sleep."

"Something troubling you?"

"Too quiet, Doc. Too lonely. I ain't used to this much silence," Molly explained.

"I imagine so, but I don't know what I can do about it."

"You can shove over, share your bed with me. I wouldn't mind that at all, Doc."

Doc Waters looked at Molly, his eyes more adjusted to the dimness of night. He thought her a handsome woman despite her being a whore. He had thought so since that first day she showed up in Calumet. He would have pursued her then but Doc wasn't the type to pay for a poke nor was he one to share his poke with half the men in town. But she had given up all that now. She had come to work with him in the medical profession. Hell, one might conclude Molly was no longer a whore at all; she was a nurse. Doc pulled back the patchwork quilt on his bed to let her in.

"Thanks, Doc," she said and snuggled in close to him.

Molly fell immediately to sleep.

Doc Waters followed suit, not waking again until just before dawn when he saw a figure standing in the doorway to his room. The aroma of fresh-brewed coffee stopped him from panicking. He rubbed his eyes to clear the sleep. He focused. Newt! It was Newton Blake standing there: back leaning against the jamb, steaming coffee cup in his hand, smile on his face.

"So this is how it is," he commented.

Doc slid from the bed, aligning the bottoms of his long-johns as his bare feet hit the floor. He stood.

"She do that?" Newt asked.

"Did she do what?" Doc asked.

"Check behind you, Doc." And Doc did. The back flap of his long-johns hung open, his backside fully exposed. Doc quickly flopped it up an fumbled for the buttons.

"How the hell can you see that in the dark?" Doc asked. The only light in the room came from a lamp in the hall.

"How could I miss it, lily white ass like that one? It glows in the dark you know."

"Must have worked open during the night," Doc admitted, referring to his open trap.

"Must have," Newt agreed. "Coffee's on. I'll wait for you in the kitchen."

"You do that," Doc insisted.

Waters was surprised to see his patient, Ransom Feltus, in his kitchen drinking coffee with Newton Blake.

"What're you doing out of bed, Rans? Thought

you'd be out of it at least another day," Doc said.

"Seems you're a better doctor than anyone thought," Newt said. "Either that or Mr. Feltus here is a fast healer."

"A bit of both, I recon," Feltus said. "I've been out here getting to know your friend, Newt, here. Seems we're kinda on the same side of things here in Calumet."

"So you are," Doc said.

"We got a plan, Doc. My plan before all of this happened," Feltus gestured to the head wound, "was to get some help in here. The Klan has no idea of giving in you know. I'm guessing Crowe will be heading out for more men anytime."

"I hear he already has," Doc said.

"Then we need to move," Rans said. "Newt has volunteered to go get a telegraph off, since I can't go for another day or two. Got any idea where a telegraph station might be, one they won't know about here in town?"

"Marble's likely got one. Not even a mile west of here."

"I'll set out right away," Newt said. "Ira and his cowboys get in here, I scouted out a camp. It's about a half-mile south. Point them in that direction, Doc, and tell them we'll meet up there. Now, Rans, just who is it I need to telegraph and what should I say?"

Feltus gave Newt the particulars, his boss' name and the union office address and the number of bodies he thought they needed, and he told Newt to make the message sound urgent.

"Doc, I may need to send the union guys here. Then you can send them on to the camp," Newt said.

"They can stay here if you want them to."

"No. That'll ruin the surprise I'm planning for Emil Crowe," Newt said. "And it'll likely put you and Molly in danger to boot. Now... be on the lookout for Ira Shank and his men. They ought to be in here any time. I'll put up in Marble for the night and wait for those union fellows. Just tell Ira I'll see him whenever the others show."

Chapter Eleven

At union headquarters in Saint Paul, Minnesota, Abraham Curran called on his secretary, Dolly Markus. "I want you to find Alexander Penovich for me, and I need him fast," he instructed.

"I'll get right to it, Sir." Dolly said. But she did not make a move to pick up the telephone. Instead she stared at Curran for a moment.

"Is there something, Dolly?" Curran asked her.

"Have you heard anything about Ransom Feltus?"

"I forget, the two of you have some interest in each other, don't you? Ransom Feltus has been injured, attacked by the Klan faction at the Calumet mine. Now don't you go getting all upset girl, he's fine. He's recovering. And I'm told by this Newton Blake up there in Calumet, he'll be back in action in a day or two. Now you go ahead and find Penovich for me. He's needed up there." Curran went back to his desk and began calling men, good strong men who were not afraid of a war. Newton Blake had wired that Ransom Feltus was requesting at least six men to defeat the Klan in Calumet once and for all. Abraham Curran would assemble twelve, and they would be led by Alexander Penovich, the meanest, toughest labor organizer he had in his employ. Curran had been up against situations like this in the past and Penovich was always his answer. And Alexander Penovich side by side with Ransom Feltus, well… that was an unbeatable combination. Curran instructed each of the men called upon to meet up at the rail platform in South St. Paul at three that afternoon and to wait there until Alexander Penovich arrived to take the lead. Penovich showed up just as Curran finished his calls.

"Where am I off to?" Penovich asked.

"Calumet," Curran said.

"Where the hell is that?"

"You'll soon know, and from what I'm told about the town and this job, you won't soon forget."

"So... it's like that again, is it?" Alexander was no stranger to the more difficult and dangerous missions of the union. He seemed always to be on the front line of this tough conflict or that one, and none of them passed without considerable bloodshed. Most did not conclude without considerable loss of life. "Who will I be up against?"

"A mining company as usual, but this one uses the KKK as its muscle."

Penovich rubbed a huge hand through his thick hair. He had dealings with the Klan before, more than once, and these things never ended well. "Will I have help?"

"Ransom Feltus is there. You'll find him at the home of a fellow name of Doc Waters on the edge of town. I'm sending twelve men, thirteen counting you, then there's a man name of Newton Blake, some sort of lawman from Missouri. He claims to have at least another seven or eight men and he's looking for more."

"Rans is a good man. Know anything about this Blake fellow?"

Curran handed him a telegram he had received a short time before from a union office in St. Louis.

"US Marshal, eh? Humph! Well... that's encouraging. Know anything about the men he's got with him?"

"Not a thing," Abraham Curran admitted. "He'll meet up with you at the train station in the little town of Marble. You can ask him then."

Penovich stood. He pulled his jacket over his broad shoulders. He slid a revolver from its holster under his left arm and opened the cylinder to check his ammunition. "Guess I'll go find out. See ya, Abe." And he left Abraham Curran's office for the rail platform in South St. Paul.

~*~

At the Marble depot, Newton Blake could not believe his eyes the next morning as he watched thirteen well armed union men disembarked the train. Should he be encouraged by their numbers, or concerned? Did Ransom Feltus' boss, Abraham Curran, know something he did not know about all of this, like a valid reason why the number of men requested should be more than double? Newt was a man accustomed to the odds being stacked against him, and if that were true this time out, it was about to be one hell of a war he was destined to undertake. "I made arrangements for horses, but not for this many. I doubt the stable has the extra, but, no matter, it's not a long walk to camp," he told Penovich.

"We brought our own," Penovich said, and motioned to one of his men to open the cattle car. "I thought Ransom Feltus might have come along to greet us."

"Rans is still at Doc's. Doc thought his injuries could use another day to heal," Newt said.

"How bad is he hurt?"

"His noggin's got a sizable slice in it. Somebody hit him with a shovel, I hear. He's been in Doc's care long enough he ought to be good to ride by tomorrow — next day, latest." Newt watched as the thirteen men mounted their horses. "I stayed at a boarding house last night, not far from here. There's a woman there who agreed to fix breakfast if you have a mind to eat before we head out. I only told her about the six I asked for though but I doubt she'll object to feeding extras."

"They usually don't. More belly's means more money. Yeah! We could eat," Penovich said. "It'll probably beat the hell out of whatever accommodations you've got at your camp for us."

Newton Blake led the thirteen men to their boardinghouse breakfast then set out on his own, leaving Alexander Penovich with a map to the camp.

By the time Blake arrived back at the campsite south of Calumet, a morning hunt had been in progress for some time. All of the Jenson men except Virgil Dare had gone off, excitement and playfulness at the thought of bagging the outfit's next several meals governing their moods, and were several miles south of the camp by the time daybreak came.

Virgil Dare drifted back in his memory to a peaceful time on the trail of his long past youth. Sleeping under the stars, the quiet of the wilderness, the smell of the open campfire, all stirred his senses and comforted him. He hated progress. He hated towns. In his younger days he had found nothing but trouble in towns: always some bastard looking to enhance his own image by taking on the fast hand of a known gunmen, most of them not living to tell. Always a kid with brute strength and quick fists hoping for a chance to display his pugilistic talents. Always a gambler with a hideout gun looking to catch a slight of hand and when none was available would see one and draw the hideout anyway. Oh… yeah! Virgil hated progress, and he hated towns because they were progress. And together they were why Virgil was this far north, and as he sat basking in his memories, he silently decided that once this was behind him, this latest brush with progress, he would head further north, and he would continue to head north so long as progress chased him, until he runs out of north. Or until he runs out of life.

Dexter Connors was Virgil Dare's reflection in the mirror. He was that kid looking to out-draw the faster gun. He was that youngster with brute strength and quick fists, that carefree reminder of what Virgil Dare had been in his youth, before the time when he came to hate progress and towns. Virgil hated and loved Dexter Connors, hated him for his youth yet loved him like a son who needed his constant eye. And he lived with a persistent fear, a reality maybe, that his abilities would one-day fall short of protecting that son from the faster gun or quicker fist they shared an unquenchable thirst for.

Virgil was so thoroughly wrapped in his thoughts he heard nothing until he heard the click of a Colt hammer being pulled back. He sat in silent thought for a moment. "Newton Blake," he finally said.

"How'd you know it was me?"

"I heard you were in these parts. You're a long way from home, aren't you?"

"I might say the same for you, Virgil," Newt said.

"So how'd you know it was me you was drawin' on?" Virgil Dare asked.

"I only ever saw one man with half his right ear missing. It had to be you."

"Guess you'd recognize it. You shot it off," Dare said. "Guess your shooting was a bit off that day."

"Lucky for you."

"Well, I'm a might tired, too tired to gab, so if your gonna shoot, I'd appreciate your getting on with it."

Newt hammered forward. He needed all the guns he could get right now. He slid his Colt back into his holster. "Not yet, Dare, but before all this is over I plan to haul your smelly carcass back to Missouri and cash it in for the bounty."

"I'll remember that," Dare said.

"You can plan on it," Blake said.

~*~

As morning came on the road from Hibbing, the nearly starved Louis Foss shoveled food in ravenously while two of his companion installed the repaired tire on the mining company's truck. Emil Crowe watched. He did not offer a hand. His treatment of Foss the night before had set him on edge. He knew better. He should never subject a man he might need to place his trust in later to a night's sleep on an empty stomach. But that was Crowe. Sometimes his meanness ran so deep he himself could not understand it, let alone control it. Now for his inconsideration of a man he had worked hard and treated poorly, he would have to remain on guard against him for their entire time together. Maybe an apology would help, maybe not, but Crowe would never know. Crowe never apologized — not to anyone.

Tully Backus, the man picked by his superiors to replace Profit as Deputy Mayor of Calumet after Crowe won the mayor's office and Profit had been disposed of, and Tully thought, would eventually come to replace Crowe as well, kept a close eye on Crowe and Foss that morning. He thought it important to keep this harbored hatred for one another from escalating into some sort of war between the two of them. Tully knew something Crowe did not. He had heard the tales of Crowe's knife fighting expertise. Hell, he had a firsthand look at it just an evening ago, one of his fellow Klansmen's sliced open shirt bearing testimony. But what he knew that Crowe didn't, Crowe was a Duluthian and new to the Klan, was that Louis Foss was considered among Klan members all over the country as a knife-fighting champion. He had never lost. And Tully Backus had seen Foss fight and thought him unbeatable. So... in these facts lie Tully Backus' problem. If he allowed Louis Foss to kill Emil Crowe, and he undoubtedly would, the Klan's entire plan for Calumet would disintegrate before all of their eyes. And all would be for naught.

Louis Foss jumped to his feet and let the metal plate he had been eating from fall noisily to the ground. Crowe scurried back a few feet and began to stand, one hand resting atop his knife. Tully Backus drew his gun. Foss grinned, spat on the ground between him and Crowe, then turned and ambled easily toward the truck.

"Jesus!" Backus said softly to himself, and shook his head. "Gonna get scary 'round here. I swear!" And he moved toward Emil Crowe's position. "What's your plan?" he asked Crowe when he got to him.

"We'll go to the mine. They'll be expectin' us. We best hide the men out there for a spell, just till we get us a feel of how things progressed while I was away. You and me ought to go into town, meet with Profit.

He's supposed to be keeping an eye on things."

Backus thought for a moment about simply plugging Profit, getting ahead of the game a bit, then thought better of it. If this Profit fellow was on their side, now wouldn't be the best time for eliminating a good gun. "He the one runnin' for mayor with you?"

"Deputy Mayor," Crowe insisted, wanting the record set straight. He was going to be the mayor, and if it was up to him there wouldn't even be no deputy, Profit or anybody else. That's a position of no value unless the mayor kicks off, and Crowe had no intention of doing so. "But I've been told you'd be the deputy mayor."

"After Profit dies," Tully Backus said. He grinned and slapped Crowe on the back. "Only after he dies, Mr. Mayor."

The comment brought a smile even to the sober face of Emil Crowe. "We best load 'em up and get on with this before we piss away another full day," he said.

~*~

In the town of Hibbing twelve men, stout, sober, and armed to the teeth, held tight to reins and listened to their leader explain the details of their mission. "The taking of Calumet," their leader began, "is a must. That town sits halfway between us and Grand Rapids and it'll be our stepping stone to gaining control of the whole iron range." The Klan's efforts seemed to be taking them east of Hibbing effortlessly enough, but attainment of ground to the west had been held at a standstill, and Isaac Burris couldn't understand why. Perhaps the culture was the deterrent, the western limits of the range being more diverse in its peoples' heritage, so many from so many different parts of the world that finding common ground and interests prevented them from achieving measurable momentum. Or possible, the fault lie with Emil Crowe and his inability to effectively communicate without out and out violence. There was a cause and Burris needed to find out what it was. Time was running out and soon his superiors on the shores of the Great Lakes would lose faith in him. But these twelve men sitting on horseback in front of him, they were his hope for answers and might well be his solution to the problem. "Crowe is no longer fitting in well in Calumet," he went on. "He's become part of the problem. I want him gone, but let's do it quietly and at the right time. He's a warrior and only a fool kills off a warrior in the time of war. But when it's done, after you boys licked them over there, I hope to hear that our Mr. Crowe was a casualty of that war. You men will ride to Marble, the little settlement a stone's throw west of Calumet. You'll set up camp there. Kaleb Pruitt, you're to go from there to Calumet and find Tully Backus. Don't go to Crowe. Crowe will likely shoot you. He has no idea who you are. You set things up so Tully can call you in when you're needed, and stay back until he calls for you. Now, remember, men, no one's gonna want you there, so be real careful. The mining company only wants a couple of Klansmen to use as muscle when needed and they'll look at more of us as a threat. The town don't want their precious election contaminated with Klan votes. The union…"

"Union, Boss?" one of the horsemen quizzed. "Is this a union battle too?"

"It has to be. If the mining company's got enough

trouble to call in someone like Emil Crowe, it means they're having trouble with miners, and you get trouble with miners when the union tries to move in. There'll be union alright, and there may be plenty of them. Be ready for that."

"Do we know how many union fighters?" Kaleb Pruitt asked.

"Nope. But we'll have nineteen men over there, and there's that constable."

"How do we know he won't fight against us?" a rider asked.

"Because there are nineteen of us. The constable strikes me as a man who'll go with the odds. Now you men best get to riding. That war isn't going to wait on you," Burris said, and then he left them.

Chapter Twelve

At the Calumet mine, orange dust spewed from the shaft and shot thirty feet into the air where breezes formed it into a shape not unlike a medieval dragon. Men working in the yard readying cars for shipment to the Duluth harbor ran, their shovels at the ready, toward the shaft. Miners were likely trapped. A dynamite blast had gone off prematurely, an altogether too often occurrence of late. The company was once again economizing at the expense of human safety. Ransom Feltus had registered his objection just hours prior to his shovel whipping by Emil Crowe, of the continued use of explosives that had gone to beading up with nitroglycerine like sweat on an overworked miner's brow. The sticks were old, dangerous, too far gone for safe use. The company chose to use them anyway, and since that decision, there had been three such poorly-timed explosions and two lives had been lost. All of the men hoped, as they ran for the opening, that this mishap would not add to the number of dead miners, for in that hole billowing orange dust were their co-workers, their friends, their neighbors, and could well have been them.

"Dig, you sons-a-bitches," one excited miner shouted. "Dig! My brother's down there."

The flatbed truck, Emil Crowe at the wheel, six men standing in the back, pulled to a halt at the top of the hill and watched the goings on below. "We should get down there and help," Tully Backus said as he leaned to look in Crowe's window." Backus was a different sort of Klansman than Crowe. He was softer spoken, a convincing orator, a negotiator first — fight only if that fails kind of guy. That's why Isaac Burris had chosen him.

"We ain't bringin' all of you down there. I don't wanna give our numbers away just yet," Crowe said.

"But there are men dying down there."

"And too bad for 'em," Crowe snorted. "Now... there's a clearing about a quarter mile north. Four of you — don't care which ones — go to that clearing and wait. Two of you stay with me. Now get to it!"

Randal Parks and Lawrence Fish, the only two company officials at the mine that day, watched the scene from the safety of their office, door bolted, shotguns loaded and leaning against a nearby wall. The miners of late, seemed to anger a bit quicker than they used to. And they were bolder. None had stormed the office as yet but Parks did not trust that they wouldn't one day soon. When Crowe and his fellow Klansmen were around, Parks and Fish felt relatively safe, but when they were not, well... that's why the locked door and loaded shotguns. Fish scanned the area. "Look!" he said. "No. Up there." He gestured toward the narrow roadway leading into the yard. Parks averted his eyes from the trouble at the shaft. "See it? I believe that'll be Crowe now. Looks like he's got new men."

"Randal Parks moved to the door, slid back the deadbolt, and picked up one of the loaded shotguns. "Come on, Fish. Let's get out there. They'll need settling down before all this is over with." It would be safe now. The miners seemed to lose their nerve once the well-armed Klansmen showed themselves.

Shovel after shovel flew into ore car after ore car

to be railed to the skip, where the materials from the cave-in would be hauled to the surface. The process would take hours, especially this time. Nearly twelve feet of earth and ore had collapsed, fifteen men, hopefully all still alive, trapped and running short of breathable air beyond it. Tons needed moved, the ceiling of the drift needed to be shored up with timbers as they progressed. Men worked in shifts of fifteen minutes, then were replaced by fresh workers while they rested. Some prayed, some cursed their mining company bosses, some paced nervously as they awaited their next shift in the hole. All at the surface studied Emil Crowe and his two new sidekicks as they rested. One of them, the man Crowe addressed as Tully, seemed far too malleable for a Klansman. Something was in the air, something different, something probably not good.

The work on the collapsed drift would take the miners well past dark, well beyond their standard workday, and for some of them, well past their own personal limits and to exhaustion. Finally though, an opening large enough for a small man to crawl through existed at the top of the pile of caved in debris. The miners sent a man to the surface for the smallest of the men. All who were down in the mine at the moment were too large for the opening. But before a smaller man came, a face, scarcely recognizable with it's crusty layer of orange paste covering everything except his eyes, appeared in the opening on their side. "Grab him. Pitch in, men," cried a tired miner now running on pure adrenalin. "Pull him out of there." Two men yanked the man through and sat him on the ground on their side of the collapsed material just as the opening filled back in with yet more earth and rock. "How many alive in there?"

"All of 'em on the other side are, some are hurt, some are not. One feller didn't make it though, just his boots is stickin' through. Rest of him is still somewhere under all of that."

"Dig careful, boys. There's one body in there."

Both Parks and Fish lit out as soon as dark began to settle in. Emil Crowe, Tully Backus, and Lewis Foss stood watch in their place. The miners, getting more and more testy as time went on, began to press the Klansmen a bit. "You fellers is with the company. Why the hell can't you do something to keep this shit from happening?"

"Ain't our place!" Crowe shouted and pushed the man off balance. The exhausted miner tripped on an untied bootlace and fell backwards to the ground. Tully Backus placed a hand on Emil Crowe's shoulder. Crowe's hand went directly to his knife, and in a split second, he had turned to face Backus, knife in hand, ready for battle.

"Easy there," Backus said, his hands held at shoulder height, palms facing Crowe in a sign of surrender. "No need for that, Crowe. Just seeing things don't get out of hand here."

"Ain't your place, Backus," Crowe said angrily.

"Think votes, Crowe," Backus warned. "Those you push around will be voting for Otis Johnson, not you."

Crowe calmed down and put his knife away. Backus and Foss lent a hand. The first of the injured men was being hauled out through the mineshaft's head frame.

"There's two more hurt, one dead man for the mortician. The two hurt both want to be brought to

Doc Waters'," a miner told Tully Backus."

"Are you going to get the truck?" Backus asked Crowe.

"Not to haul 'em to Waters'."

"Think votes, Crowe," Backus warned once again.

~*~

At the Campsite south of Calumet, Alexander Penovich asked excitedly as he felt the earth move beneath his feet and heard the distant blast of dynamite at the mine, "What the hell was that?"

"Never been around mining country, eh?" Dexter Connors said.

"And you have?" Virgil Dare teased.

"As a matter of fact, I have," Dex boasted.

"You have." Virgil's response was filled with sarcasm. "When?"

"Before you knew me. Before I came to work for Jenson."

"You never worked any mine," Dare pressed.

"I never said I worked one. I robbed a bank once in a mining town."

Dare shot a glance in Newton Blake's direction. Blake was a marshal. Smart folks didn't go shooting off their mouths about robbing banks in front of a marshal. Then he shot a look at his young friend that told him caution needed to be observed. Dex stopped talking and Virg pressed no further.

Newt Blake vowed silently that, once all of this was behind them, he would check into the possibility that Dexter Connors had been telling the truth, although he thought Dex was simply bragging.

Alexander Penovich joined Newton Blake at the fire. He picked up a twig and began poking at the coals. "It'll be dark soon," he said. "The boys bagged a deer this afternoon. I suppose we ought to build this fire up and start roasting us a hind quarter?"

"Not a bad plan, I recon," Newt said and threw a couple logs on the fire. "Who's cooking, one of yours or one of these loggers?"

"Well… not that one for sure," Penovich said gesturing toward Dex Connors. "He's all talk, not likely a cook."

"I recon you're right about that." Newt agreed.

"Ever see him shoot? He any good?" Penovich asked.

"I've seen him draw. He's fast as hell. I haven't seen him shoot though."

"What the hell you two talking about over there?" Virgil Dare asked.

"I was just telling Alexander here, how I was intending to haul your ass back to Missouri and cash in on a whole bunch of reward money once this is over. That's what we're talking about."

Dexter Connors' gun appeared immediately. "You're right," Penovich whispered. "Fast as hell."

Virgil Dare reached a hand out and laid it gently on Dex's gun-hand. Dex returned his gun to its holster.

Later that evening at Doc Waters' place, the mining company's truck pulled up in front. Two men approached the door, one on either end of a stretcher. "Bring him in here," Doc Waters said leading the way to the room Ransom Feltus had occupied for the past several days. Rans threw a fresh sheet over the makeshift gurney in the corner of the room. Doc patted its surface. "Lay him up here. Molly, go get some water boiling. We'll need to clean out his wounds."

"Where you want this one, Doc?" a miner carrying one end of a canvas stretcher asked.

"Christ sakes," Doc said. "How many of them do you have?"

"Just these two, Doc," the miner answered. "All the other injured will heal on their own, just scratches a stuff. Lucky this time."

"What about you," Molly asked as she passed by with a stack of clean linins. "What's that red all over your face?"

"Shucks, Ma-am. That there ain't nothin', just good old ore mud, that's all."

"Put that other fellow over here," Doc ordered as he swiped everything off the kitchen table. "Rans, throw one of those sheets over the table here."

Soon Molly stood behind Doc who was wiping at the injured man's face, the one in Rans' room, to see the extent of his injuries. "Plenty of cuts and bruises on this one, Molly, clean him up while I check on the other one. Call me if you come on one that won't quit bleeding. Oh! And Molly. Careful of that right arm. It looks to me to be broken."

"Doc!" Molly yelled before Waters could clear the doorway. He turned and looked. Blood spurted high into the air. "I just cleaned off a clump of mud, Doc, honest."

"Move!" Doc shouted as he shoved Molly out of the way. Doc poked a finger over the man's artery at the side of his neck. "Get my bag, Girl," he shouted excitedly, then, "Move, Molly!" And when Molly returned with the bag, Doc instructed her to thread a needle, then began carefully sewing the miners artery back together. "Lucky for him," Doc said, "he got covered with mud so quick. He would have bled to death otherwise." Doc worked steadily while Molly shook. "There, now. That'll do nicely. Might as well set that arm now, before he wakes up and starts thrashing around. Hold him here Molly. Rans, you hold him down on the other side." CRACK, the bone objected as Doc set it back to right. Waters sent Rans out for a couple pieces of kindling wood to use as splints, and set Molly to tearing bandages from a bed sheet while he checked the miner over for any other wounds or breaks that might need immediate attention. He found nothing, and when Rans returned with the kindling he used them and Molly's bandages as a makeshift splint. "Let's see to that other fellow," Doc ordered.

The man in the kitchen was coming around when Doc, Rans, and Molly got to him. "Easy there," Doc said. "That is a nasty gash on your head. You best let me have a look before you get to moving around too much." He helped the man to a sitting position on the edge of the table. The man wobbled. He was weak, maybe dizzy. Doc couldn't tell which it was or if it was both. He laid the wounded man back down and stretched him out on the kitchen table. "Molly, you stand over there." He swung a hand to indicate the other side of the table. "Best we don't have this fellow falling off on the floor."

Chapter Thirteen

Shortly after dark at the campsite south of Calumet, Ira Shanks whispered to Newton Blake, "What the hell was that?"

"Sh!" Blake cautioned. He listened — riders — maybe a hundred yards south. Maybe closer.

Alexander Penovich quietly approached. "Quite a batch of them," he whispered.

"Dozen or so," Virgil Dare whispered from behind. "Want me to send Dex? He's real good at sneaking up on folks in the dark."

Newt looked at Penovich. "Don't look at me. Your the one in charge here, Blake," Penovich whispered. Newt nodded to Virgil Dare and Dare started for Dexter Connors' position.

"Virg," Newt said just loud enough for Dare to hear. Virgil stopped. "Have Dex come right back with a count, then send him out again to see where they're headed." Virgil Dare nodded his understanding, then continued.

Soon Dexter Connors was back. "There's twelve of 'em, all on horseback, all heavily armed. It made the hair stand up on the back of my neck. I don't like the look of that bunch. If I didn't know no better, I'd say they were a posse."

"They're Klan," Newt said.

"Still want me to follow them, see where they land?" Dex asked.

"Yeah! Follow! But not too far. They go past

Marble and they're not here for us."

~*~

Dexter Connors lay on his belly atop a small knoll looking down on a campsite a half-mile west of Marble. Twelve men had strung a rope between two oaks and tethered twelve horses to it. Now they sat in a circle around a campfire, the smell of beans filling the night air. They posted no sentry, apparently unafraid of intruders. Dex guessed none of them suspected that he had followed. Should he move closer? Should he see if he could hear their conversation? He looked out over the area — no cover but the cover of darkness. He would not risk it. He slid down the backside of the knoll and mounted his horse. He would return to camp before he was out of night.

~*~

As morning broke, Newton Blake nudged Dexter Connors' leg with the toe of his boot. Dex's gun hand went for the draw. Newt's was quicker. "My. My. Aren't we jumpy this morning?"
"You ought to know better than to wake a feller like that? You could get yourself shot."
"Could be," Newt agreed. "Just not by you."
Dexter Connors narrowed his eyes and Newton Blake knew the chance of the kid trying him before this was all over had just doubled. Perhaps the glory days of gun slinging wasn't over after all. The twentieth century maybe had its own breed of them.
"What do you want, Blake?" Dex asked.
"I want to know where that little army settled in

last night."

"Marble. They're Klan, sure enough. They had Klan written all over 'em." He stopped talking and listened for a time. "Someone's comin'," he said and jumped to his feet. He headed to the brush line. Newt took up a position in the woods across the fire pit from Dex. They were the only two in camp, the rest, some having gone on a morning hunt, others on an expedition to assess activities nearby, and a few over at the mine for a look. The sound of horse and rider came clear. "Just one," Dex said softly as he held a finger in the air. Newt nodded his understanding. The horse broke into the clearing, Newt and Dex both popping out of the brush, guns aimed at its rider as it cleared the tree-line.

The rider reined in and the horse reared. "Put it away, Dex. He's one of us," Newt said as he studied the shock on Ransom Feltus' pale face. "Should you be out yet, Rans? You look a bit ghostly."

"Doc said it ain't nothing. He said I'd come around shortly."

"Doc's a horse doctor. Ever think about that?"

"You got a point, Blake, but I'll stick out here with you just the same. Doc's place kinda filled up last night with the explosion at the mine and all," Ransom Feltus said.

"I take it that wasn't a regular explosion."

"Nope," Rans said. "It was supposed to be, but the company's been using old dynamite. The shit goes off when it wants to. Last night it killed one and stove up two others pretty good. And this isn't the first time. Newt, I'm guessing this whole thing is going to blow and nobody's going to be ready. Those miners are mighty stirred up."

Newt mulled the new information over in his mind for a time. He knew Feltus was right. He had been around the miners long enough to know that. They were a spirited lot to begin with, the miners. And any good feeling they might have had for the company predated Newt's arrival on the Range. The Klan... well... the only thing the Klan had been capable of is stirring the pot and making or keeping nobody happy. The time had come. There would be a war here, Newt knew that from his first day in Calumet, with his first fight with Emil Crowe, and that war was about to begin. "Well... there are two things we can count on: us knowin' what's up just like everyone else, and we're just as ready for it as everyone else. It'll be a fair fight."

~*~

At another campsite, this one on the north side of Calumet, Keleb Pruitt rode cautiously in. He knew most of his fellow Klansmen who would be there but he had never met Emil Crowe, and from what he had heard of the man he did not care to. "Tully Backus around?" he asked of the four men sitting around the campfire.

"He's with Crowe. Crowe keeps Backus and Foss with him; Backus, because he's our leader and Crowe wants to be sure he don't do any leading. He's a bit that way, that Crowe, scared somebody's going to take his place."

"What about Foss? Crowe got reason to keep him close too?" Prewitt asked.

"Oh... yeah," the Klansman said, and proceeded to tell Pruitt all about Crowe sending Foss for the tire repair and how when Foss returned after walking ten miles round trip, lugging a heavy truck wheel, Crowe did not see to it the man was even fed a meal for his efforts.

Kaleb Pruitt knew Louis Foss. He knew him well. They had been friends for years. "Funny Louis Foss didn't kill Crowe on the spot."

"He can't. We're all under orders, direct from Isaac Burris himself. We have to protect the son-of-a-bitch. After the elections though, we get to kill him; win or not, makes no difference. That Profit, that Calumet Constable, we kill him first no matter who wins. He's a clever one. You know he's got himself set to be the mayor's deputy no matter who wins. Tully's supposed to work his way in with Crowe's opponent so that, when we kill Profit, he gets Profit's job. If Crowe wins, we kill Profit and Tully still gets his job. After that I guess we kill whoever's mayor, and Tully Backus is the new mayor."

"Yeah," Pruitt said. "I guessed all of that. Listen," Pruitt picked up a twig and began drawing in the red earth, "I need to get back. This is where the rest of us are camped. Tell Tully Backus we made contact and to send somebody over to fill us in on the plan." Pruitt mounted his horse, touched the brim of his hat, reined the animal around and headed off in the direction of Marble.

~*~

At the Klan's headquarters in Hibbing Isaac Burris paced the floor of his office. He had made an error, or at least, the Klan had made an error. His soldiers shouldn't be on the side of management, they should be backing labor. That's where the votes were, with labor, not management. He paced more. He sat behind his desk and closed his eyes for a time. His head began to pound. *How the hell do I fix this*, he asked himself silently. Then it came to him, the idea that might just solve all of the problems his people in Calumet faced.

He picked his telephone from its cradle and pressed it to his ear, then clicked the cradle up and down several times to get the operator's attention. "Put me through to the Calumet mine office," he said when the operator announced their connection.

"Do you have that number?"

"417J1," Burris told her.

"In Calumet?"

"That's correct, operator, 417J1 in Calumet," Isaac Burris confirmed. He waited. It seemed to take an eternity. Then someone picked up. "Is this the mine over in Calumet?"

"Yes it is."

"Is this Randal Parks?"

"No, Sir. This is his assistant, Lawrence Fish."

"Would Parks be around?"

"Yes, Sir. Would you like me to put him on?"

Who is this fool? Of course I want you to put him on. Why else would I call? Burris was thinking. "Yes, please. You can tell him it's Mayor Burris over in Hibbing."

"Isaac?" Parks answered.

"Randal. I thought it wise to let you in on something. You got big trouble coming your way — union trouble."

"I guessed that already, Isaac. The natives have been uprising all season. Your guy Crowe hasn't done much to quiet them, I'm afraid."

"Listen, Randal, I want you to know something. You got Crowe because you went to Duluth for help. If you'd have come to me, you'd have Tully Backus the negotiator, not Crowe the agitator."

"Well... why not get me this Tully fellow and take Crowe back."

"Too late in the game, old friend. But I think I may have the next best thing. I think we can solve both of our problems."

"I hope so, because right now, I can't even define the problem."

"Let me help. First, you got a bunch of unruly miners. Among them, and you probably don't know this, you got one or two agitators from the union in St. Paul. And just recently I'm told, St. Paul sent in a dozen more."

"I haven't seen any new bodies around." Parks said.

"No. But they're there. When I heard they were coming I sent men your way. They reported in this morning. It seems they run across those union fellows in the middle of the night, saw their campfire and sent a man for a look. Later, those same union boys sent someone to spy on my boys."

"Why don't you send your boys to kill them union boys, and all this will be done with," Parks suggested.

"I could, but that wouldn't get my people elected, now would it? I have a better plan. I have twelve men over in Marble, and four more near you. Crowe's got two with him and he needs to keep them to keep up his tough guy image — can't break from that now. So you put all sixteen of my boys to work in the mines, let them get to know those unruly miners of yours, maybe sway some of them to our side. It's a good plan, Randal. At least we'll have sixteen more votes come election time. You know how it works, you got a job, and you got a vote. And make no mistake, my friend. You want us to win. We're the only ones with the power to keep those union fellers off your back."

Chapter Fourteen

Doc Waters entered the Red Rose with Molly Carpenter on his arm. Even though it was a saloon it was still the only place in Calumet where one could order a nice juicy steak and have it arrive nice and juicy. So… if a couple wanted a meal out, it was the Red Rose or nothing.

"Look, fellers," a patron shouted. "Molly's back."

"How's about a poke for old time's sake, Molly," another yelled.

A young man stood at the end of the Red Rose's bar staring wild-eyed at both of the rowdy miners. "What're you lookin' at, Boy?" one of the miners snarled.

"Not much, I fear," the youngster said.

"You'll be needin' to fear," one of the miners said as both of them stood. The youngster stood, a six gun appearing magically in his hand, aimed directly at the miners. The youngster grinned. The miners sat and turned their attention away from the gunman and away from Doc and Molly.

The young man slid his gun back into its holster as he approached Doc and Molly's table. "You be Doc Waters?" he asked quietly.

"I am," Doc answered. "Who are you?"

"Dexter Connors. Newton Blake sent me to find you. He says I'm to give the two of you a message, that is if you're Miss Molly, Ma-am."

"I'm Molly. Not so sure about the Miss Molly.

That's a bit formal now, isn't it?"

"What's the message, Son?" Doc interrupted.

"Blake says for the two of you to head out of town. He says you'll likely be welcome at Libby Tilden's farm, 'bout twenty miles south of here. He says it ain't gonna be safe 'round here shortly. That war ain't gonna hold off much longer, Newt claims."

"Well, you tell Newt thanks for the warning, but if there's a war, I, me and Molly that is, we'll be needed. There's bound to be injured and dead. Yes, sir, there'd be a couple of folks you don't want to run off at a time like this. Those would be the doctor and the undertaker. You tell Newt that."

"You sure, Doc?" Dex asked.

"I'm sure."

"He told me you'd say that." Dex got up and walked out of the Red Rose, just as Henry Holland delivered steaks to Molly and Doc.

"What do you make of it all, Doc?" Molly asked and took a sip of her wine.

"Not much to make. War's coming and that's all there is to it." Doc answered around bites of his meal.

"Maybe we should skedaddle like Newt says."

"You know, Molly, I've come to like that Newton Blake. I liked him the first time I laid eyes on him. You recall that day." Molly nodded. "Sure you do." Doc took the last bite from his plate, chewed a moment, then continued. "Me and you patched him up after his fight with Crowe."

"I remember," Molly said.

"He whipped Crowe. I feel almost like I owe him for that. I'm not deserting Newton Blake, Molly. Not now, not ever." He looked her in the eye, then he checked the time on his pocket watch and slammed the rest of his whisky. "Now, my dear, I'll walk you home, then I have a meeting."

"It's only a short walk, Doc. I can manage by myself."

"It may be short, but it's past ten more saloons. Dangerous. I'll walk you."

Later that evening with Molly safely deposited at Doc's home where she would spend the remainder of her time before bed seeing to the needs of Doc's two wounded iron miners, Doc set out for the first council meeting ever to be held in the town's meeting hall. Otis Johnson once again headed the proceedings, but Amos Profit would not show up to act as master at arms. "The ballots are in and there appears to be an issue," Otis said.

"What issue," Henry Holland asked.

"Amos Profit shows up in the deputy mayor slot on both tickets."

"Well… how the hell did that happen?" someone asked.

"Don't know. When we sent them to be printed, this being our first election, we hand wrote in the slot on both tickets, 'deputy to be chosen by winning candidate'. Somehow, Profit must have gotten to them between us and the printer." Otis looked around the room. "Anyone know what we can do about this?"

"Print new ones," Mathew Gray, the livery stable operator, suggested.

"No time," Otis said. "These took the biggest share of a month. Elections are coming up fast,"

"Do nothing," Doc threw in.

"We can't just do nothing," someone said.

"I have it on good word," Doc said, "the man isn't going to be trouble. The simple truth is, he won't be around by the time all this is over with."

"Well, Doc, that's interesting," another of the saloon owners commented. "Where's he going to be?"

"In the hands of the undertaker. At least that's what I gather." The town's undertaker looked at Doc curiously and Doc nodded knowingly at him. "That's right," he added. The door to the hall creaked open, drawing everyone's attention away form the current issue.

Amos Profit entered, a stranger with him. "You're late, Amos," Otis Johnson reprimanded. "And you know these meetings are closed to strangers."

"This here's Tully Backus, a newcomer to Calumet. I brought him along because he's got something he wants to tell us."

"I'm sorry, Profit," Otis objected. "That is just not how…"

"Ah, let him say his peace, Otis," Holland insisted. "This man has been in my place a couple of times now. He seems a good sort."

"Thank you, Henry," the stranger said. "My name is Tully Backus. I just arrived in your friendly little town recently."

"Friendly? You sure you got the right town, Mister?" a saloon keeper shouted out. Laughter filled the room.

"Okay," Tully continued. "Maybe not so friendly yet, but we'll make it that way. Now I know none of you know me so let me fill you in. I come from Duluth where I worked the docks and dabbled in politics a bit."

"What kind of politics?" Doc asked.

"The kind you got here. Setting up towns with their own government. That sort of politics."

"Well… Mr. Backus," Otis said. "It might just be we could use some of your knowledge. I invite you to stick around a bit, that is if no one here objects." No one did.

While the town meeting was going on, Molly Carpenter's trouble at Doc Waters' clinic far exceeded her abilities. One of the injured miners took a drastic turn for the worse. He began a coughing fit which soon turned into convulsions. She panicked. She cried out for help when she knew none would come. She tried holding the man still but he would not quiet. Blood began to flow from his mouth, small amounts at first, increasing as he shook.

"He's biting his tongue," a soft, weak voice came from behind her. "You need to put something between his teeth. I got a boy who has fits like that."

Molly turned to see who was coaching her. It was Doc's other patient. "What should I put in his mouth?" she asked.

The man approached slowly, and handed her an old wallet Doc had left laying on the dresser. "Try this. Here. I'll help." And he began prying the man's mouth open. "There. Stick it in. Let him clamp down on that." And soon the convulsing man settled while Molly cleaned the blood from his mouth. Her helper took a chair in the corner of the room, exhausted from his efforts.

"Thank you," she said looking at him over her shoulder. She continued wiping at the blood.

After she finished she helped the other injured man back into his cot, then went to the kitchen to calm herself with a stiff shot of Doc's whisky and to have herself a well earned cry, her final assessment being that she was a whore, not a nurse. She would later confess this to Doc Waters who would do his best to convince her otherwise. "It was one more step on the road to switching from whoring to nursing," he would tell her.

~*~

"You find Doc?" Newton Blake asked Dexter Connors as he stepped down from his horse back at the camp.
"Yeah. I found him, the whore too."
"Watch your mouth Connors or…"
"Or what, Blake?" Connors snorted emphatically.
Virgil Dare, self appointed protector of the sometimes far too imprudent Dexter Connors, jumped to the young gunman's side, not to side with Dex on this one, to side with Newt. "Back down, Dex. We're all in this together. You'll save your fight for after, and if you're as smart as I think you are, you'll forget about taking on Newton Blake altogether, son."
Blake wished Virgil hadn't said that. He knew many young men like Dex, and almost always, they would take exception to a warning such as this one.
"Why? Don't ya think I can take him?" Dex snorted.
Virgil grabbed Dex's elbow and led him to the tree line. "I've known Newton Blake for a dozen years or more. You can't take him."
"Is he that fast? Or are you protectin' him, Virg?"
"He's that fast," Virgil Dare affirmed. "Fastest I ever saw."
"Faster than you?"
"Do you see this ear?" Virg said pointing at his missing lobe. "Newt there's the one who shot it off."

"Well… seems he's not that good a shot, fast or not, Virg." Dexter Connors grinned. "Or else you'd be dead!"

"Oh… he hit where he aimed. Make no mistake about that. Newton Blake wanted me dead that day and we wouldn't be standing here talking right now."

Chapter Fifteen

When morning arrived at the Calumet mine it came with fifteen new workers — softies — new blood the veteran miners would call them. They would wear them out by noon. Then they would steal their lunches and eat them in front of them. And there would be the fight over who's in charge. It was always that way when a new crew arrived. If there were one or two, sometimes even three, it would be no problem, but fifteen, well... that many always came with their own leader. And that leader would be a challenge to the leader who was already in place, Lucien Locke.

"No need in you tryin' to throw your weight around," Locke warned when a man named Otto Pavlic, one of the newcomers, issued an order to one of the other newcomers. "I'd be the one who gives the orders down in this here hole in the ground." He poked a finger into Pavlic's chest.

Otto Pavlic, despite his orders to shy away from any fighting, raised his arms chest high, palms out, and slammed his hands into Lucien Locke's chest knocking Locke into the rock wall of the mine. The fight was on, seasoned miner against newcomer, pushing, shoving, slamming one another into rock, pounding at each other mercilessly with bare closed fists until blood ran freely from cuts over swollen eyes and lips that had been split wide open. A pause in the action came with the sound of the winding tower kicking into gear. The cage was being lowered. All fighting stopped and men listened as the cage came to an abrupt clattering halt at the floor of the tunnel thirty feet away from the drift they were to work that day, the drift they were now using like a Roman coliseum; their battle being not Christians vs. lions, rather seasoned miner vs. newcomer. Each group silently assisted their fallen partners to their feet and waited for the rider or riders of the cage to show themselves. They did not wait long.

"What the hell is going on down here?" Emil Crowe demanded, looking from one miner to another. His expression — surprise — came from his having recognized faces he had seen in Hibbing. No one had informed him he'd find Klansmen in the drift. He looked them over. Other than Lucien Locke and Otto Pavlic who seemed to be equally battered and bruised, the Klansmen seemed to be the victors of the ongoing battle for pecking order. Crowe decided to stay out of it. Tully Backus and Louis Foss, the two who replaced Crowe's two sidekicks who were killed by Newton Blake at Libby Tilden's place, received stares from the veteran miners and nods from their fellow Klansmen, the newcomers to the mine.

"We're just getting acquainted, Mr. Crowe," Lucian Locke explained.

"The company ain't payin' get acquainted time, Locke. Get your asses back to diggin' before I have to do something you might not want to have done to you."

"Yes, Sir."

"You men are expected to produce and you know how much. I expect every one of you," He looked at Otto Pavlic and his companions for a moment; this was not a time to play favorites, "I expect you all to stay down here until you produce all the ore that's expected of you. You got that?" He stepped into Lucien's space and poked a finger into his chest.

"Yes, Sir," Lucian said and backed into a wall of the drift. Sharp points of ore poked into him. He winced. Crowe took it as a sign that he had been understood and feared.

"I'll be leavin'," Crowe said. "But I'll be back, so best you get the work done down here."

Two men had been injured in the fight, one, a seasoned miner beaten unconscious, and one newcomer — not hurt badly. The rest of them moved the injured men to the safety of the tunnel then went about their work. "We'll be doin' extra to make up for them," Lucien Locke said.

"Alright by me," Otto Pavlic said. "My men can handle it. Can yours?"

~*~

Keleb Pruitt was the one man Isaac Burris had sent to Calumet who did not go to work in the mine. He walked past the undertakers door four times before he dared enter. When he finally did he was met with anything but kindness. "What the hell do you want?" the enraged undertaker asked.

"How are you, Brother?"

"Don't you dare call me brother," Owen Pruitt objected. "After all you've done to this family, don't you dare, Kaleb. Now you get the hell out of here and don't you ever come back."

"Owen." Kaleb Pruitt begged.

"I mean it, Kaleb. You get gone. I want nothing to do with you. You're dead to me. Dead!"

"The Klan…"

"I know all about you and the Klan, Kaleb. That's most of the reason I'll have nothing to do with you," he said although it wasn't really the case. The trouble between Owen Pruitt and his brother, Kaleb, ran much deeper. It all happened a few years back, when the two of them and Owen's wife, Abigail, moved to Calumet in search of a new life. They had come from the city where they had a run-in with a rough gang, the Klan to be exact, and as a consequence of that encounter Owen had run out, deserted his business, and lessened himself in the eyes of his wife. But somewhere in the process Kaleb had made friends with a couple of Klansmen. Owen was furious when he discovered it. Abigail turned to hating her husband for giving in to the pressures and moving her to what she termed 'the god-forsaken wilderness that was Calumet'. Owen, now on the outs with brother and wife equally, became angry and withdrawn. Soon Kaleb chose to leave. Abigail begged Kaleb to take her with, and Kaleb, although reluctant, was angry enough with Owen at the moment that he allowed it.

"You don't know this, Owen, and you need to," Kaleb insisted.

Owen Pruitt did not care to hear what his brother had to say. But he did want the answer to a question that had plagued him for a very long time. "Is she still with you?

"Owen," Kaleb pleaded. "Don't."

"Is Abigail still with you? Is she here in town?"

Kaleb looked down and away.

"Really, Kaleb. I'd like to know where my wife is. I'd at least like to know if I'm going to run face to face with her in the middle of Calumet's main street. I don't need this turning into some ugly scene."

"That won't happen."

"How do you know that?"

"Owen, I know you don't believe me and I don't blame you. But honest, Abigail only rode with me to Hibbing. She stayed in the hotel for a couple of nights. We had dinner together and she cried on my shoulder, cried over you, my brother. Then she took a train out of town. I don't know where she went and I haven't seen her since. And that's the whole ugly truth of it, Owen. Honest."

"Honest, hell. Nothing about you is honest."

"Well, you still need to hear what I have to tell you about the Klan. It isn't information for you alone; it's for the whole town." Kaleb had always been true to the Klan, but this move, this plot to take over the Calumet somehow settled wrong with Kaleb Prewitt. He didn't know why. Perhaps it was because of what he had done to his brother. Perhaps it was atonement. But whatever the cause, Kaleb was working against the Klan in this one.

"Very well. If listening to you is what I have to do to get you to move on, out with it," Owen finally said.

"There's a man in town, a real slick fellow, name of Tully Backus," Kaleb started.

"I met him at the last council meeting."

"Yeah, well, like I said he's real slick. He's also Klan."

Owen Pruitt's chin dropped. "How do you know that?"

"Because I'm Klan." Kaleb turned toward the door. He grabbed the handle and pulled it open, then turned to have a last look at his brother. "Tell the rest of them, don't tell the rest of them, Owen. It's up to you." And he was gone.

~*~

It was nearly eight p.m. when the miners finished digging out their expected tonnage and gathered their tired bodies and injured comrades to the surface, a fourteen-hour day with no lunch break. That was the cost of battle and the price for doing without two of their men. Now they had to see to it their injured received medical attention. The veteran miner who had been hurt could barely answer when he was asked to which doctor he wanted to be taken. "Water," he whispered scarcely audibly. He was asking for a drink, not expressing his choice.

"Bring 'im to Doc Waters' place," Locke ordered. "What about your guy?" he asked Pavlic.

"Wherever you're takin' yours."

"Doc Waters is only a vet," Locke warned.

Pavlic was aware of Doc Waters' background. He was also aware Doc was aligned with those who opposed the Klan's involvement in Calumet. So… he wanted his man in Waters' clinic, not so much for the care he might be given — his injuries were scarcely bad enough to justify medical attention anyway — but because they needed someone on the inside — to spy. The fight had been the perfect opportunity for that. Hell, it even afforded Pavlic himself an in if it became needed, as a visitor of one of his men.

They loaded the injured onto the flatbed company truck.

~*~

"I'm kind of full-up in here," Doc waters complained when the first stretcher was hauled into his living room that night. "How many injured men do you have?"

"Two," Lucien Locke told him.

"Very well, bring them in. I have room for two I guess."

~*~

At the camp south of Calumet, as Ira Shank watched the western sky just moments before it was to turn dark, all he could say was, "This ain't gonna be good." Black storm clouds gathered on the horizon and rolled out toward the camp like a thick blanket of doom, shards of lightning scattering in all directions throughout its dense interior. A distant rumble followed the shards, seeming to chase them. "Thunder, lightning, looks like the rain's gonna be heavy, and hail, there's gonna be hail."

"Oh, how the hell would you know all that just by lookin' at some clouds twenty miles away?" Lucas Mann, one of Ira's old partners from his logging and farming days asked. Lucas thought Ira correct in his assessment of the oncoming storm, but he so missed the arguments the two of them shared over the years. He thought this an excellent chance to get one going.

"What are you now, a weather-witch?" Lucas prodded.

"There they go again," Virgil Dare said and pulled his hat down over his eyes, his sign that something long and boring, possibly even annoying was about to take place.

"Is this a regular happening?" Newton Blake

asked as he stirred at the ashes of the campfire.

"Them two been at it for years," Dexter Connors told Newt. "They're like man and wife. He says this, she says that, only nobody seems to know who's he and who's she."

Ira pitched a rock in Dex's direction. Dexter's quick hand caught it and threw it back in the blink of an eye.

"Well…," Newt said as he looked toward the west, "I do believe Ira's right. Those clouds look a touch menacing. We're going to need to button up." Newt had snuck into town and paid a visit to Otis Johnson's general store a day earlier and had thought to gather up a large chunk of canvas and other materials to make a make-shift shelter from for just such an occasion. Men had been laboring on the project for most of the day, just a few final adjustments to go.

Ira Shank had gone back to work on the shelter. His argumentative partner had gone off to the other side of a patch of trees to relieve himself. "Best get a move on," he said upon his return. "That there wind's a comin' on strong — nearly blowin' the bark off the birch, it is."

"That right?" Ira asked.

"That's right," Lucas Mann insisted, and threw a sheet of birch bark at him for effect. "Brung ya some. Knew ya wouldn't believe me."

Virgil Dare groaned and pulled his hat further down his face.

Chapter Sixteen

"I'm terrified of storms, Doc," Molly said. She had come from a different world. She had no idea what was to be expected from a Minnesota thunder storm. "This place got a cellar?"

"A cellar?" Doc Asked.

"A storm cellar," Molly said.

"Now what on earth would we need with a storm cellar?" Doc frowned.

"Where I come from, Doc, a storm cellar is where everyone goes to wait out a storm." She had always lived in the Missouri and Kansas area of the country where a storm usually came with tornados. Molly had seen too many of them in her youth, one of them taking both her parents from her and sending her to live in home after home, strangers and relatives who seemed not to like her very much, and finally to the streets where she took up her career as a whore at far too young an age. She blamed tornados for her lot in life. "Tornados, Doc."

"We don't have them here, well… maybe once in a great while. Not usual though."

"Well I don't care. I'm scared to death, Doc. Do we have a cellar or not?"

"There's a trap door in the floor of the pantry. It leads to a small cellar, just shored up dirt walls and a dirt floor though, not much for comfort."

"I don't care. I'm going there when the storm

comes and that's all there is to it."

"You do that. Now! If that's all settled, Molly, I'd like for us to get back to the task of treating our patients." And they returned to bandages, broken bone setting, ointment administering, etc, on the seasoned miner, and to popping in a slightly dislocated shoulder and cleaning up a few scratches on the newcomer.

Later in the kitchen, out of sight and hearing of the two injured miners, Doc had something to say that he knew Molly wouldn't like. "I'm going to be gone a spell, Molly. You'll need to see to our two new guests."

"You just gonna leave me here in the storm? Where ya goin', Doc?"

"I have to ride out and see Newt. That one fellow, that new miner, he isn't hurt, not hardly at all. And he's a big fellow, a tough sort. I just can't see somebody like him showing up for medical treatment in less than unconscious condition, but for one reason."

"What's that?"

"He's a spy. I need to tell Newt."

"What's he got to spy on here?" Molly asked.

"I have no idea, but Newt will know," Doc answered as he slipped a raincoat over his shoulders and headed out the back door. "I shouldn't be long."

A slight drizzle came as Doc just finished saddling his horse. *Damn!* he told himself. *One of these days, I'm going to learn to drive. Then I won't be messing with smelly animals in the middle of a rain like this.* He thought back to his old days when he had been just a veterinarian, not a real doctor like he was now, and how he had always thought of himself as more. For even then, when he actually prospered at it he had hated the odor of horseflesh and cattle manure and all that came with it. He looked at the small shelter that housed the animal and imagined it as a garage. Perhaps it was a bit small, but with minimal modification, it would do. *I'll start shopping as soon as this is all behind me,* he silently told himself. *I'll be needing an automobile to make house visits in sooner or later anyway.* He hoped for sooner. He mounted the horse. He headed for the camp south of Calumet.

"Hold up there!" a raspy male voice ordered as Doc Waters approached the camp. "Who the hell are you?"

"Doc Waters. I'm here to see Newton Blake."

"He know you're comin'?" The sentry was one of the union fellows from the big city, likely accustomed to an office atmosphere where folks made appointments with other folks rather than just showing up.

"What're you? His secretary?" Doc looked down at him. "Just tell Newt I'm here, and hurry. I'm getting goddamn wet sitting up here on this smelly critter."

Soon Doc was under the shelter of the makeshift canvas quarters, sitting on the ground across the campfire from Newton Blake and Alexander Penovich, leader of the union fighters from St. Paul. Ira Shank and Virgil Dare, sharing leadership of the loggers, joined them. "The one fellow, I can't think of the name but he's a local — I've seen him around here plenty — he was hurt bad. The other one's a new face. Now… there's something wrong with him. He wasn't hurt much at all. My guess is he's been sent to learn from us." Doc looked from one to the other to the other, until he had gone around his whole audience, reading their expressions. It appeared he had done the right thing. Concern shone on all of their faces. "What do you want me to do?" he asked.

"I recon," Penovich offered an opinion, "just watch him. See who comes to see him, listen to conversations, that sort of stuff."

"Let's do more than that," Newt suggested.

"What's your plan, Blake," Virgil Dare threw in.

"Let's work this. Somewhere along the line this war's gonna commence. Why not get it going so we can be done with it. The longer we stall, the worse it'll be?"

"Doc," Newt said. "You best be on your way. That sky's going to open up any time now. You can tell your house spy there's a... No! Tell Molly. Let that fellow overhear. Make it sound like there's a group of men, say a dozen or so, coming from the north and they should be hear within a day or two. Make it sound like you're not sure how long. That'll keep 'em lookin' the wrong direction — away from us."

~*~

Benjamin Dawes, Doc Waters' mining incident patient, the one suspected of being a spy, had his fill of laying in bed and went to the kitchen. He heard Molly. She was making herself a cup of tea. "Wouldn't mind a cup of that myself," Dawes said.

Molly jumped at the surprise. "Are you sure you should be up?" she asked once she got over the freight.

"I needed to stretch. May I know your name, Ma'am?" he asked

"If I may know yours," Molly said and handed him a cup of tea.

"Fair enough. I'm Benjamin Dawes."

"I'm Molly Carpenter. I'm Doc Waters' nurse."

He knew who she was. She was that whore who

worked the Red Rose. He had passed through Calumet not long ago, a month or two at the most. He had stopped in to wet his whistle on a hot afternoon on a ride from Hibbing to Grand Rapids where he was checking out the paper company for his boss, Isaac Burris. Lucky he was in a hurry then, or she'd certainly know him now. Molly was a looker that day, still is. "Good to meet you Miss Carpenter," he said and held out a hand.

Molly wondered, *Where have I seen this man before.* She hoped it hadn't been at the Red Rose but feared it had been. His face was familiar, especially now that she had cleaned up his cuts and bruises. "Good to meet you, Mr. Dawes," she said and took his hand.

"Where'd that doctor get off to?" Dawes asked.

"I don't quite know. He had some errand or other I expect, maybe a town meeting. Doc seldom lets me in on his whereabouts." She didn't know if Doc had been right about this Dawes fellow; he seemed nice enough, but then, what would be the purpose in not being nice, especially if he was some sort of spy. Doc was probably right. "How are those injuries, Mr. Dawes?" she asked.

"I don't suppose you folks have a telephone," Dawes asked ignoring Molly's question.

"No we don't. Why?"

"Where would be the closest one?" Dawes asked.

"Constable Profit's office has one. Then there's one over at Otis Johnson's place."

"Otis Johnson. Is he that feller who runs the general store?" Dawes asked.

"That would be Otis," Molly said.

"Isn't he running for mayor?"

"Yes."

"Somebody said he's a Catholic. Is that true?" Dawes asked.

"I wouldn't know about that, Mr. Dawes," Molly said but lied. She knew. She knew full well Otis Johnson was Catholic as Catholic could be. And now as Benjamin Dawes pried for information she knew Dawes was Klan. Doc had told her that the Klan hates Catholics and that anyone coming around asking about Catholics would have to be Klan or Catholic. This Dawes was no Catholic. "So how are those injuries, Mr. Dawes. Anything I can do to ease your pain?"

"No. I'm coming around just fine. A little trouble low down in my back where one of those boys kicked me, but other than that I'm healing up. I'd appreciate it though, if you'd have that Doc feller look in on me when he gets back." Benjamin Dawes downed his tea, sat the cup on the table, then turned from Molly and went back into the room he shared with the other patient from the fight at the mine.

It was nearly midnight when Doc returned. Molly was fast asleep in a chair in the kitchen. Doc tried to wake her to get her off to bed but she would not come around. It was when he picked her up from the chair to carry her to the bedroom that he smelled the faint sweet odor of chloroform. "Son's-a-bitches," he whispered and hauled her to his bed. He tucked blankets around her then left the room to check on his patients.

Benjamin Dawes pulled the quilt up to cover all but his face. He hoped that Doc Waters hadn't noticed that his boots were not on the floor by the bed. He hoped he had gotten them covered by the blanket as well. That was close. Dawes had been climbing the steps to Doc's front porch just as Doc was putting up his horse in the lean-to out back. Dawes should have been back sooner, long before Doc Waters, but with the rain and all, he and the other fellows had a time of it getting the cross to burn in front of Otis Johnson's place.

~*~

Constable Profit did not like what he was now witnessing. Otis had called him when he heard the disturbance in the street in front of his store. He had looked out of his upstairs window and he saw the half-dozen men, flower sacks covering their cowardly faces, as they hoisted the cross and set fire to it, and he had made a call to Profit's office immediately. Lucky for Otis, the constable had been in his office so late. Coincidence, really. Profit had just arrested a drunk and was locking him down in a cell as the phone rang.

"Now... isn't this something?" Otis said as he came up beside Amos Profit. "I never thought I'd see this sort of thing in Calumet."

Amos Profit spat chewing tobacco into the wet dirt of the street. "Me neither," he said. "Me neither."

"Got any idea who did this, Amos?"

"There's a whole batch of new miners in town. Likely it was some of them." Amos shook his head. He wanted progress in his little town and he wanted to be a big part of it and until now he hadn't cared how or on whose side he had to be to get there. Now, all of a sudden, it mattered. This was over the limit. Burning crosses, for Christ sakes. Otis was not someone Amos Profit particularly cared for, but he was a town official, and one who could easily become mayor. These Klansmen were here to give Crowe votes and maybe defeat Otis and that would be alright, but this, this was too far.

"What's next? Tar and feathering and lynching like someone did to Carl Tilden a while back? Not in his town. Not no more. You have to do something, Amos. It's your place," Otis insisted. He was unaware that Amos Profit had been in on what had been done to Tilden, and equally unaware of what had happen to Newton Blake and Profit's involvement in that as well. Newt hadn't seen Otis when he came in for supplies and canvas for the camp, and his clerk had said nothing about Newt having been there. So far as Otis Johnson was concerned, Newton Blake had gone missing, Profit and the two volunteers he took with him did not find Newt, and that was the end of it.

Rain had taken most of the life out of the fire, a few flames high up still flickering when Amos Profit suggested he get his truck and pull the cross down. Mathew Gray, the livery operator and the town's only mechanic, even though still awaiting some parts, had been successful in temporarily repairing the damage Otis Johnson's horse had done to the truck and Amos once again had use of it.

"What'll you do with it?" Otis asked.

"I'll pull it out of town. No need for folks who ain't seen it to see it. The rumors are gonna be enough trouble," Profit insisted and went for the truck.

~*~

Emil Crowe and Tully Backus jumped to their feet. The ruckus outside the window of the mining company office, even the noise of the storm took a back seat to. They had been going over plans with

Randal Parks, the mine boss, of how to best handle the discipline that morning's fight in the tunnels had brought the need for. But now, outside, Amos Profit's truck circling, wooden cross dragging in the mud behind it, seemed much more urgent. Their meeting could wait. They peered out the window. Parks came up beside them. "Is that a cross?" Parks asked.

"Looks like it." Backus said.

"You're new hereabouts, Backus, so I don't expect you to know this. But I told your superiors when I first talked to them about getting some help out here, that it was policing help only, and that I would not tolerate this here sort of activity. Crowe, you knew it."

"I'll see to it," Crowe said.

"Crowe!" Backus broke in. "Things are different."

"How do you figure?" Parks asked.

"You got union problems now. You didn't have them before."

"They'll be gone soon. That's why you're here," Parks insisted.

"We don't stay, and they won't stay away, Mr. Parks. You know that's true, you might as well get right with it," Tully Backus insisted.

Parks stared out into the rain and watched Constable Profit spin circles for a moment. He didn't like the turn things had taken but suddenly he knew he was powerless to change it. "Do something about him," he said and left the office.

Backus looked at Crowe. Peace had to be kept, at least for a time. "I didn't mean to overstep, Crowe," he said apologetically. "I just thought I'd better be able to handle Parks. He thinks you work for him. He's not so sure about me." He studied Crowe's expression. No trouble coming. "You expect we better stop that crazy constable before he gets stuck in the mud?"

"I recon so," Crowe said and headed out the door.

Amos Profit's blood boiled. It boiled even harder as Tully Backus pulled him from his still moving truck and tossed him like a rag-doll into an iron ore orange puddle. He gasped, cold water bringing his ability to breath to a standstill for a moment. He tried to sit, his efforts stopped by the kick of a boot to his midsection. "You goddamn moron," Backus shouted and kicked him again.

Emil Crowe caught the constable's truck just shy of the cliff's edge. He threw the shifter into neutral and pounded a foot hard on the brake peddle. The front wheels lunged into the soft earth at the edge of the bank and settled in the mud to the axle. Crowe killed the engine, then went back to see what Backus was doing to Profit. He was missing the fun. He and Profit had been on the same side of attacks like the ongoing, but of late, Crowe found himself more and more hoping for an opportunity to lay into Profit himself. Profit had been wearing on his nerves, just like the rest of this shit-hole little town on the edge of nowhere. *Calumet. What a name. Hardly one for a town—means ceremonial pipe according to local Indians*, Crowe silently reminded himself, then, "Welcome to peace pipe," he said and grinned. He approached Backus just as Profit was on the receiving end of yet another kick. Crowe joined in. He planted a boot into the small of Profit's back. Then another. Then another. Profit let out a weak groan, then passed out. Crowe smiled and asked, "Now what'll we do with him?"

"How about we leave him here in the rain?" Backus suggested. "Maybe the son-of-a-bitch will drown." Then the two of them joined forces, cut the cross loose from Profit's truck, and rolled it over the bank where it would be out of sight of the men when they came to work the next morning, not that either of them cared if it was seen, they just didn't want their hand tipped this early in the game. "I think we need to find whoever burned this thing and stall them a while longer. After the elections will be soon enough for this."

Chapter Seventeen

Ten men, some veteran miners, some newcomers to the Calumet mine, gathered around the muddy and battered body of Amos Profit. One of them pushed at him with the toe of his work boot. "Is he alive?" he asked. Profit began to moan and his legs seemed to automatically draw up into a fetal position. "Oh, yeah! He's alive." The miner studied Profit for a time. "Ain't this feller the local lawman?"

"He is," someone offered. "That there's his truck," the man added and swung and arm in its direction. "Best we get it over here and load him on it, get him to one of the docs." He knelt beside Profit.

The eight men standing by moved toward the constable's truck to push it free of the mud while two other men, one veteran miner, one not, stayed with Profit. "I'm August Cole," the veteran miner announced.

"Kaleb Pruitt," the newcomer came back.

"Any relation to Owen, the undertaker here in Calumet.

"Sort of."

"What do you mean, sort of? Either your related or your not."

"Owen is my brother, only he don't like to admit it," Kaleb said.

"Got some kin like that myself. Here, help me get him sitting so we can tell how bad he's hurt," August Cole suggested. But Profit gave out quite a yell when they pulled on his shoulders. "Broke collarbone I recon. How about you getting a stretcher. There'll be one in the winding house."

"The what?" Kaleb asked.

"You sure ain't no miner, son. The winding house. It's that shack where the cable that raises and lowers the cage is at. Over there," he pointed, "other side of the steam engine." August Cole watched Kaleb Pruitt for a moment, then turned his attention to the rest of the crew's efforts to free the constable's truck. Only moments, it seemed, and the stretcher bound Profit was loaded on the back of his own truck and on his way to Doc Waters' place. He wouldn't have been welcomed at the company clinic. He was no miner, and no friend to the company.

~*~

"Well…. it's about time you come around," Doc Waters told Molly Carlson as she broke through the doorway to the kitchen from the stairwell at a dead run.

"Get out of my way, Doc. I'm gonna throw up." Doc stepped quickly aside, letting her escape out the backdoor. The outhouse was her target. Doc hoped, they had been getting mighty close lately, that her condition was due to having been hit with too much chloroform and not morning sickness. He followed her. He waited for her outside the outhouse. When she came out he placed an arm gently around her and helped her back to the house. "Jesus, Doc. I feel like crap," she complained.

"Who hit you with chloroform last night?" he asked and pulled a chair from the table for her.

"Is that what happened?"

"It was. I smelled it on you when I got back last night. Do you have any idea who did it to you?"

"They came from behind, Doc. I didn't see a thing. I didn't hear anything either until just seconds before it happened. Then it was only scuffling sounds — boots across the floor." She looked up at him with pitiful eyes. "Got anything for this headache, Doc?" she begged.

"Laudanum. But I'd rather you try good old strong coffee first." He turned his attention to sounds on his front porch. As he passed from his kitchen into the living room, the front door opened.

"Doc! You in here? It's Amos Profit. He's hurt real bad." Amos's stretcher bounced off the doorjamb and Amos let out a moan.

"Careful of that jamb," Doc scolded and walked over to the doorway to check the damage. He had never given two hoots for the likes of Amos Profit in the past, and now that he knew Amos had something to do with the tar and feathering of his friend, Newton Blake, he cared even less about the man. "What did you bring him here for?"

"Company doc won't take him," August Cole said.

"Well... I don't much want him either," Waters complained.

"C'mon, Doc," Cole pleaded. "You gotta take him. I gotta get back to work." Cole said, walked out the front door, and pulled it shut behind him. He left Profit's truck in front of the house and walked back to the mine. Kaleb Pruitt went with him, leaving Amos Profit's broken body in Doc and Molly's care.

"What now, Doc?" Molly asked.

"How's that headache?" Doc asked her.

She smiled. She did not know when it had let up, possibly it was the coffee as Doc had suggested, but had let up. "Much better," she admitted, and took another sip of the coffee.

"We'll look him over. I'm guessing we'll find some bruised or broken ribs. Looks to me like the clavicle might be broke. I'd say, patch him up and send him on his way."

"You can't do that."

"Do you remember what this culprit did to Newt? Of course I can patch him and throw him into the street. And he can consider himself lucky to get patched up first."

"I see your point, Doc. Speaking of Newt, what'd he say last night?" Molly asked.

Doc looked at the open door to the room where his two other patients rested. He peaked in briefly. The miner who was genuinely injured lay completely still, breathing steadily and deeply — obviously still out of it. The other man, the one Doc suspected of being a spy, breathed shallowly, like he was awake and listening. Doc pulled the door most of the way closed. "He said there's a bunch of men coming from the north. They'll be here within two days, about a dozen of them." He looked at the partially open door. "The constable here looks more beat up than seems necessary, but not really broken badly."

"Are his ribs okay?" Molly asked.

"They're bruised. That's all."

"How about the collar bone?" Molly asked.

"Shoulder's out of the socket," Doc Waters said. Just then the stranger came out of the bedroom, fully dressed, boots and all. "Feeling better?" Doc asked him.

"Pretty good," he said. "What do I owe you?"

"Five dollars, stranger."

The man frowned and pulled a five from his pocket. Doc smiled. This fellow wasn't bright or he would've known no miner had five dollars in his pocket in the middle of the week. "Anything else?"

"Yeah. Can you drive?" Doc asked.

"I surely can."

"Good. Then you can hold the good constable here while I set this shoulder. After that, I'll ask you kindly to help load him on that truck out front and drive him to his office. Now hold him." Doc yanked the shoulder brutally and Profit screamed and passed out. "That ought to do it. Let's get him out of here."

~*~

At the Tilden' farm, Libby had been up a good share of her nights for quite some time now. Clara would awaken in a cold sweat, crying uncontrollably. It was her dreams. She had them for a time after she and her mother found her father tarred and feathered and hung in the front yard of their Calumet home, and now they were back. They returned the night after Newton Blake left and were with her every night since. Libby was at her wit's end. Even when it had been her own father, the dreams didn't persist, not like now.

As daybreak came, Libby hoped for sleep. She was exhausted. Clara, on the other hand, was not all that affected by her dreams. The sleep she lost was minimal. She would whimper, sweat, toss and turn, but she would fall off to sleep easily. It was Libby who would remain awake. And this morning, with Clara sitting on the edge of her bed moving back and forth while she tried to quietly draw in a sketchbook without awakening her mother, Libby kept waking up. Soon she gave in. She got out of bed and went to her kitchen to prepare a breakfast for the two of them.

The two-rut dirt trail that ran past the farmhouse two hundred feet to the south was shielded by a thick stand of pin cherry and chokecherry trees. Most noises this time of year were blocked and passersby normally passed without notice, but this morning, as Libby fried bacon in a cast iron skillet, the rare sound of an automobile turning from the roadway into her property stood out like thunder. Perhaps it was because her lack of sleep was promoting a more acute sense of hearing, perhaps the car was just noisy. She ran to the window and looked out. The automobile was a dark, shinny blue. *A Ford,* she thought, *a Model T.* She didn't know why she thought it. She knew little of automobiles. All she remembered about them is that her late husband, Carl, had dreamed of one day owning a Ford Model T, and that the family would ride in it to church on Sunday and to picnics throughout the week once he figured a way to make them wealthy. Libby wiped the bacon grease from her hands and opened the front door for a better look. She stood, half admiring the car and half fearing it, on her front porch as it stopped fifteen feet from her. A woman got out, a handsome woman, thirty-five years old Libby guessed, well-dressed for these parts. The woman rounded the front of the Model T and approached Libby. "I'm your new neighbor," she announced. "I'm Abigail McCain. My husband, Thomas and I just moved into the old Jonas place, about a mile west."

"I know where it is, Mrs. McCain," Libby assured her.

"I just know we're going to be great friends," Abigail said. Libby was not so sure. This woman seemed to forward for her tastes. "Are you Mrs. Tilden, Mrs. Libby Tilden?"

"Yes, I am."

"Phew!" Abigail said as she wiped a white gloved hand across her brow. "For a minute there, I thought I might be at the wrong farm."

"I don't see how that could be. There're only two farms still standing around here." Libby studied her guest briefly. Then she considered what she had just said, that this was one of only two farms around here. They would become friends, like it or not. They were after all, each other's only option. "Won't you come inside, Mrs. McCain? I'm putting on breakfast for me and my little girl if you care to join us."

"Only if you call me Abigail," she said and smiled.

"Where do you hail from, Abigail?" Libby asked over a cup of coffee. Clara had gone outside in search of an adventure.

"Most recently, Thomas and I moved here from Michigan."

Libby looked out the window, keeping a cautious eye on her daughter, a habit she had developed since the day Crowe's man had taken her from her fishing hole. She looked at Abigail's fine, shiny automobile. "Are you rich, you and your husband?" she asked without turning around.

"Oh! Heavens no! Thomas just had a dream and a way of getting it. You see, he worked for the Ford Motorcar Company in Michigan. We always wanted a place of our own in the country so Thomas worked and worked and saved and saved. We bought all we thought we would need, even the Model T, then we came here."

"Why here?" Libby asked.

"Because this is home," Abigail said.

"Thomas' home?"

"No. Mine. I was born here—Abigail Jonas."

"Why… I'll be damned," Libby said and smiled.

"Excuse me?"

"You've changed." Libby said.

"I don't understand," Abigail said.

"I'm Libby Castle. You and me were children together. Right here on these two farms."

"I'm turned around," Abigail said. "I was positive your homestead was west of ours. No wonder I couldn't find it." She grinned and stood. "You see? We are going to be friends." And she approached Libby and embraced her.

"Do you have children, Abigail?" She hoped for a companion for Clara way out here in the wilderness.

"No." A deep sadness filled her pretty face. "Not any more."

Chapter Eighteen

Otis Johnson watched the street in front of his general store, his curiosity brimming. Amos Profit's truck had just come to a full stop in front of the jail, a strange man got out and walked off heading north toward the mine, and someone appeared to be spread-eagle on the back of the truck. Otis thought of going down to check on the peculiar sight, then chose not to. He returned to his bookkeeping. A full half-hour would pass and his curiosity would once again get the best of him. He looked out — still there, a silent and motionless body. Was it alive or dead? He decided to check it out.

Downstairs, in his store, Otis came face to face with Owen Pruitt. "Might be some funeral business down the street, Owen," he told the undertaker.

Owen did not respond.

"Owen?" Johnson called. "Owen!" he said a bit louder.

"Oh! Sorry, Otis. Guess I was a bit lost in my own thoughts."

"Something troubling you?" Johnson asked. He was genuinely concerned. He and Owen had been friends for years.

"It's my brother, Kaleb. He come for a visit yesterday."

"I thought he was dead."

"He was," Owen said. "At least to me he was." Owen looked at Otis. He saw no good coming from plaguing Otis with his troubles. "Were you about to tell me something?"

"Yes. I think there might be some business down in front of Profit's office. It appears there's a stiff on the back of his truck."

"I already had me a look. He's not stiff yet," Pruitt said.

"Do you know who it is?"

"It's Amos Profit," he said and donned a grand smile. "Looks like somebody has beat the shit out of him. I'll see you later, Otis." Pruitt said. Then he left.

Otis Johnson looked up the street at Profit's truck and shook his head. Then he returned to his room above his store and continued with his bookkeeping.

~*~

"You just getting here?" Lucien Locke asked Benjamin Dawes when Dawes finally arrived at the shaft station of the mine.

"Sorry I'm late. Doc had me take that policeman back to the jail," Dawes explained.

"So… that old constable survived, did he?" Locke more commented than asked.

"He was alive when I left him," Dawes said. "Can't speak to his condition now, though."

"What'd you do, throw 'im in one of his own cells?"

"Nope!" Dawes said. "I left him on the bed of his truck. He's resting now I recon."

Dawes and Locke rode the cage to the bottom in silence. Miners and foremen seldom talked unless it was about work, besides, the ride was always too noisy for hearing. At the bottom, each man went in opposite directions; Dawes toward the drift being worked that day and Locke in the direction of the next area to be mined. Otto Pavlic asked Benjamin Dawes when they came face to face in the tunnel, "Did you learn anything over at the doc's place last night?"

"There's supposed to be a dozen or so armed men, coming in from north of the camp, tonight, maybe tomorrow night," Dawes explained. The conversation stopped for a time. Dawes finally broke the silence. "We working peacefully today or we fighting more?"

"Peaceful. We made enough of an impression on these fellers yesterday — showed 'em we can fight and we can dig. Now we need to make some friends down in this hole in the ground." Footsteps in the distance caused them to quiet. They listened as someone came closer.

"Best get to it," August Cole suggested as he approached their position in the tunnel. That drift ain't gonna mine itself. C'mon fellers. We got a lot of catching up to do today."

~*~

"Will you settle down?" Newton Blake demanded of Dexter Connors. Dex had been pacing back and forth in the camp south of town, kneeling at the fire, poking at the ashes, then standing and pacing more, for hours — almost since daybreak.

"Let him be, Blake," Virgil Dare protested and pushed his hat brim up to expose his eyes. He had been laying in the dirt all morning, head propped against a fallen tree, legs crossed. No one even knew he was awake, or alive for that matter. "He's just the nervous sort. We got nothing to do, and when we got nothing to do Dex paces. That's all."

"Well it's driving me nuts," Newt said.

"Nervous energy. Pay it no mind. You'll be glad for it soon," Dare promised and pulled his hat back down over his eyes.

Newt went back into the canvas shelter they had erected to keep them safe from the storm. Maybe a conversation with Alexander Penovich and Ransom Feltus, the two labor leaders, would relieve his anxiousness. Maybe it would lead to some planning. Anything but this silent stillness. It was maddening. Newt wanted the battle to just begin. Get on with it, was his wish and by now — everyone's.

"You two fellows ready for the fight," Newt asked as he approached Penovich and Feltus. He had his pistol out, checking to see if it was loaded.

"Is it time?" one of them asked.

"No! No! I'm just getting in the right mind for it," Newt said. He had led many a posse over the years, and always, not long before the posse was to set out, or a battle was to begin, Newt filled himself with nervous energy and anticipation. He used to have to work at it, but these days, it seemed to come upon him naturally. Whatever. Either way. If he had to make it happen or it came by itself, the nervous energy always fired the men up and, (he was sure) assured success.

Penovich looked at Feltus and smiled.

"What?" Newt asked.

"Nothing really. It's just… well… I don't believe I've seen a man wound so tight as you, that's all," Alexander Penovich said. "How about you, Rans?"

"Me neither," Feltus agreed. "All except old Emil Crowe when he gets all riled up at Constable Profit."

"Are you comparing me to Crowe?" Newt asked,

his hand on his gun.

"Not so close as I could get shot for it," Feltus said with a smile.

"Listen, Newt," Penovich said, his tone turning more serious. "I really think it's time for a plan. What do you say?"

"I say it's a little early for a plan. I wouldn't want someone listening in and giving us away before it's time."

"Well... you got an idea when you want this battle to be fought?" Ransom Feltus asked.

"Election day," Newt proudly offered.

"Election day?" Alexander Penovich hadn't expected that one. "Why election day?"

"None of you vote here, least none of you union boys."

"I can," Rans offered.

"Other than you, Rans. And the only miner we have with us is Ira Shank. The rest of these guys are cowboys and loggers from the north. Then there's me. I have a vote of course. That makes just three votes in our camp, and we can somehow figure out a way to get those votes cast. Now... those Klan fellows, they all work at the mine. There going to be considered citizens because they work in Calumet. Those are the men we need to keep from voting. We'll fight them on election day. And we'll start before first light."

"When's election day?" Virgil Dare asked. He had been standing in the opening to the canvas shelter listening to the conversation.

"Eight days from now. Ira go into the mine this morning, Virg?" Newt asked.

"Yep!"

"Good. He'll likely have the lay of the land for us

when he comes in."

"Something's been bothering me about all of this, Blake," Virgil Dare said. "Ira Shank is my good friend, and me and the boys, we got other friends around the area. What's to keep these Klan fellers from coming back and raising holly hell once we leave?"

"Anyone know anything about tar and feathering?" Newt asked.

~*~

Tully Backus had reeled in many of the town leadership with his smooth personality and easy-going ways, and had taken it upon himself to convince the council to hold a special meeting to deal with Amos Profit's mishandling of the printing of the ballots, Profit having had put his name on both tickets as deputy to the mayor. Backus had been successful in convincing the others that any election they held would be unlawful until the matter was resolved. His objective, of course, was to get Profit's name removed from the ticket with Otis Johnson and replace it with his own. He knew that if Crowe won the office, Amos Profit was to be killed and Backus was to be appointed in his stead. Either way, Tully Backus would be deputy to the next mayor, and of course, according to the Klan's agenda, would be sworn in as Mayor of Calumet upon the assassination of Calumet's very first mayor. The plan was set. All Tully had to do was play the game.

"Mr. Backus," Otis Johnson started. "We're pleased you joined us, but a matter has arisen that's a bit on the confidential side, so I'm afraid I have to ask you to step out of the meeting for a time."

"Perhaps it's something I could assist you with,"

Tully Backus said.

"Nope!" Owen Pruitt threw in abruptly. It was, after all, in answer to his request that Backus was being removed from this meeting. He had information for the council, and that information was about this newcomer to the Calumet. "This here's a private matter for the ears of council members only. Sorry! You'll have to leave." Backus rose, stomped out — clearly displeased with having been ousted from the hall — and slammed the door behind himself. Pruitt, already having taken the floor began his drawn out speech. "This Backus fellow. Anyone here know anything about him? I recon not, at least not what I know. I'm sure you all remember my brother, Kaleb. Well…Kaleb paid me a visit…"

"He bring your wife back?" someone in the hall shouted. Several laughed.

"Think this is funny?" Owen blurted. "Wait'll you know the truth. Some of you men have been cozying up to the K.K.K. That's the truth of it." The room silenced. "That's right! That Mr. Tully Backus, that feller is Klan. That's what he is. He come over here with Crowe. Now I know he hasn't been hanging around with Crowe and his boys, at least not where any of us can see him, but he's Klan sure enough. He's from Hibbing, same as my brother, Kaleb. And Kaleb told me all about him."

"You're sure about all of this?" Otis Johnson asked.

"Positive," Owen Pruitt insisted.

"Well… what'll we do now?" Otis Johnson asked of anyone who'd answer.

"What if Pruitt's wrong?" someone yelled out.

"He's not," Otis said. "I was hoping Tully was for

real, but I pretty much suspected he wasn't from the start. Think about it. Nobody of value just happens along just when he's needed. Not like this. Backus was sent to us by somebody, somebody hoping to gain from our little town election. Might as well be the Klan." Otis looked around the room — reading faces — looking for silent objections. He found none.

Tully Backus listened beyond a closed door. He heard all he needed. It was only fortune he hadn't heard the name of the turncoat Klansman who had ratted him out. He would ask around. He would find out who the traitor was.

Chapter Nineteen

Tully Backus nearly knocked the door to Constable Profit's office and jailhouse from its hinges. Profit let out an annoying moan from a bunk in one of the two cells. "Who's out there?" he asked weakly.

"I need your telephone, Profit," Backus demanded.

Amos Profit grunted.

"C'mon! Get up! I need to make a call, now!"

Profit's every muscle cried out as he rolled onto his side and let one foot touch the floor of the jail cell. The beating he took at the mine felt as though it may never wear off. His ribs hurt. His backbone seemed to catch as he moved. One eye was swelled shut, the other bruised. A shoulder sent pain like a bolt of electricity through his entire body at the slightest movement. He struggled to sit and when he finally did he recognized Tully Backus as one of the two men who had done this to him. Immediately, automatically, his pain eased — powered by rage. He felt for his gun. It was still strapped to his leg. He stood, wobbled a bit, then headed to his office, pistol drawn and cocked. He stuck the barrel in Backus' face. "In the cell." he said softly.

"What?"

"I said, in the cell," Profit said, his tone stronger, louder. "Now, git," he waved his gun in the direction of the cell he had just vacated, "before I shoot you."

Backus slowly lifted himself from Amos Profit's

desk chair, turned away from the gun being held on him, and walked into the tiny jail cell. "What's the charge?" he asked.

"Assault! On an officer of the law."

"I want a lawyer," Backus demanded.

"Tough shit." And Amos Profit lit out in search of Emil Crowe, his intent — when he finds Crowe, he'll shoot him. *Why take the chance of having your belly laid open at the tip of Crowe's knife,* he silently decided.

~*~

Abigail McCain appeared at the Tilden farm just in time to breakfast with Libby and Clara every day but one over the past week and a half. It had become ritual, one that Libby did not regret although she often wondered how she would break the habit once Newton Blake came back, if Newton Blake came back. Abigail, of course, did not want it the way it had become, her doing all the traveling and eating free off her friend, but Libby had insisted. "What am I to do, put a leash on Clara and walk all the way to your place?" she had reasoned. So Abigail found equality in bringing food, bacon, eggs, the occasional loaf of bread, and had come to grips with always being the guest and never the host. She did, however, collect Libby and Clara one morning in her Model T, and drive them to brunch at her home.

Both Clara and Libby smiled broadly with the excitement of their first ride in an automobile. "Nearly as rough as a buckboard," Libby commented.

"But much softer seats," Abigail said and straitened her hat.

"How far can you go in one of these?" Libby asked.

"We came all the way from Michigan in this one. It took us nearly a week."

"My goodness. Where did you sleep?"

"Right here. In the car mostly, outside when it was nice. Thomas hauled a tent along," Abigail told her.

"How long would it take to get to Calumet in this?" Libby asked.

Abigail's face paled for a moment. "Where's Calumet from here?" she asked.

"North. About twenty miles."

"I don't know of a road north from here. I'll ask Thomas this evening."

"Where is Thomas?" Libby asked. She was curious. She had never met Abigail's husband. *Odd,* she thought suddenly.

"He's in bed." Abigail said. She looked at Libby and recognized there in her eyes the need for further explanation. "Thomas works at night in the paper mill in Grand Rapids. That's why I come to see you so much. It's just too big an effort on my part to let him sleep all day, and if I wake him for the company he'll be too tired and he'll get hurt at work."

Libby understood. She recalled many times when Carl had been forced into longer shifts and needed daytime quiet following them. Other wives had not been generous enough to allow their husbands to recover from these grueling episodes. It seemed to Libby they were the husbands who would be hurt on the job, or even killed.

"Why ever would you want to go to Calumet Libby?" Abigail asked.

"I'm concerned about Newt," she said. She had

told Abigail much about Newt: the way he arrived, her initial distrust of him considering how Carl had died, how they came to love one another after a time, how Clara came to think of him as a father image. And now she went on to tell her how worried and restless she had become lately over his long absence.

"You poor dear," Abigail said. She rose from the table and placed the dishes in the sink. When Libby got up to help her, Abigail explained that she always did any cleaning at night, after her husband was up. "Less noise," she added. "Best be getting the two of you back so I can get home in time to make Thomas' supper."

It was not until the girls reached Libby's drive that she summoned up the courage to ask Abigail for the favor, or at least hint that there would be such a request coming. "Couldn't one simply follow the train tracks north to Calumet, I mean, with a car?"

"Look, Libby, if you're so determined to go to Calumet, why don't you just come out and say it?"

"Okay. I want to go to Calumet — to see if Newton Blake is alright. I just must. I'm so worried. Abigail, I just need to get close enough to get a look at him. For all I know he isn't even alive."

"I'm sure you have plenty of reason to be concerned, Dear, and I'm also sure there's nothing to be concerned about. These men can take care of themselves. They're rugged and can't..."

"Abigail, you weren't here. You didn't see him tarred and feathered. You didn't see the men who came here looking for him and what he had to do to protect himself, to protect me and Clara. It was all so... so horrible. And he went right into a whole town filled with men like those who came for him. I'm worried — not just concerned." Tears began to run down her cheeks as she spoke.

"There, there," Abigail consoled. She patted her friend's shoulder. "If it's that important, I'll take you to Calumet. You just tell me when."

"Won't you have to ask Thomas," Libby asked.

"Not really," Abigail said, then added, "I will, of course, but I don't have to."

Libby found that interesting. She had never met a woman who did not feel the need to check with her husband, even though this was 1909 and things were changing. She supposed it was just another sign of the times. But then, Libby did not know women who drove, other than her friend, Abigail, in the first place. "When would you feel comfortable to go?" she asked.

"Whenever you wish," Abigail told her.

"Are you certain this will be alright?"

"I am."

~*~

Ira Banks returned to camp drained of ambition, scarcely able to hold up his tin dinner plate let alone a full coffee cup. "Rough day?" Lucas Mann asked.

"Don't start on me, Lucas," Ira warned.

"Hear they go again," Dexter Connors leaned in and whispered to Virgil Dare.

"Yep!" Dare said and pulled his hat down to show his lack of interest in the ongoing friction between these two.

"What?" Mann said. "I ain't said nothin'."

"That don't mean you're not gonna," Ira said.

"So…rough day?" Lucas Mann once again asked.

Ira remained silent. It had indeed been a tough day at the mine. Lucian Locke put him and August Cole on opening the new drift at the end of tunnel four, the north tunnel. Tracks needed laying. Shoring had to be placed. Lights had to be strung. And near the end of their shift, drill holes for dynamiting seemed to use up every tired muscle leaving behind nothing but excruciating pain. Then came the time for blasting.

The very first stick of dynamite ignited prematurely and sent August Cole flying twenty feet down the tunnel and half-buried him under dirt and rock. Ira, although he had called for help, dug him out alone. No coworkers showed, probably hadn't heard him or the explosion above the noise of their own duties. Had more than one stick gone off they would have but that wasn't the case. And to make things worse, as if all of this was not bad enough, they had struck water with the blast — not a heavy flow, just a trickle. But it was enough, and both men were sufficiently experienced that they knew where it would lead. Not real soon but soon enough, there would be flooding. Maybe it would be gradual, maybe all at once — difficult to predict. "Are you hurt?" Ira had asked August Cole. Cole told him he thought not and began helping Ira by pushing whatever rocks within his reach off of himself, and soon, August was free.

As he struggled to his feet though, Ira noticed an obvious limp in his partner's slow walk. He watched him for a time as they worked at clearing the rubble from the explosion so there would be easy access for a crew with a pump to get in and handle the water situation. "You did something to your leg," Ira said.

"Just a scratch," August insisted.

"Le-me have a look," Ira said.

"It ain't nothin," August told him.

"A look!" Ira said. It was his responsibility just as

it would have been August's had it been the other way around and Ira had been hurt. Miners were partnered for a reason — safety. An uninjured man had accountability for an injured man, and authority over him as well. It was the law of the mine and a miner who breaks it is no longer a miner. "Pull up that pants leg. I'm gonna have a look, like it or not." And August Cole pulled up his pants leg exposing a deep crimson, two inch wide, six inch long gouge in the calf of his leg. "Jesus, August!" Ira said and curled his lip. "You gotta have the doc look at that. That'll turn putrid on you in no time."

"Ah, it ain't nothing!" August argued.

"That isn't for you to say. Not down in the mine it ain't. We'll be hauling you to see the doc. Now... which one do you want to see, Waters or the company doc?"

"Waters," was all he said. Then he pulled the pants leg down to cover the injury and winced.

Ira shank and August Cole rode the cage to the surface long after everyone else, and shared Ira's horse for the ride to Doc Waters place. Ira thought of having the doctor look his partner over, patch him up, and then Ira would take him to the camp with him. But as he rolled over the day in his mind he thought better of that plan. The two men had engaged in conversation as they worked. They had been friends for years, closer lately since Locke had been pairing them up more and more. Their conversation took a course that morning that Ira hadn't expected. It seemed his old friend was being led in an undesirable direction.

"Who you votin' for, Ira," Cole had asked. "Otis Johnson or Emil Crowe?"

"Johnson," Ira had said.

"I planned on votin' for him too, but I've been talkin' to that new feller, that Oscar Barlow, and he makes a good point," Cole said.

"He does, does he?" Ira said.

"Yep! You heard of a man called Tully Backus? He's hereabouts now too, not a miner though, somebody who's helping get the elections organized."

"I heard of him. He's making quite a stir around town with his fancy ideas about politics." Backus' name had come up in conversation around Newton Blake's camp on more than one occasion. Ira knew full well that Backus was Klan, and thought of clueing his old friend in on that fact, but he also wanted to know how much influence these so called new miners were having, so kept quiet for the moment. "But what's he got to do with Crowe?"

"Rumor is if Crowe gets in, Backus will be Deputy Mayor," August said.

"I thought Profit had that all sewed up."

"Not any more. Profit's out. Backus is in. Yes, sir! My vote goes to Crowe and Backus," August Cole said. "And that's where yours should go too."

"Me? Vote for Crowe? Hell no! Crowe's a bully. He ain't no mayor." Ira was insulted. He thought his friend smarter than all of this.

"Crowe's just doin' his job here, keeping the peace. He don't go 'round bullyin' good miners. He just goes after those union fellers. You know. Ransom Feltus. That Tilden before him. The rest of us he leaves alone. Besides, it's not Crowe we want. It's Tully Backus that'll do somethin' for the town, and everyone thinks he can handle Crowe. Then there's the Company."

"The Company? What's the Company got to do

with it?" Ira asked him.

"Oh. I forget. You were gone a few days. You missed the speech Mr. Parks gave us. He told us we back Crowe in the election, 'cause if Otis Johnson gets in, the company's gonna close down," August said. "No mine and we ain't gonna need a mayor. There won't be no Calumet."

It had been that discussion which caused Ira Shank to rethink his original plan — to invite his friend, August Cole, to join him and the others at the camp. He dropped him at Doc Waters' and went on his way.

His labors and his responsibility toward August Cole and his injuries brought Ira into the camp later than usual and more tired than ordinary, so prodding from Lucas Mann, as much as he had enjoyed their arguments in the past, Ira was in no mood for. And the third or fourth attempt by Mann to get his goat sent Ira into a fit. "Goddamn it, Lucas. Can't you see I'm in no mood for your bullshit tonight?" he shouted.

"Jesus, Ira! Touchy!" Mann responded.

"Just... leave me be." Ira insisted. And Lucas Mann left the tent.

He met Newton Blake coming in. "Oh... Ira's back. Why didn't somebody tell me?" Newt asked of anyone who'd answer. Nobody did. "What's the goings on at the mine today, Ira?" he asked.

"Trouble!" Ira gave his one word answer.

"What kind?" Newt asked.

"Parks, the mining company official is stirring things up. He's giving orders to the miners to vote Crowe in the election, telling 'em if they vote for Otis Johnson he'll see to it the mine is closed down. Can he do that?"

"I don't know," Newt answered honestly. He

lifted his hat and ran his fingers through his hair.

"He can't if he ain't there," Virgil Dare offered.

"And how are we to get him out of there?" Newt asked.

"Kill him!"

Chapter Twenty

Doc Waters' place had cleared out. The last patient, although not quite in the condition Doc wanted to see him in, felt strong enough just the same, to return to work — or maybe broke enough. Whichever it had been, the man left Doc's clinic early in the morning leaving the place private for Molly and Doc. Molly wanted a picnic. "C'mon, Doc. It's gonna be a bright, warm, sunny day, and it's just us. We're alone for the first time since I moved in here."

"So… what of it?" Doc asked. He knew full well what she was getting at. Sex, with a houseful of recovering injured from this mining accident, that mysterious mugging in the dark of night, or even the occasional vomiting woman or child needing attention, had been nonexistent. It wasn't that they did not have privacy for such things; they did, after all, enjoy a bedroom on the second floor of the story and a half far away from the ill or injured below, but the incessant screech, screech, screech of worn out bedsprings seemed to ruin the mood. Doc also knew Molly was a bit addicted to sex, a side effect of her former life, and he knew that it would be in his best interest to administer whatever might need administering to satisfy that addiction if he wanted her to remain his. It didn't stop him from picking on her however.

"So… I want to go on a picnic, Doc. I want to get away from here before anybody else can show up."

"What if someone gets sick and needs me?"

"I need you!"

"What if there's an accident at the mine? You know they're having trouble with defective dynamite."

"Let the company doctor deal with it."

"What if…"

"Doc!"

"Yes?"

"Picnic!" Molly ordered and picked up the basket she had already packed. She went to the back door and opened it for him. "Now!" she said.

Doc Waters smiled and headed to the lean to. They would ride double, which was just fine with Molly.

~*~

Dexter Connors was the chosen one. It had come to a vote, Newton Blake, Ira Shank, Virgil Dare, and Alexander Penovich each having a say so in the matter. And that vote had been unanimous. Randal Parks had to go. It could not be allowed. Any one who dared to stand in the way of Calumet's first election being free from outside influence of any kind would be dealt with in whatever way seemed the most expediently effective. In the case of Randal Parks, a mining company official, the highest ranking one at the Calumet Mine, who had issued or else orders — you vote for the candidate I tell you to vote for or else — removal would not be sufficient. An example must be made — a public example. Randal Parks would be executed.

"Why not just get him out of town until the election is over?" Newt had argued.

"They'll all know he'll be back when it's over,

and it could be just as easy for him to fire men or even do as he's threatened, close the mine and put everybody out of work," Ira Shank explained. "The miners are afraid of him. Most of 'em will vote his way anyway knowin' he'll be back. Nope! I think he's gotta be shot, and some of 'em's gotta see it."

"Well, what about that assistant of his?" Newt asked.

Ira laughed. "Fish? Ha! Ain't nobody fearin' 'im, not out at the mine."

"I might be a little lost here," Alexander Penovich said, "me being an outsider and all. But why do we have to kill Parks. Wouldn't it serve us just as well, maybe even better, to shoot that Crowe fellow and be done with it."

"Won't work," Virgil Dare said. "I heard a rumor this Parks might be connected to the Klan too. Maybe not directly, but if he's the one who got Crowe and his boys here in the first place, he's connected at least a little. Besides, Newt here wants to get rid of folks standin' in the way of an honest election. We kill Crowe, him bein' the other candidate, and ain't we in the way of that ourselves?"

Newton Blake scratched his head as he thought. "I recon Virg is right. I recon Ira's right too. So…who do we send?" Everyone looked at Virgil Dare.

"Dex," Dare said.

~*~

Molly Carpenter had a blanket stretched out on the soft grass of a clearing in the pines before Doc could get their horse tied to a tree. She sent him off in search of firewood in spite of his complaining that he hadn't planned to build a fire. "C'mon, Doc. It'll be romantic," she insisted.

"Romantic... we could have done at home," Doc said. But as she put on her very best pout and batted her eyelashes, then followed it up with a lick of the lips, all of Doc Waters' objections seemed to fade into the surrounding pines. And Doc was off to gather firewood. But when he returned with a healthy armload of birch and pine, Molly was nowhere in sight. He called out for her. No answer. He called louder. Still no answer. He began to panic.

These were bad times — unsafe. He feared she might have been drug off. Then, just as he was about to run off in search of some clue as to which direction she might have been dragged, he felt something at the nape of his neck. He shuddered. Then he felt arms reach around him, slowly, softly. And he felt a kiss on the back of his neck. "There's something you need to see," Molly whispered.

He turned. "What? What do I need to... Holy Shit, Molly." She stood facing him, completely naked.

"You like?"

"I... I like! B-but what if someone should c-come?" he stammered.

"You mean other than you and me?" Molly asked with a smile. Then she began pulling at the buttons on his jacket, then his vest, then his shirt and belt and before Doc knew it he lay on his back on the blanket, nude as Molly, birds singing gleefully overhead, receiving his first ever girl-on-top sex. And as he climaxed, he did so with a loud cry of, *"Goddamn, Girl!"*, his eyes held tightly shut, and he did not hear Dexter Connors horse walk slowly by. Molly looked at Dexter Connors and smiled.

"Ma'am," Dex said and tipped his hat. He rode on without looking back.

~*~

Emil Crowe and Louis Foss were just clearing the crest of the hill coming out of mining company property as Dexter Connors arrived. Crowe slammed on the brakes of the company's truck, sending a cloud of red ore dust into the air around Dex and his horse. The horse bucked. Dex, not expecting it, was thrown clear and bounced off the hood of the truck. Foss jumped out and grabbed Dex's arm. "You alright young feller?" he asked.

"What the hell you want around here?" Crowe yelled out.

Dex stared long and hard at Crowe. Lucky for Crowe, Dex was under orders from Virgil Dare not to harm Crowe should they happen to meet. Dex thought briefly about ignoring that order and plugging this son-of-a-bitch right where he sat behind the wheel of the mining company's truck, but, he had never gone against Virgil Dare before and thought it a bad idea now. "I'm huntin' a job."

"I doubt there's any here," Crowe said. "They just put on a bunch of miners, less than a week now."

"You the man hiring?"

"Nope. That'd be a feller name of Curtiss Clay. Don't think 'e's down there though," Crowe said motioning toward the building at the bottom of the hill.

"Mind if I take a look?" Dex asked.

"Suit yourself," Crowe said and drove off in another cloud of red dust.

~*~

Emil Crowe and Louis Foss drove directly to Amos Profit's office. Crowe had had enough of Profit. Crowe was not a part of the cross burning in front of Otis Johnson's general store and he resented Profit's subtle allegation that he might be involved in the burning by dragging the charred cross around mine property while he and Tully Backus were conducting business with mining company officials. The incident left Crowe in a position where he either took the action he did or lose his influence over miners whose votes he needed. The election was coming — rapidly. Profit, by his actions, was effectively throwing in the towel for them. Crowe had no time at all to get Profit back in line and smooth over the situation, at least where the voters were concerned. They needed to look like a team. He would talk to Profit, let him know he had nothing to do with the cross burning, and between the two of them, devise a plan to convince the voters of Calumet that incidents such as that one would not be allowed to happen in Calumet in the future, not so long as Crowe was their mayor and Amos Profit was their deputy mayor.

Crowe pulled the truck to the side of the street in front of the constable's office. The constable's truck was not there. He went inside, looked around, and decided to go looking for Profit elsewhere. He did not bother with the cells, although he did see someone laying on one of the cots covered by a blanket. Probably some drunk.

"Not in there?" Lewis Foss asked when Crowe got back into the truck.

"Nope!"

"What now?"

"Can't be too hard to find. Just look for his truck. We'll try the Iron Man Saloon. Profit hangs out there most of the time when he isn't harassing some citizen. Ever been in the Iron Man, Foss?" Crowe asked.

"Heard plenty about it, enough so I've stayed clear of it."

"Yeah, the place is a bit on the low-life side, but buy a low-life a whisky and you buy yourself a vote. That's how I look at it."

Foss was surprised. He hadn't credited Crowe with enough intelligence to buy votes with kind acts. He saw Crowe as the typical bully, both him and Profit. He saw them as gaining votes with sheer intimidation, not with the kindness of a free drink to the less privileged of the community. "Is that what you think Profit's doing right now, setting up drinks for the voting dredges?"

"Nope!" Crowe said. "I think 'e's huntin' me and Backus right now. He'll be lookin' for a way to get even. We need to find him and settle him down, so voters don't get the sense we're not all on the right side."

"Mind if I offer a suggestion, Mr. Crowe?" Foss asked. He saw in this whole scenario an opportunity for him to get even with Crowe after too long a wait. Crowe still needed paying back for the night on the road, the night he (Foss) came back to camp after a long and hard day with a repaired tire, and did not get fed upon his return.

"Go ahead," Crowe said. He had been wondering what the best way to deal with Profit might be. This Foss, he seemed fairly bright. Perhaps his ideas were worth a listen.

"Leave your knife and whatever weapons you have in the truck. Show Profit he has nothing to fear from you, or you from him."

"I'm not sure that's a good plan. We did beat the shit outta him, you know."

"Blame that on Backus. Profit's probably figured out by now he had it coming anyway, but just in case he's still a little sore about it, blame Tully Backus," Foss told him with a reassuring smile.

Crowe bought it. He laid his pistol on the floor of the truck, his sheathed knife on the seat, and pulled to a stop in front of the Iron Man Saloon — right next to Constable Profit's truck. He walked proudly into the saloon.

The moment Profit saw Crowe coming he got up from his barstool. He walked rapidly and purposefully to Crowe. He saw no gun. He saw no knife. His first swing landed on Crowe's chin with the power of an anvil, rendering him unable to retaliate. Then Profit pummeled him bloody right there in the Iron Man, in the presence of fifteen of their votes. Louis Foss looked on, arms folded across his barrel chest, broad smile on his face.

"C'mon." Foss said pulling Crowe to his feet by a limp arm. "Let's get you back to the mine."

~*~

Dexter Connors tipped his hat as he rode by the same truck he had met on his way to the mine, at least he imagined it the same truck. The driver was different but how many could there be. No matter. He tipped his hat just the same.

At the base of the hill, Lewis Foss stopped the

truck in front of the mining company office. Emil Crowe was just coming around. "What the hell happened?" Crowe asked.

"You got your ass kicked. You must've pissed that constable off way farther than we thought, Boss," Foss said and smiled.

"Think that's funny, do you?"

"I apologize," Foss told him. "I missed my guess. That's all. And you got yourself blindsided for it. C'mon. We'll go in here and we'll do our damnedest to patch you up."

As the door to the mine office opened, Randal Parks' dead body rolled out onto the board sidewalk in front of the building, one bullet hole in his forehead, a pool of blood and a whimpering Lawrence Fish inside. "Jesus Christ!" Crowe said.

"Yeah!" Foss agreed.

"Crowe looked at Fish huddling in a corner. "I recon this makes you the new mine boss," he said.

Chapter Twenty-one

Six in the morning seemed to come in a flash to Libby Tilden. Perhaps it was because she had slept so soundly. Perhaps it was the excitement of what she had planned. Whatever the cause it was uncharacteristic for her. She had been an extremely light sleeper ever since the morning she awoke to find Carl, her tarred and feathered husband, hanging from the tree in their yard. She reasoned when she first began planning it that her get-even agenda would put an end to her restless nights for good. And — she hoped — would put and end as well to the vivid image of Carl's lifeless body tumbling to the earth when she cut the rope from his neck that morning. She only wished she had courage; not for killing Amos Profit, she had plenty of courage for that, courage driven by hate and vengeance. What she lacked was the kind of courage that would allow her to be honest with her friend, Abigail. She detested having to lie to her. After all, should something go wrong, and it easily could, she would be putting Abigail in as much danger as herself. She hadn't been totally dishonest with Abigail though. She did want to see Newton Blake again, see if he was alright, see if he was still alive. She simply neglected the part about wanting to shoot Amos Profit, maybe others, but she doubted the need for that. Newt, provided he was alive, had gone to Calumet to take care of Crowe and the Klan element. She should not have to deal with that. It was just Profit.

He was the one with involvement in the death of her late husband and Clara's father who might go unpunished. Libby would see to it personally that did not happen. She wiped excess oil from Carl's old six-shooter, checked to see it was fully loaded, wrapped it in a hand towel, and stuffed it in her handbag.

"What are you doing, Mama?" Clara asked as she rubbed the sleep from her eyes.

"Good morning," Libby said and snapped the flap of her bag down. "We're going on a long ride today, with Abigail. Won't that be fun?"

"Where are we going?"

"Well… me and Abigail need to take care of some business in Calumet. But… you… you get to visit Annie. Won't that be exciting?" Annie had been Clara's very best playmate when both families lived in Calumet. Now Annie lived in Marble, next door to Calumet yet far enough away that Clara would be untouched by any of her mother's actions in Calumet that day. Clara donned a enormous and brilliant smile and Libby knew she was pleased.

~*~

Abigail McCain stuffed a derringer wrapped in a handkerchief under the seat of her Ford Model T. She hadn't slept well at all. She wondered to herself why she had even agreed to such a thing. Calumet was the last place on earth she wanted to visit. But Libby had been so intent, how could she tell her no? It wasn't in her. A friend in need was what Libby Tilden had become. And Abigail would give her what she could. This time it would be a ride into Calumet. As she drove the distance between her farm and Libby's she wondered how she would handle things. Should she tell Libby? She hadn't let on that she even knew where Calumet was prior to this day, let alone that she had once lived there. She began to question why she hadn't ran into Libby or Carl when she lived there. Calumet wasn't but a few blocks long, not big at all. Not that she knew Carl, she didn't; and wouldn't have known he was Libby's if their paths had actually crossed. But she had seen photos of Carl at Libby's, and she did not recall ever having seen him. Did they move to Calumet after Abigail left? Maybe she would ask. Maybe it would ease her into the conversation that would lead to her being honest with Libby about her past. It bothered her having deep secrets from her best, actually, only friend.

~*~

Libby and Clara were anxiously waiting on the front porch of their farmhouse when Abigail drove up. They were in the car seconds after it came to a stop. "In a hurry, are we?" Abigail asked.

"We weren't sure how long this was going to take. I want to be back before dark. I imagine you'll need to be home when Thomas get's up this evening," Libby explained.

"It's not going to take as long as we thought," Abigail said. "We can follow the railroad north and it'll connect with the main road just west of Calumet a mile or so."

"Is that what Thomas told you?"

"Mr. Tyler. The mail man," Abigail said.

"Do you know where Marble is?" Libby asked.

Abigail thought for a moment. There hadn't been

a town called Marble when she lived in Calumet, but there was talk of one and she knew where it was to be built. "No," she said not wanting to get into a conversation in which she would have to tell Libby about her past, not with Clara in the car. Too many questions to answer.

"It's a rather new town, just west of Calumet. We'll stop there. I have an old friend we can leave Clara with while we go looking for Newt," Libby said.

Abigail was glad for it. She really wanted to let Libby in on her plan for the day, her private reason for choosing to take Libby to Calumet in the first place, a confession of sorts. It gnawed at her, this deceit. But with Clara listening in it would just have to gnaw. With the little girl away from them, however, she was free to tell her friend anything. She silently prayed Libby would not think poorly of her once she opened up. That would be worse than what had brought on the need for her actions in the first place.

"I want to see Newt," Clara said.

"Not this time, Clara," Libby told her.

"When, then?" Clara asked.

"Soon," Libby promised.

Abigail turned the Ford onto a dirt pathway barely wide enough for a small wagon alongside the train tracks. "You certain we can drive this all the way to Calumet?" Libby asked, looking down the two-rut road with grass cropping up in its middle.

"Mr. Tyler said we can. He said it was narrow but smooth. He said we can make pretty good time too. The only problem we'll have is one creek crossing. We'll need to go down in the water, but Mr. Tyler says automobiles make it all the time and not to worry about it."

"I don't know, Abigail." Libby looked into the back seat at Clara. "Maybe we should take the long way through Grand Rapids."

"Nonsense. That'll take twice the time, maybe more. Mr. Tyler said we'll be just fine."

Thirty minutes into the trip came a trestle. Tracks only. No room for a car. Creek far below. Abigail pulled to a stop, set the brake, and got out to have a look. "That little trail we saw just back there," she said, gesturing back up the narrow roadway as she talked, "I'll bet we need to follow that."

"Let's walk it first. I'd feel more comfortable," Libby suggested. She instructed Clara to stay in the backseat while the two women scouted the trail. Abigail had been right. The road snaked through a patch of woods and sloped gently down to the water. They could see tracks from other vehicles and wagons crossing the creek and coming out on the other side to another gentle slope upward to the roadway beside the tracks again. Soon they were on the other side, making good time once again. The closer they came to Calumet the quieter the women got.

As they reached Marble, Libby was first to speak — a necessity — she needed to give Abigail directions. Once Clara was safely in their friend's home, the two women set out for Calumet. The time had come for Libby to come clean. "I don't want you to drive into Calumet."

"Of course not. Where's this friend of yours, this Newton Blake? I imagine that's where you wish to go."

"No!" Libby said. "I'm afraid I haven't been honest about my reason for this trip, Abigail. I'm going into Calumet. I want to walk in so I can arrive unnoticed."

"Do you think this Newton Blake of yours has another girl?" Abigail asked.

"Oh heavens no! It's just that… oh… how do I tell you?" Libby questioned.

"Oh for pity sakes. Just come out with it. How bad could it be?"

"Alright then, I didn't come here for Newton Blake at all. I mean, I do want to see him, but that isn't my real reason. I came here to shoot the man who killed Clara's father," Libby said and pulled the towel-wrapped gun from her purse.

Abigail slammed on the brakes and began to laugh uncontrollably.

"Is that funny?" Libby asked her.

"Hilarious!"

"Why? Is it because you don't think I'll do it?"

"No! No! Not at all! It's because that's why I agreed to bring you," Abigail said.

"So I could shoot my husband's killer?"

"No! So I could shoot my ex-husband," she said as she reached beneath the seat and pulled out the handkerchief wrapped derringer. She laid the gun on the seat and pulled the Model T into the brush. "We'll walk from here," she said.

"Who is your Ex-husband and why do you want to shoot him?" Libby asked as she stepped from the car's running board.

"Owen Pruitt. And I want to kill him because of what he did to me many years ago. He's the mortician in Calumet."

"I know that. He buried Carl. I still owe him," Libby told her.

"You won't after today."

"So what did he do to you, beat you?"

"Some," Abigail admitted. "But that's not why he deserves to die. He deserves that because of those other things he did. He was a perverted son-of-a-bitch, pardon my French. He made me make love to him in the coffins. It was horrible. He did it that way for years and I dreaded it. But that's not why I left."

"That would have been enough for me," Libby told her. "So… what did make you leave?"

"He tried to make me do it with a corpse. It was a young man who had been shot trying to escape the bedroom of an early home from work miner. The stiff was stiff, if you get my meaning, and Owen ordered me into the coffin with him. That was the end of it for me."

"So… what did this dead man look like?" Libby asked.

Abigail smiled, then giggled a bit. "Honestly? Not bad as I recall," she said and broke into laughter. When she calmed she asked, "Tell me Libby, what would you do if it was your husband?"

Libby chuckled a bit under her breath at the though of it all, knowing of course that it had to have been devastating at the time, but funny now. "You go ahead, Abigail. You shoot him. He has it coming."

"So… who's this killer your after?" Abigail asked as they came into a clearing. They silently studied it in all directions for a time, then crossed.

"Amos Profit, the constable," Libby told her.

"Oh, dear! Yours is dangerous. Mine won't even be armed, but yours can shoot back. You sure you want to do this?"

"Are you?"

"Hell, yes!" Abigail said.

"Well... so am I."

The two women found Owen Pruitt behind the mortuary cleaning his first ever motorcar hearse. They had planned. Libby would distract him. He was considerably larger than his former wife, and strong. He would easily overpower her if given the opportunity. Libby came up the alley walking straight at Pruitt. He kept his eyes glued on her. Abigail approached from behind him, derringer at the ready. "Can I help you, Ma'am?" He asked pleasantly.

"Probably can't help her, you bastard," Abigail said from behind him. "But you can help me by turning around so I can see you die." He turned.

"Abigail?" he asked. And she shot, once in the chest. He gasped for air, fell to his knees, then bounced up and rushed her. She aimed, pulled back the derringer's hammer, and pulled the trigger. Nothing. Then she heard the shot from behind her and saw the bullet pierce Owen Pruitt's forehead. She turned.

"Kaleb?" she asked as she recognized her former brother-in-law.

"You girls best get out of here. Profit's gotta be on his way. He'll have heard the shots." And the two women fled around the corner.

They were back on the street in front of the mortuary in seconds watching the constable duck into the alley where the shots came from, gun drawn, hammer back. "Let's go," Libby ordered. "We'll follow him into the alley and get this over with."

"You sure that's wise?" Abigail asked. "He's armed."

"He'll always be armed unless we catch him in his sleep," Libby said. "Now is the time. It may be cowardly but I think I'm just going to shoot him in the back." And they ducked into the alley where Profit had just gone.

"What the hell happened here?" Profit asked Kaleb Pruitt. He looked down at Owen's body. "You shoot 'im?"

"No! He's my brother, Amos. You remember that."

"Sure I do, but did you shoot 'im?

"No!"

"Then who did?" Profit asked.

"I don't know. I heard the shots and came running," Kaleb explained.

Amos Profit stooped down over the body. "There was two of 'em," he said. "Two holes—different sizes—two different guns. He say anything?"

"He murmured something, sounded like Abigail," Kaleb said.

"Poor son-of-a-bitch," Profit said as he slid his six- shooter back into its holster. "His dying words and he calls out for the bitch who run out on 'im. Pity."

"He wasn't calling out for her, Constable," Libby said. Profit stood and turned to look into the barrel of Libby's handgun. "He was telling on her."

"Now… you just hold up there, Missy," Profit ordered and held out a hand, maybe to catch or stop a bullet that might be headed his way.

"You killed my husband. Now I'm going to kill you." and she pulled the trigger. Profit fell to his knees.

"Shoot him again," Abigail said. And Libby did. In the forehead. Then Abigail looked at Kaleb? "You going to tell? Do we have to shoot you too?"

Kaleb looked down at his brother. He looked at the dead constable. "Who would I tell?" he asked and tipped his hat. "Ladies," he said and walked off.

They looked both ways, the two women, before they walked into the clearing and proceeded toward the Model T hidden in the brush. Their missions had been completed. Their silence told each other their deeds were not going down well.

"Can I stay at your house tonight, Libby," Abigail asked softly. But she would not; Thomas would need her.

"Of course you can."

Chapter Twenty-two

"You hear 'bout the shootings in town?" Ira Shank asked his companions around the campfire that evening. "Owen Pruitt, the undertaker. He's deader than a doornail. So is old Amos Profit."

"Profit?" Newton Blake asked. "Amos Profit, the constable?"

"The same," Ira said.

"Who killed them?" Newt asked.

"Nobody knows, at least, nobody's sayin'. Otis Johnson said he saw a couple of strange women in town. Doubt it was them though."

"Why?" Virgil Dare asked.

"Why what?" Ira asked.

"Why would you doubt it might be a couple of strange women?"

"Strange women don't go 'round shootin' folks," Ira said.

"The hell they don't," Newt said. "I knew one who shot a cattleman right in the throat, then watched him bleed to death. Took quite a while for him to die too."

"And you know this gal?" Ira asked.

"Sure do. So do you, I recon."

"I recon I don't know any such gal," Ira argued.

"This one you do," Newt said. "I know. It's Molly Carpenter. She shot a cattleman in the throat down in St Louis, just before she came here to Calumet. I outta know. I was the marshal down there at the time."

"Really?" Ira asked.

"Honest!" Newt said. "Now… what about the two women? Otis get a good look at them?"

Ira described them as Otis had when he came out to the mine looking for Kaleb Pruitt to tell him his brother had been killed. Newton Blake had no idea who the one woman could be, but the description Otis had given of the other and was now being repeated by Ira Shank, was sure a close description of Libby Tilden. But how could that be? Libby was twenty miles south and stranded. Impossible. He put it out of his mind. "That sound like anybody any of you fellers know?" Ira asked.

No one answered him.

"Anything else happening in the mine today?" Rans Feltus asked Ira.

"Old Crowe and his boys…Oh, did I mention Profit beat the shit outta Crowe? That was before he got his self shot of course. Anyway, Crowe and the rest of them boys is all upset over the shootin' of Mr. Parks. And now, none of the miners is afraid of votin' whichever way they want to. Nobody's scared of old Fish, ya know.

~*~

The news of Randal Parks' death was a blow to Isaac Burris, Hibbing's Klan leader and mayor. Without Parks in place, the task of taking the town of Calumet under the rule of the KKK seemed enormous. It was Parks who led the mine and held influence over miner's votes. Fish was nothing. Fish wasn't even a good assistant to Parks. Burris had told Parks as much;

he had told him to find a replacement for Fish, a man who possessed leadership qualities, not butler qualities like Fish. What if something happened to Parks? Who would lead? These were the questions Burris had asked. And, guess what? Something did happen. Burris should have known. Parks was insecure — couldn't deal with having an equal at his side, someone who might go over his head with his superiors or go behind his back with the men, someone who was able to out-lead him. And now… it was too late. Burris should have forced Parks' hand long ago. He should have insisted Parks replaced Fish. But he hadn't.

"Elections are less than a week away," Tully Backus told Isaac Burris when he telephoned with the news. Profit had a change of heart once he whipped Crowe in the Iron Man, and had let Backus out of his cell. "I don't see what we can do. Without Parks, the miners will vote their minds, and I'm afraid that'll be Otis Johnson. The only way Crowe will get in is through intimidation, and sadly, no Randal Parks holding their livelihood over their heads, no intimidation."

"What about that constable, that Profit fellow. Can he help us?"

"He might have been of use. But he's dead!" Backus informed Burris.

"Dead? How?"

"A couple of pretty woman walked into town, shot the undertaker, shot Profit, and then left town quick as they come. Everyone figures they were after the undertaker and Profit kind of got in the way."

"Christ!"

"Yeah!" Backus agreed.

"Well… what about that man who does the hiring out at the mine, that Curtiss what's his name?"

"Curtiss Clay," Tully told him.

"Yeah, Curtiss Clay. He in any position to bump Lawrence Fish out of the way and lead the mine?"

"I don't know. But I don't think he'll help us."

"Why not?" Isaac Burris asked.

"He's a Catholic," he almost whispered. Clay was in the next room. That answered all questions. The Klan would not use Catholics, and Catholics would not do for the Klan, and that was all there was to it.

"Shit!" Isaac said.

"Shit, is right."

"Well… you say elections are a week away," Burris said.

"Yes, Sir. One week less a day," Tully Backus confirmed.

"What if this Otis Johnson wins the election? Wasn't the dead constable on the ticket with him?"

"He was," Backus said.

"Any chance you're in position to slide in under Johnson? If you can, if you've made good enough friends with the man, we can still win in Calumet."

Tully Backus went silent for a time. He hadn't wanted to tell Burris, but now it appeared he had to. "Otis Johnson found out I'm KKK. I don't know how, but he found out."

Now it was time for silence from the Hibbing end of the telephone conversation. Finally Burris spoke. "It's time for war," he said.

"Are you sure? I mean, we're working in the mine, many men, all saying they're making friends and making progress winning over the minds of fellow miners. Isn't that something that'll help?"

"Help? Yes. But it'll only help. It won't do the whole job. I'm afraid without Parks and his threats of closing the place down if they vote wrong, it'll only do half the job," Isaac Burris said.

"Well... why don't we supply the intimidation?" Backus suggested.

"I couldn't agree more. But like it or not, that'll be the war I'm talking about. Get it started," Isaac Burris said and hung up. He would call the mining company to see if a suitable replacement for Parks was available, one who would be sympathetic to the cause, but he knew it would be a shot in the dark. Time was too short.

Tully Backus left the mining company office in search of Emil Crowe. This would be an order suited to Crowe. He was the type of man who'd rather win a war than win an election anyway.

Curtiss Clay watched Tully Backus mount a horse and ride up the hill and away from the mine. He set out as soon as Backus disappeared from sight, on his way to the shaft. As much as he hated the thought of lowering himself into a black hole in the earth — Clay was a more than a touch claustrophobic — he needed to find Ira Shank. He needed to report this latest development, or at least as much of it as he got from one side of a telephone conversation, to Shank so he could take it to Newton Blake. If forewarned is truly forearmed, his message was valuable. If not, then no loss.

August Cole had undergone serious grilling from Ira Shank while they worked. Ira wanted to know, now that Parks and his undue pressure on the miners to vote his way was out of the picture and Amos Profit's candidacy was as dead as the man, was Cole still determined to cast his vote for Emil Crowe? Hours of Ira's time had gone into this. August Cole was a friend, more than that, August was pretty much Ira's best friend. But either Ira had been unconvincing or August was simply hard headed. No progress was being made.

The abrupt sound made by the elevator cage falling the last fifteen feet and the cloud of dust that all but filled the tunnel they were shoring up, the tunnel leading to the new drift Ira and August had spent the better part of a week opening up, brought an equally abrupt end to their work. They were closer by half to the cage than any of the other miners. They ran. As the dust settled onto the floor it also settled onto the figure of a man laying prone and still inside the cage. Ira and August pulled at the wire door to the elevator. Immovable. Like it was welded in place. They jerked harder. Nothing. Then the dust covered figure inside the cage began to stir. He looked around, bright blue eyes, looking larger than life, peering eerily from beneath an orange mask. Ira and August backed away several steps. They looked at one another. They looked back at the man. Eerie had turned to panic. The man began bouncing off the walls of the cage trying to break out. Ira and August, once again pulled at the door, this time their effort timed with the man inside throwing all of his weight at it as well. When it gave way, all three men landed in a heap far out in the tunnel. "Mr. Clay?" Ira asked as he recognized the new arrival.

"What the hell happened?" Curtiss Clay asked.

"The cable gave out I recon," Ira told him. "What're ya doin' down here?" Clay's fear of tight places was well known. Anyone who came across him in the tunnels would take a second look to see if their eyes had been playing tricks on them.

"I came searching you out, Ira. I need to talk to you."

"Down here?"

"Of course not," Clay said. "Now… how the hell do we get out of here?"

"We climb."

"Climb?"

"Yeah! We climb. There's an emergency ladder that leads to the top. We climb the ladder," Ira said.

"Should I come?" August Cole asked.

Curtiss Clay looked at Ira Shank. Ira Shank looked at August Cole then back at Curtiss Clay. The look on Clay's face along with his silence told Ira that this conversation would be a private one. "I'll be right back," he told August.

Otto Pavlic, leader of the men who recently joined the miners at the Calumet operation, the men who had been sent by Isaac Burris, Hibbing's mayor and Klan leader, to infiltrate and convert miners to the Klan's service, approached August Cole from behind. "What was that all about?" he asked.

The sudden intrusion in the otherwise silent tunnel startled August Cole. He jumped. Pavlic laughed, then offered a feeble apology in a joking manner. "What's what all about?" Cole asked once he regained his composure.

"Mr. Clay there. And your partner, Ira. What are they doin'?"

"I don't know. Mr. Clay just come down here, the cable holdin' the cage snapped, the cage fell, me and Ira sprung 'im from the cage — the door was stuck — then Ira and Clay, they climbed to the surface and that's all I know."

"Clay didn't say anything?"

"I think Mr. Clay was too scared to talk much. All he seemed to want was for Ira to take 'im back to the surface. That's all," August told him. All the while he was moving toward the ladder and pointing up animatedly.

As Ira Shank cleared the top of the shaft ladder and stood on solid ground he came face to face with Emil Crowe. Crowe grabbed him by the arm and flung him aside like a rag doll. Curtiss Clay popped his head out of the shaft. Emil Crowe kicked him hard in the face. Clay clung to the ladder. Crowe kicked again. Clay lost his grip. He plummeted down the shaft, bouncing from wall to wall to ladder and screaming helplessly as he fell, finally landing right on top of August Cole. Clay cracked his head open on the cage at the bottom and bled to death rapidly. Cole died instantly from a broken neck. Otto Pavlic shook his head. "Jesus Christ, Crowe," he said and walked off toward the drift he had been working.

When Crowe looked around, he found no Ira Shank in sight. When he flung him, Ira kept on going. He had cleared the hill, and was well on his way back to Newton Blake's camp.

Chapter Twenty-three

Aside from short but pleasant conversation when they picked Clara up from her play date in Marble, the two women, Abigail McCain and Libby Tilden, made the journey home in silence, each of them going over in their minds their deeds of the day, both of them looking inwardly for absolution that did not seem to come. Tears were held back for Clara's sake.

"Will Thomas be upset with you?" Libby asked Abigail as the Model T came to a stop in front of her farmhouse. They were back much later than either of them had guessed they would be.

"No! Heavens no!" Abigail answered. "Thomas understands," she added with a forced smile. "I best hurry on home just the same." She did not wish to be invited in and she felt her friend was about to do just that, out of politeness of course. She imagined Libby had as much a need for quiet aloneness as she did.

Libby welcomed Abigail's words. She did not want company tonight. She wanted to think, to dwell — more or less — on what this day had brought. And she wanted to find a way that would let her live with herself for the rest of her life, a way to deal with the guilt, which seemed unbearable at that moment. And she thought her friend needed to do the same. "Good night," she said and closed the car door.

~*~

"Home kinda early, ain't ya?" Ransom Feltus asked Ira Shank. "Trouble out at the mine?"

"Might say!" Ira admitted. He grabbed a cup and poured himself coffee from a large steel pot hanging above the campfire. He sipped in an obnoxiously loud slurping noise.

"It ain't soup, fool," Lucas Mann offered.

"Don't mess with me today, Lucas — I ain't in the mood."

Newton Blake's ability to read faces had developed throughout his substantial career in law. As he entered the area and squatted to fill his own coffee cup, he focused in on Ira Shank. He could see there in Ira's eyes the need for intervention. Clearly, the beginning of Lucas Mann's effort to get one of his little comical 'pick on Ira for his own amusement' conversations going, needed suppressing. "Lucas, find Dexter Connors. The two of you ride in and sniff around the Iron Man for a bit. See if you can pick up on any news we can use." Then Newt looked at Ira. He watched Lucas Mann disappear from sight out of the corner of his eye before he spoke. "Out with it, Ira. What's happened?" And he took a sip of his coffee. "Burnt," he snapped. He curled his lip and pitched the coffee into the fire.

"Curtiss Clay's dead," Ira said.

"Are you sure?" Newt asked. It wasn't good news. Not at all. Clay was the one mining company friend to his side of the upcoming battle, him being Catholic and anti Klan. And he was all that was left of mine management. There was, of course, Lawrence Fish, but Fish was a nobody, even worse, Fish was a nobody who would be easily used by whoever might be the major influence at the mine and right now that was not

Newt and the boys. It was the Klan.

"Sure as I can be," Ira said. He went on to describe Curtiss Clay's trip into the tunnel to seek Ira out. He told Newt of the collapse of the cage due to the cable giving out, and the fifteen or twenty foot drop the cage made with Clay onboard. He described the extreme effort it had taken to free the jammed cage door and the panic the whole idea of entrapment brought out in the claustrophobic Curtiss Clay. He went on about their climb to the surface through the shaft station and up the ladders. He told Newt that he had gone first and that he came face to face with Emil Crowe, and that once Crowe had cast him aside, how he kicked Curtiss Clay in the face until Clay lost his grip on the ladder and fell back to the bottom of the shaft. "I just kept on runnin', I did."

"Well... that don't mean he's dead," Newt argued. He had seen falls in his lifetime, many of them. Some much farther than fifteen or twenty feet. Hell, once when he was young and the family farmed a small place over near the Kansas border, he and his brother got into a scrap in the hayloft. They both fell. The drop was eighteen feet. He got a broken wrist and his brother got a scratch, that's all. "Many a man's fallen twenty feet without injury," he added.

"Fifteen or twenty was his fall — inside the cage. This one was all the way down. And it was different. He didn't fall. He was shoved, and it was Emil Crowe who shoved 'im. Now when Crowe does something like that, he aims to kill. You can bet he scooted down that ladder to see, and if Clay wasn't dead, Crowe finished the job. That's how I see it."

Ira made sense. Newt had to concede. He had to figure Curtiss Clay was a goner and the outfit no longer had a friend in the mine's management. He thought about the elections and wondered if Clay or Parks would even be replaced before then. Not likely, and probably not worth much if they were. It takes time to make good relationships with officials, months, sometimes years, and time was not on their side. "I wonder," Newt said to all who were gathered: Ira, Rans Feltus, Virgil Dare, and Alexander Penovich, "I wonder should we attack now?"

"Without a plan?" Virgil Dare asked. He pulled out his six gun and spun the tumbler. "Risky. Dangerous. A real challenge. I say yes!"

"Well, as much as I can see your spirited desire to throw yourself into the heart of danger, Virg, I vote no," Penovich said. "I like the element of surprise an immediate attack would have, but that's only useful if we ain't surprised right along with the enemy."

"Why would we be surprised?" Feltus asked.

"Why? I'll tell you why." Hell, I'm surprised we're even considerin' it. That's why," Penovich answered. He looked around at the others. He too possessed the ability to read people. He dealt with union business, with getting workers agitated enough to vote against everything they had previously known as normal, and getting them to vote in favor of what appeared a whole new, braver world than the one they had been so comfortable in all their lives, and it all required the ability to read men. You read wrong and the bottom falls out. And now he saw the thoughts of those around him. Newton Blake was anxious, he wanted it over and done. Ira Shanks wanted it done as well, but Ira was afraid. Ransom Feltus seemed void of expression, like his opinion could run uphill or down, depending on how the others voted. Virgil, on the other hand, was unafraid and rather calm, too calm. Virgil Dare just wanted to die in a blaze of glory. Alexander Penovich shrugged his shoulders. "Whatever the rest of you decide," he said.

"So is that a yes vote?" Ira asked.

"I'm abstaining."

"Oh, no you don't," Newt said. "We go unanimously or not at all. That's our best chance of winning."

"Well then, I suggest we all vote. I don't mean just the five of us, the whole unit. Then let's go for a majority vote. We go for unanimous and we'll be here through the winter," Penovich said.

"Agreed," said Newt Blake. "Anyone else got something more to say?" None did. "Alright then, we'll get 'em all together tonight and take the vote."

~*~

Libby Tilden cried her eyes out as she fixed supper for her and Clara. She thought this was what she had wanted. It was, after all, something that was on her mind like a bad angel talking in her ear since the day she had been forced away from her life in Calumet and into the weeds of her old family spread, a woman alone with a child. It was that vengeance she had thought would be so sweet. But it had turned bitter. So she wept, and when her daughter came in from playing in the yard and asked why her mother wept, Libby blamed it on the onions.

"What's that for, Mama?" Clara Asked pointing at the counter beside the sink.

Libby looked. There laid Carl's gun rolled in a towel, barrel poking out two inches. *Cripe sakes,* Libby silently scolded herself. "Oh, I just thought I'd give it a good cleaning, that's all."

"So Newt can use it when he gets back?"

"That's right, Dear. So Newt can use it. We'll clean it up real nice, and then we'll hang it on the wall by the door for him. How's that?"

~*~

Abigail McCain had forgotten to feed the chickens that morning, and now, late in the day when she should be inside cooking Thomas' supper, there she was, doing morning chores. But this was important too. What would Thomas say if he knew she had forgotten the chickens? She swung her arm across her body scattering seed in an arch and watched the hungry chickens sort out their pecking order. She would see to it now and none would be the wiser. She took a moment to gather a few eggs and lay them softly in her apron, then headed for her kitchen.

Abigail, potatoes boiling atop her wood-burning cook stove, flour-coated chicken frying in a pan next to them, set the table to serve two, her and Thomas. He would awaken anytime. Suddenly she remembered. She had forgotten about the derringer. It still lay wrapped in a handkerchief under the seat of the Model T, where she had put it before she and Libby went to collect Clara in Marble. She should have thrown it away. Thomas didn't even know she had it in the first place. Now, though, it might be possible for him to find it and that would lead to questions she cared not to answer, even dared not to answer. She ran from her table setting, pulled the door to the Ford open, reached under the seat and collected the tiny handgun, and walked it to the chicken coup where she pushed it to the bottom of a nearly full pail of chicken feed. He'd not think to look there. She always fed the chickens and so long as Thomas did not discover she hadn't that morning, it would go on being that way.

    Supper was a silent time. Abigail so loved fried chicken that whenever she fixed it she ate in silence. Generally, she did not think, she enjoyed it so much. But this night, she would think. She would go over and over in her mind the shot she had made to the midsection of her first husband, Owen Pruitt, with the derringer, the clean and neat shot her friend, Libby, made to the forehead the constable who had been responsible for her husband Carl's death, and the final execution of Owen by his own brother. Suddenly she smiled — just a tiny smile of course so Thomas wouldn't see it. She had been sad earlier, on the trip home, but now, somehow everything seemed alright. *Libby and me are alike. We're both widowed by our first husbands and now we can go on with our lives,* she thought. She smiled again, this time larger. Then she looked across the table to Thomas' chair. "What?" she asked.

    Thomas did not answer.

Chapter Twenty-four

It would not be until morning that everyone at the camp could be gathered for a meeting. Four men were told of the plan to attack, asked to submit their vote on the idea, then sent off to guard the camp so that none of their meeting risked the chance of being overheard by some spy in the woods.

Doc Waters joined them. Dexter Connors had been sent to Doc's to inform him of the meeting, to tell him the war was coming. "Things are getting a little spooky in town," he told Newton Blake as he climbed down from his saddle.

"How so, Doc? Newt asked.

"Parks is dead, both Profit and Owen Pruitt were shot to death by a pair of strangers — women at that, and if that isn't enough, Curtiss Clay got himself shoved down a mine shaft and died. Now just to make the whole thing more interesting, when Clay landed at the bottom, he landed smack on August Cole. Cole's dead too — broken neck — I saw it myself. They brought them all to me since we no longer have an undertaker.

Virgil Dare got to his feet. "Where's the closest telegraph?" he asked. Doc's report reminded Virgil that he had left instructions with a compadre back at the logging camp to send his best suit to the undertaker in Calumet should something happen to him. He dusted off his britches. A cloud of red puffed from his hand. *Can't let 'em burry me like this,* he thought.

"Marble," Newt offered. "That's the one I used to send for Penovich and the boys."

"There an undertaker in that Marble?"

"I recon there is. There is in most towns these days."

Virgil Dare saddled his horse.

"What about the meeting, Virg?" Newt asked.

"You got my vote," he said. "Let's ride on the sons-a-bitches." And he rode off for Marble.

"So… what are you hearing, Doc? Any rumblings that might tell us something about what they're planning?" Newt asked as Virgil Dare rode out of sight.

"Lucian Locke stopped by last evening. He seems to think Crowe and his boys might just go after Otis Johnson. It seems with all the killing that's already gone on, Crowe's concluded that the only way he has left of winning is if he has no competition. Now Locke also claimed the newest miners are doing a pretty good job of swaying men to the Klan's way of thinking. Even so, they can't count on that happening in time. They'll send someone for Otis."

"How the hell can they sway men?" Alexander Penovich asked. "They're the Klan for Christ sakes. And these are reasonable men."

"You know, Penovich," Doc started, "you union boys see like you're in a tunnel. You think nobody else can be as convincing as you. Hell, the Klan's been influencing folks for longer than the union has existed, and that's a fact. Don't ever think they're not persuasive. They wouldn't be as many as they are if they didn't have that ability. Best you consider that, mister union agitator. You're not all that different when it comes right down to it."

Penovich stood. He spat tobacco on the ground in front of Doc Waters, clearly taking offence at Doc's words. Newt stood. Rans Feltus stood. Ira Shank stood. "Doc's right," Feltus said. "He might not say it so pleasantly, but 'e's right. I been down there in the mine. I heard some of 'em talk, and most of 'em, not them like Crowe of course, but most other Klansmen talk like us — they make friends — and they do that just like us. They don't go right up front with their ideas 'bout Negros and Catholics and Jews and settlers from the wrong parts of Europe and that sort of thing. Hell, most of them miners have no idea of what the Klan is all about yet. Some of 'em never will, some will find out too late. And some of them boys down in the drift think of those Klan fellers as religious. Some of 'em figure the union's the devil."

"Alexander Penovich sat back in the dirt. "I suppose that's true enough," he said.

"Tell me, Doc, when do you think they'll go for Otis?" Newt asked.

"Well, today's Friday. Election's Tuesday. If it were me, I'd be on my way now. But those boys like to work at night. It think I'd start planning something to protect Otis Johnson immediately, just in case they make tonight that night. And a couple things you probably should consider," Doc said. "Profit's dead. His office might be a good one to use to watch the general store from. Mathew Gray down at the livery, he's one of us, we can put a couple men in his place I recon. The other thing is, you might want to close down the telephone and telegraph wires into Calumet. All them Klan fellows came here from Hibbing. That mayor over there, that Isaac Burris, he's Klan as Klan gets, and he's likely in charge of these boys. They send a message to him and we'll be up to our ears in Klan before we know it."

"Good suggestion, Doc," Newt said. "Anyone know where all the telephones and telegraphs are?"

"There's one at the mine, a telephone that is," Ransom Feltus said.

"You outta know," Doc said. "You took it out once and nearly got yourself killed for it."

"Well... that might be so, but I ain't dead, and I still know how to take it out. Want me to do it, Newt?"

"No, not you. I need you with me. Who's the sneakiest son-of-a-bitch we got?"

"Dexter Connors!" three men called out at one time. Virgil Dare was among them — fresh back from his ride to Marble. He had just dismounted his horse as Newt asked the question.

"Why?" Dare asked, having missed the preceding conversation.

"We need someone to shut down the telephone at the mine," Ransom Feltus said.

"He'd be the man. Want him to kill somebody over there for you while he's at it?"

"Just the telephone. Have him get with Rans. He'll tell Dex where to hit it," Newt said. "Now... what about other's. What else is in Calumet? You know Doc?"

"Let's see. There's the mine. You got that one covered. There's Otis Johnson's general store. There's the fire station, and Profit's office. I believe that's it." Doc thought for a moment, thoughts that soon began to develop into an alternate plan.

"I remember one time back at the St. Paul union office," Alexander Penovich butted in. "Something went haywire with the telephone. We could call around the neighborhood, but not out of the city. Anybody know how to make that happen here?"

"That's what I was thinking, something along that order anyhow," Doc said. "I was thinking, what if we could let those boys think the telephones are still working. We'd need to kill the telegraph of course. But why couldn't we leave the phones working. All the calls go through the switchboard. They can't get nowhere if the operator doesn't plug in the right plug to the right hole. Anyone know the operator?"

Ira Shank knew Mary Belle Clausen alright, but he fought hard against enlisting her help. She was from Hibbing, just here in Calumet less than six months, and didn't seem to have local friends.

"What if we put somebody at the switchboard, one of our own?" Rans suggested. "Would that work?"

"We could. But who?" Newt asked.

"Molly sounds a bit like Mary Belle with a cold," Doc offered. "I'll talk with her. She hates the Klan enough to go for it, I'll bet." And Doc got to his feet. He brushed the dirt from his trousers, straightened his jacket, and excused himself explaining that he should be getting back and that he'd talk with Molly and send word whether she would be willing to help or not.

The remainder of the meeting laid the groundwork for the group's plan for defeating the Klan and putting the proper officials in place to ensure that Calumet would be free of unwanted influence in its future. Their first step, all agreed, was to get Otis Johnson to a safe place. Ira Shank, one of the few among them who could show himself at the mine, in any one of the many saloons in town, or at the general store without drawing suspicion to himself, was selected to ride in and see to it that Otis was protected. No other man seeking office would need it. The Klan, when it first arrived, included Emil Crowe and a small number of strong arms who were all dead now, so the only office with a KKK member opposing was the mayor's office — the office Crowe himself sought. Now, as Newton Blake and his men sorted things out, all began to look frighteningly simple and funneled down to one main issue. Protect Otis Johnson.

~*~

Mathew Gray was meticulous when it came to shutting down his livery stable at the end of a day. Always, he locked up the front first, where most of his patrons entered, then the back. Then he would spend an entire hour cleaning and straightening and seeing to anything he hadn't had time to get to if he had a particularly busy day. The only access to the place during this last work hour was through a narrow man door behind his desk, an area he kept a close eye on, so he was amply surprised when he turned and came face to face with a total stranger, a cowboy sort packing a pair of six-shooters. "Can I help you?" he asked.

"Name's Dexter Connors," Dex said. He was shocked that he didn't know Gray. Virg, well really Newton Blake since he was the one giving the orders, had sent Dex out among the population on several occasions. This Gray must not be a drinker. Dex hadn't run across him. "You Mathew Gray?"

"I am." He sized his visitor up. The non-serious type. He looked harmless enough aside from the tied down guns of course.

"Newton Blake sent me."

Mathew Gray knew Newton Blake. Hell everyone

knew Blake, him being the only man in town to stand up to Emil Crowe. But he hadn't seen Blake since the night he disappeared from Doc Waters place above the Red Rose. "Thought Blake might be dead," he said.

"He thought you might think that so he give me this to give to you, so you'd know he sent me." He handed Gray Newt's marshal's badge.

"Hell," Gray said rolling the badge around in his hand, "you could have pulled this off his dead body." And he handed the badge back.

"He also give me this," Dex said and handed Mathew Gray a note.

Gray unfolded the paper and looked at it for a time, then handed it to Dexter Connors. "Can't read," he said. But he guessed Dex was on the level. Who would bring a badge and a note if he wasn't, unless they knew he couldn't read. And damn few knew Gray couldn't read. Certainly not a stranger. "What's Newton Blake want with me?"

Dex went about explaining. He told Gray of the likelihood of Crowe and his men coming after Otis Johnson and killing the competition, literally, so Crowe would be voted in as mayor, and how Newt felt Mathew Gray's livery was an ideal spot to place two or three men as lookouts. "You got a couple barn sashes on the front. Perfect for watchin'." He went to one of them and looked out. Gray joined him and together they watched as Ira Shank banged persistently on the door of the already closed for the day general store. Then they watched Otis Johnson open that door and pull Shank inside, looking both up and down the main street as he did. "Looks to me like Johnson's already been threatened."

"Looks like it," Gray agreed. "When do you boys

want in here?"

"Tonight. Leave that little door unlocked. Can our men hide out in one of those pens?"

"Might be better up there," Mathew said pointing out a ladder leading to a loft. "There's a couple of windows up there too. View might even be better."

"I'll tell them. They'll show after dark. Don't let 'em shoot ya in the morning," Dex said and left.

Mathew Gray finished his evening chores and left the livery without locking the man-door behind his desk.

Chapter Twenty-five

"You gotta go, Otis," Ira Shank said. "You don't get it. These fellers are serious. They're plannin' to kill you if they have to, if it's the only way of gettin' Crowe into the mayor's office. You know that's true, Otis."

"Well... I hear the miners are leaning toward throwing their vote Crowe's way anyway," Otis said.

"Crowe ain't gonna wait for that," Ira said. "And if you stay here, they'll kill ya."

"So what am I to do, Ira? Close my store? Hold up someplace until the election's over? Hell, people don't see me and there's no way they'll vote for me anyway. They'll think I'm dead."

"No, they won't, Otis," Ira Shank assured him. "Newt says..."

"Newt says! Newt says!" Otis paced the floor and shook a finger at Ira. "Newton Blake was brought here to get rid of Crowe and his boys. That should have happened long ago. Where's this Newt been anyway?"

Ira hadn't thought of it — nobody had. The only time Otis could have seen Newton Blake since he got himself tarred and feathered and dumped in the woods near Libby Tilden' place, was when he came in to buy canvas for a tent for the boys. So far as Ira knew, Newt hadn't even seen Otis then. He could have dealt with Otis's girl, or John Pearson, the preacher who watched the store from time to time when Otis' girl was unavailable. He filled Otis in on the details. He told him all he knew about the night Newt disappeared from Doc's. He told Otis about the tar and feathering Newt suffered, and about him not quite all healed up and Crowe and his two thugs coming for him. He filled him in on why Crowe had to send for replacements from Hibbing after Newt killed those two thugs. "He's been a busy man, that Newton Blake, doin' what you brung 'im in fer. You just didn't know how much 'e had to do, that's all, Otis. Now, fer Christ sakes. You let me take you where you'll be safe before it's too late." And he grabbed Otis by the arm. Resistance seemed unwise, Otis being a small man and Ira, although not a large man himself, being quite strong from years of shoveling ore and swinging an axe. Otis did as he was asked. They left out the back door and headed for Doc Waters' house on the edge of town. They steered clear of the main street to avoid being seen.

~*~

Doc Waters nearly had Molly Carpenter convinced to impersonate the telephone operator when a knock came on the back door. "What're those fools doing?" he asked. It had to be miners coming for the bodies of Curtiss Clay and August Cole. Doc still had the two stiffs in a room in the front of the house. Men were to come for them and take them to the undertaker in Marble, Owen Pruitt no longer being available. "They know those body's are in the front." Doc pulled the door open. "Otis?"

~*~

Oscar Barlow was about to climb down Emil Crowe's throat. He had enough. Crowe pushed people past their limits, and to suggest that he (Barlow) had not been loyal to the brotherhood was far past his. "You son-of-a-bitch," he shouted and got to his feet. Crowe's knife appeared like magic. So did Louis Foss's.

"Simmer down," Tully Backus ordered. "That ain't what we're here for."

"To tell the truth, Backus, I don't know what we're here for anymore," Barlow objected. "It sure can't be to put a moron like Crowe in the mayor's seat. I say we kill 'im right now, then we go for that Johnson feller, then we wait for the new election."

Crowe stepped forward, moving on Barlow. "I said simmer," Backus ordered once again. "We got real business to tend to. We can't spend all our fight among ourselves. Save it. Save it for them union boys. Save it for taking care of the likes of this Otis Johnson."

"And just when do we get to do that?" Benjamin Dawes asked. "We can't hold out too much longer. That election ain't that far away."

"I know. I know," said Backus. "But we make a move too fast, and the voters could turn on us." it was an excuse. He didn't know at the moment which direction to take, and he doubted Crowe ever did.

"How is it you seem to be the one in charge, Backus?" Crowe asked.

"Because that's what I was told by Isaac Burris himself the day he sent me with you. Isaac said if things got too sticky over here, I was to take charge. Thing's are sticky, Crowe. Even you can see that. Profit's dead. He was supposed to help you carry the election and he sure can't do that now, can he? And all this killing in the mine, now that's got the miners thinking there won't be jobs after all is done. Parks is dead. We don't even know who killed him. Clay is dead, thanks to you, Crowe. And all those miners have is Lawrence Fish and Fish couldn't lead horny men to a whorehouse let alone lead miners in their work. And has anyone thought about the union? Why aren't they around any longer? I'll tell you what, they didn't disappear just because we come along. The union don't work that way. Once they bite down on something, those boys intend to finish the meal. They're still around. You can bet on that. My guess is they're who killed Parks."

"So what's your plan?" Otto Pavlic asked Backus.

Blood shot from the back of Pavlic's head just as he spoke the last word. Then the sound of a bullet came. The shot had been taken from a distance. Then another man fell. Men ducked into the shadows and waited for the next shot, to see if they could locate the shooter. But none came.

~*~

"I recon you boys can relax for the night," Lucas Mann said, as he climbed the ladder to the loft above Mathew Gray's livery. "I took out two of them Klan boys. They'll be combing the woods lookin' for me most of the night." Mann was a rifleman, an expert, something left over from his mountain days. He could take a man down from so far away with a single shot that he'd be back home in his bed before anyone could figure out where he had been. And he wasn't squeamish about it. He enjoyed his art.

"Why didn't you take out more?" one of the union men from St. Paul asked.

"Newt said just two. Hell, I could have taken half of 'em from where I was. Probably still would have got away too."

~*~

"What in God's name has happened now?" Doc Waters asked, his voice an octave higher than normal as he stared past the two men standing in his open door at the truck in the street out front. From his vantage point, Doc thought the entire flatbed of the truck was loaded with bodies. "How many?" he asked.

"Just two," one of the men answered.

"Both dead?"

"Both of them."

"Then why did you bring them here? They're past helping," Doc insisted.

"Crowe told us to."

"Well, you can tell Crowe…"

"Please, Doc. Just drive 'em to the undertaker in the morning for us. We come back with 'em and we'll get a bullet for our trouble. Please, Doc."

Doc mulled it over for a time. Were they Klan or miners? Miners, probably. Poor bastards. Goddam Crowe. "Leave 'em be. I'll see to them soon as I can," he said, and slammed the door. "Christ," he murmered to himself. "I don't even drive."

"How'd we get so lucky as to become the dropping station for the dead?" Molly asked.

"No clue, Molly. No clue. You get Otis settled in?"

"Sure did, Doc. He ain't none too happy with the

accommodations, though."

"Our cellar ain't good enough for him?" Doc asked. He smiled as he recalled the night in the storm when Molly wanted to hide out down there. He had a hell of a time convincing her that Minnesota storms were not to be feared, at least not to that degree. He thought for a time that she'd make him go down there with her. She even tried bribery, offering to make love to him in the cellar. Luckily, he needed to see Newton Blake that evening, so declined her offer. "Do you suppose Otis can drive?" he asked.

"The real question is, will he after spending the night in the cold dark cellar?"

"I suppose not," he admitted. His look turned suddenly serious. He glanced out one of the kitchen windows, then the other.

"Something wrong, Doc?"

"Sh!"

"What?" Then she heard. The truck out front was running. They rushed to the window in the living room and looked out in time to see the truck pull away.

~*~

Isaac Burris went to the window of his second story Hibbing office as his secretary requested. "Jesus Christ!" he said as he looked at the street below. The truck outside was rigged with framework, two tarred and feathered Klansmen hanging from it. He stared for a bit. He looked at his secretary. He looked back at the truck. "Get somebody to clean that mess up, Doris."

"Yes, Sir."

"Then find Backus for me. Try the Calumet mine. Try that constable's office. Anywhere. Just find him."

Chapter Twenty-six

Breakfast at Doc Waters' house was met with immense gratitude from Otis Johnson, who had been trapped in the cellar since the last evening. The odor of damp sand from the floor and moss from the timber walls clung in his nostrils with such dominance even the delightful aroma of Molly's biscuits and gravy could not completely clear it away. Later he would learn that the objectionable smell was not entirely from the cellar. No one had come for the bodies, those of Curtiss Clay and August Cole, which still lay in one of the rooms and which were beginning to smell, well… dead. Doc closed the door on them, but too late. He could not eat. Molly could not eat. Otis could. The bodies hadn't registered as corpses yet for him. As luck would have it, Otis was just finishing with his breakfast when two men from the mine came for Curtiss and August, to take them to Marble's undertaker. Otis went to the outhouse and threw up his biscuits and gravy. "Goddamn it, Doc," he said upon his return. "Why didn't you tell me? I thought it was the sand."

"I didn't want to ruin your breakfast," Waters told him.

"I need to get to my store," Otis said.

"Someone will come for you. You'll have company at work from now until the election is over," Doc told him.

"Do you really think that's necessary?"

"Maybe not. But let's not take the chance. Somebody kills you or even just hauls you off someplace until the voting's done, and this town ends up with the likes of Emil Crowe running things. It's not worth the chance, Otis. It's not you we're trying to guard. Not entirely. It's also Calumet's future we're concerned with."

Otis Johnson was an animated little man. He pulled his spectacles from his face, wrinkled his lips enough to cause a squint and a frown, rubbed a hand over his balding head, then smoothed his waxed mustache ends between forefinger and thumb. "I suppose you might be right," he said.

Simultaneous knocks on both the front and back doors brought a halt to all activity for a moment, Doc looking unblinkingly at Molly then Otis, Otis swinging his head from side to side to get a look out all windows, Molly dead in her tracks trying to decide which door needed answering first. "Upstairs, Otis," Doc Commanded. "Molly, get those dishes off the table, then get the back door. It'll be someone for Otis. Hide him in the pantry." And Doc ran to get the front door.

It was Mathew Gray. "Seen Otis Johnson this morning, Doc?" he asked.

Doc Waters did not know what to answer, so stared at Gray.

"Doc?"

"Oh, yeah. Otis is here. Been here all night and had breakfast with Molly and me. Otis," Doc yelled out. "Matt Gray is here looking for you."

"Good morning, Mr. Gray," Molly said as she entered the living room.

"Ma'am," Gray said and touched the brim of his hat.

"What do you need with Otis so early, Mathew?"

Doc asked.

"Early? Folks are linin' up in front of the general store. I thought Otis might want to know."

Otis Johnson pulled a pocket watch from his vest pocket and studied it as he entered the room.

"Christ, Otis. You sleep in those clothes?" Mathew Gray observed. He was used to the little man looking fresh pressed and formal as a judge.

Otis stared. Molly jumped in. "I told those two to go to bed. But no! They kept it up all night."

"Kept what up, Ma'am?"

"Their card game. That Otis is quite a gambler. Took Doc here for almost all he had."

"I never thought of you as a gambler, Otis," Mathew Gray said.

"I'm not, really. But I'm better than Doc. Now… he's about the only man in town I can beat at poker. That's why folks never see me play," he told Gray. Then he turned to Doc and Molly standing side by side. "I thank you for the game, Doc, and I thank you for the fine breakfast, Miss Molly, but I really must go open my store." And he left with Mathew Gray.

Doc and Molly hurried to the pantry where Dexter Connors waited. "Best follow them for protection," Doc suggested. "Bring him back this evening, if you like."

"Newt thinks we shouldn't. He thinks Otis will be best off if we move him around." Connors said.

~*~

Alexander Penovich picked up the telephone in the deceased Constable Profit's office on the second ring.

"Who is this?" the operator, Mary Belle Clausen asked. "I didn't think anyone was there to answer."
"Why'd you call then?" Penovich demanded.
"It's the Mayor's Office."
"We don't have a mayor," Penovich insisted.
"Not Calumet. Hibbing."
"Well put them through." And Mary Belle did without further question.
"I'm trying to reach Tully Backus," the female voice told Penovich.
"Did you try out at the mine, Ma'am?"
"I did, but Mr. Fish told me Tully hadn't showed up out there yet today. I thought he might show up at your office, Constable."
Alexander Penovich figured that no one over in Hibbing had gotten news of Profit's murder yet and he decided to take advantage of it. "I'm sure he'll show sooner or later," he said. "Usually does. Want him to call somebody?"
"Oh, that's very kind of you." She was surprised. She had been told Amos Profit could be inhospitable, especially to women. Today he seemed quite polite, or so she thought. "Would you ask him to call Mayor Burris' office?"
"I surely will, Ma'am," Penovich said and hung up. He turned to Ira Shank. "We have to get Molly Carpenter to take over the operator's switchboard before they catch on." He peered out the window. He looked up the street then down. All attention seemed on the general store at the moment. Otis Johnson had just arrived. "Go to Doc Waters' place, Ira. Tell him to speed it up. We need Miss Molly on these lines, not that other woman."

~*~

"But, Doc," Molly complained. "I've never been a telephone operator. I wouldn't know what to do."

"How hard could it be? There's only a handful of telephones in Calumet."

"What'll I do if a call comes from Hibbing, or some other town, or somebody wants to call someplace else? What'll I do then, Doc?"

"If someone calls in, you're to tell them that phone is out of order, or there's no answer. No answer will work good for the mine. There's only Lawrence Fish out there now. And if someone wants to call out you tell them all the lines out of Calumet are down. They'll believe it. It's happened before. Can you do it, Molly?"

"I guess," Molly said.

"Good. Ira, you going to take her?"

"I'll report to Newt. Somebody will be back fer her shortly," Ira said then he went out the back door.

~*~

Newton Blake, Doc Waters, and Molly Carpenter sat patiently for more than an hour outside the telephone operator's tiny office above the bank. They listened carefully to each call that came through the switchboard so Molly could get a sense of how things are handled. When she felt ready, she nodded to Newt. They entered the office. Newton Blake flashed his badge at Mary Belle. "Mary Belle Clausen? You're under arrest for the murders of Owen Pruitt and Amos Profit. This here gal will take over your switchboard for you. You will come with me."

"But I didn't kill anybody," Mary Belle cried out.

"Why would you think it was me?"

"Well... Ma'am, you match the description of the woman who was seen coming out of the alley just after it happened."

"I didn't come out of no alley. I didn't kill anybody."

"I'm sorry, Ma'am. You'll still have to come with me. If there's some mistake, we'll sort it all out, don't you worry." Newt looked at Molly. "You need any information from her?" he asked.

Molly looked at the switchboard. Everything was labeled — Calumet Mine, general store, constable, etc. "No. I won't have any trouble."

Newt escorted Mary Belle out the door and down the back stairs to the alley behind the bank where two saddled horses waited. He helped her onto one of them, tied her hands to the saddle horn, took the reins and mounted his own horse. He took her to the constable in Marble who, despite his not wanting anything to do with holding a woman, agreed to out of fear of the United States Marshal badge Newton Blake had flashed in his face. The constable was told that Mary Belle was only a suspect in a murder case and that she was to be held with the respect and kindness of an innocent until Newt came for her no later than Tuesday next.

Molly Carpenter settled into her role as telephone operator nicely, having to hookup only three local calls for the day, and one call for Hibbing in which the caller bought the line problem story readily. Tomorrow would be Sunday. Molly expected calls would be scarce. Behind the tiny office was a small room with a table and two chairs, an icebox, a two burner kerosene stove, and a cot. Everything was lovely but the cot. She and Doc would be a tight fit in it.

Chapter Twenty-seven

Aside from an hour or so when he was out removing two sections of telegraph line, one on either side of Calumet, Dexter Connors spent his entire Saturday with Otis Johnson in his upstairs quarters over the general store. He was about to go crazy from being cooped up when Otis informed him it was closing time. Dex looked out the window into the street below. Two men, strangers to Dex, sat in wooden chairs in front of the Red Rose across the street, noticeably focused on the general store's doors. "Would there be a back way out of here?" he asked.

"There is. The door's downstairs," Otis said.

Dex checked out the back wall of Otis' quarters. No window. "Is there a window downstairs so we can see out back?"

"No! It's a storeroom. A window would invite break-ins."

"Now you're not plannin' to live here once you're mayor, are ya?" Dex asked.

"I am. Why shouldn't I?"

"Because the security here is a criminal's haven, that's why. I tell you what. You go down and close the place up if you want to, but we ain't steppin' out the door for a while."

"Why not?"

"Because those two fellers across the street, right in front of the saloon, they'll shoot you down like a wild bobcat. And I recon if we went out that back door of yours, we'd find two more just like 'em," Dex said and started down the stairs. "You stay behind me, Mr. Mayor."

Otis curled the waxed tips of his mustache and tilted his head back with pride. He followed Dexter Connors down the steps. He remained behind him when they passed from the storeroom section of the building into the main store.

Lucas Mann was in the general store, stroking a large braded oval rug everyone around him knew he could not afford. He just had that look, soiled breeches, tattered shirt, uncombed hair. It was the rug, not Lucas Mann that got Dex's attention. "Ain't you got a telephone in here, Mr. Johnson?"

"Right there behind the counter," Otis said and pointed.

"Ain't there one at the constable's office?"

"There is."

Dex walked to the phone. He picked it up and asked Molly Carpenter to connect him to the constable's office. When Alexander Penovich answered, Dex told him of the problem and asked for his assistance.

"Can't leave," Penovich said. "Who'll watch my prisoner?"

"Prisoner?"

"Yeah! That Klan Feller. That Tully Backus come in looking for a telephone. I just locked him up." The air between telephones went dead. "Just joshing ya, son. I'll be along to help shortly. You and Otis and Lucas stay put." Alexander Penovich knew Lucas Mann was in the general store because he had sent him.

"Bring a buckboard."

"A buckboard?" Penovich asked.

"Yeah!" Dex said and hung up.

The two men in front of the Red Rose watched Otis' store as the buckboard pulled up. "Now… just who the hell is that?" one of them asked. His partner did not answer. He got up and disappeared into the saloon. Moments later he returned with two glasses, obviously unconcerned and unimpressed with the buckboard or it's teamster. He did however take notice as the teamster coaxed the team to sidestep, then back up until the wagon sat perpendicular to Otis's front door. It blocked their view completely.

Alexander Penovich's sudden appearance inside the store put an end to the argument Dexter Connors was having with Otis Johnson. "I won't do it, I tell you." Otis was saying.

"What won't you do?" Penovich asked him.

"This fool," Otis began as he gestured at Dexter Connors, "wants me to let him roll me up in that rug."

"Hum! Not a bad plan," Penovich said. "But it might not be necessary. The wagon's blocking the view of the door. I think we can have you in that wagon bed and covered and out of here before anyone knows it. C'mon." And Penovich, a large man and easy for Otis Johnson to hide behind covered him from one side while Dex and Lucas Mann shielded him on the other. Once in the wagon, canvas was used to cover Otis and Lucas returned to lock the door. Alexander Penovich drove the wagon, Dexter Connors road shotgun, and Lucas Man took a position on the tailgate, feet dangling, rifle at the ready in case they were followed. They were not.

~*~

Libby Tilden was concerned. She hadn't seen her friend, Abigail, since the evening she dropped her and Clara off after their eventful trip to Calumet. It had been too long. Something had to have happened. Perhaps Abigail's husband, Thomas, hadn't liked the fact that Abigail had carried her and Clara on a trip he might have considered unnecessary and dangerous for two women and a little girl. Perhaps he did something to her. Perhaps Abigail became withdrawn and did something foolish to herself, after all, Libby knew how she had felt, the guilt that seemed to build and gnaw at her each and every day since, how she could barely look at herself in the mirror and not see the bullet penetrating Amos Profit's forehead. Abigail McCain surely had similar visions.

Libby set her mind. If Abigail did not show herself today, Libby would ride one of the dead Klansmen's horses to her farm and find out for herself what had happened. The only thing needed now was for her to decide what to do with Clara. If she found what she envisioned as the worst, Clara should not see it.

Libby went to her porch to sit and rock, to think, to plan. Clara busied herself swinging from a tree near the woods line. She did not know how long it had been, but she had fallen off into a gentle sleep, waking only as she heard the sound of an automobile approaching. *Mailman?* she thought. *No. His auto rattled from many miles of use over washboard roads.* She rubbed her eyes. She looked for Clara — still swinging in the willow. The auto turned into her yard, a Ford, a Model T, Abigail. Libby rose from her rocker and stepped down into the yard as Abigail pulled to a stop. Clara came running.

"My goodness," Abigail said trying to break loose

from Libby's grip on her. "I guessed I'd be missed, but not this much. Abigail had friends before, back in Michigan, coffee clutching hens married to Thomas' coworkers, but never any she could consider close. This was new to her.

"Where have you been, Girl?" Libby asked, now holding her by the shoulders at arms length while Clara clung to one of her legs.

"Oh! Thomas insisted I stay at home for a time. He thought I might be making a nuisance of myself."

"Nonsense! I was worried to death over you. As a mater of fact, I had it in my head to ride to your farm this very afternoon. I just couldn't figure what to do with Clara, or I would have been there by now," Libby said.

"Do with Clara? Why wouldn't you bring her along?" Abigail asked. Libby did not answer.

"Come. Let's make tea," Libby said and headed for the door. But Abigail did not follow.

"Libby," she said. "I have something to ask of you. And I know it will be hard for you to do."

"What is it?"

"I want to go back to Calumet. And I want you to go with me."

"Okay... I guess? When? Why?"

"First thing in the morning," Abigail said. "Do you think we could stay a day or two at your Marble friend's place?"

"I'm sure we can. But why so sudden?" Libby asked, not that she objected at all. After all, she still hadn't laid eyes on Newton Blake for weeks, and she wanted to. She wasn't even sure if he was alive.

"Election day is Tuesday. I just thought I might like to see that. One more thing," Abigail said. "Can I stay here tonight?"

"Certainly you can. Come. Help me pack a few things," Libby said and disappeared into the house.

~*~

As dusk approached, Alexander Penovich sat, feet propped up on Amos Profit's desk, eyes closed, hat tipped forward covering them.

"Who'd you say you were?" Tully Backus called out from his locked cell.

"Why?" Penovich asked without moving.

"Because I want to know who to send my men after when this is over."

"You won't have any men when this is over," Penovich said. He pushed his hat back, settled his feet to the floor and sat up straight. *Horses,* he thought. *Plenty of them.* He stood and went to the window.

"That my men now?" Backus barked. Penovich ignored him.

He watched the riders pass the constable's office. He counted eight, all carrying lit torches, all of them wearing hoods, some made from gunnysacks, some from flour sacks. He hoped the boys over the livery were ready. He supposed they were. They were a good crew, hand selected, all with superb rifle skills. There was Lucas Mann who could pick a rider off a horse or out of an automobile from so far away he'd never hear the shot that got him even if the first one missed. A St. Paul union man named Steadway, once a lawman, thought to have been a train robber at one time, was nearly as good as Mann. Rex Hartley, a former miner who had been convinced to join up by his friend, Doc Waters, was above the livery. And another of the union boys, Gordon Pratt had just joined the detail that afternoon. Pratt was just a youngster, but it had been said that he could part the hair on a tomcat at a hundred yards with a long rifle.

Eight riders, four marksmen, this had the makings of an eventful night. Penovich opened the door and stepped onto the boardwalk in front of the constable's office. He spat into the street. He pulled the revolver from his shoulder holster and checked his ammunition. He watched the eight hooded Klansmen stop their horses in front of Otis Johnson's general store. "JOHNSON! OTIS JOHNSON! COME OUT OR DIE!" one of them yelled out. Then they waited.

"What'll we do now," Steadway asked of Lucas Mann. "Just start shootin'?"

"Nope! Our orders is to wait for 'em to start somethin'. Then we shoot."

"Do we shoot to kill or just to wound?" Hartley asked.

"Kill, I recon," Mann said. "But we don't shut up, we'll be the ones gettin' shot."

"Okay!" one of the raiders in the street below said. "Burn it!" And eight burning torches flew in unison at the front of the general store. Shots rang out from above the livery stable. Four horses reared and bucked. Four riders fell motionless to the ground. Four riders rode off rapidly in four different directions. Alexander Penovich's gun came from its holster at lightning speed and the horseman who chanced his direction fell. Penovich ran toward the livery to check on his men.

They were in the street when he arrived. "How many got away?" he asked.

"Four," Steadway said.

"I got one down by the constable's office. That

makes three still living. That's all those boys will try tonight. Might as well head back to camp."

"What about that one you got locked up?" Lucas Mann asked.

"We'll pick him up — let Newt and Dare deal with 'im." And together they walked to the jail. Inside, Penovich shoved the key at the cell door lock. "Shit!" he said. Apparently one of the riders had circled back. Tully Backus was gone.

Chapter Twenty-eight

Libby Tilden and her daughter Clara, along with Abigail McCain spent most of a day on the road, the Model T having overheated and them having to walk to the creek and back several times for water. When they arrived in Marble just before dark, they arrived exhausted. As Libby awoke the next morning, her surroundings seemed strange. But her night's sleep — curiously enough— was the best she had experienced since before Newton Blake had left her place. She listened to the sounds outside her window, birds whistling, voices, the whinny of a horse in the distance, the pop-pop-pop on an automobile engine. *Where was she? Yes. of course*, she thought as she sat upright in the bed, *Marble.* She swung her feet over the edge of the bed. Clara came in as they touched the cool floor.
"Good morning, Mama," she said.

Abigail entered before Libby could respond. "Good morning, she said. We were beginning to think you might sleep the whole day away."

"What time is it?" Libby asked.

"Why…it's half past eight already," Abigail said. "Clara's gone and fixed you some breakfast. Best you get out of that bed and eat it now."

Half past eight, Libby thought. *Newt! I need to find Newt.* She sprang from her sitting position on the edge of the bed and went for her clothing. "I'll be right down," she told Libby and Clara.

Her breakfast was scrambled eggs with a modicum of tiny shell pieces mixed in, which lent truth to Clara's claim that she and her friend, Annie—short for Annabel, had made the meal on their own, with no help from Annabel's mother or Abigail McCain. Clara watched her mother eat. "What are we going to do today, Mama," she asked.

"You're going to play with Annabel," Libby told her.

"She doesn't like to be called Annabel."

"I'm sorry, Annie then. You're going to stay here and play with Annie," Libby corrected.

"Are you going to find Newt?" Clara asked.

"I will try."

"Can I come with you?"

"No, Clara. I don't even know where to find him," Libby said.

"I might know," Clemma Clery, Annabel's mother and Libby's long time friend said as she entered the kitchen. "I've heard talk of a camp of cattle people, some say they're loggers, whatever, the camp is just south of Calumet a mile or so. Can't be far from here. I heard a man in town talk about someone named Newton being in that camp. Could that be your feller?"

"It could," Libby agreed casually. She did not want to bring a sense of urgency to this, not in front of Clara. "Have you a horse, Clemma?"

"That old nag we've had forever. You're welcome to her. Just hope she don't die and leave you stranded in the woods," Clemma said.

"I'm sure she'll do me just fine."

~*~

The bodies of the Klansman who were shot while

torching Otis Johnson's general store by the logger Lucas Mann, union men Pratt and Steadway, miner Rex Hartley, and Alexander Penovich, had all been taken to the undertaker in Marble. Dexter Connors was sent with a buckboard to retrieve the corpses, the same buckboard used to get Otis Johnson from his store without being seen. Newton Blake and Alexander Penovich wanted all the Klan's dead together for a specific purpose, and they did not want anyone looking for next of kin or anyone else to claim them. They knew the undertaker would look if only as a way finding someone to claim the price of burial from. The undertaker fought. "I get them in here, then turn them over to you, and I go broke." Dex thought of drawing his gun, maybe even shooting the undertaker, then thought better of it. He opted to use diplomacy, or bribery, whichever might work.

"The union will pay you for your efforts, Sir," he told him.

"That'll be sixty dollars. Ten for each body and another ten for my trouble."

"But you didn't have to do anything," Dex objected.

"Sixty dollars!" the undertaker repeated.

"Write a bill. I'll see to it they get it."

"Sixty dollars — cash!" the undertaker said.

He was lucky, at least in the eyes of Dexter Connors, that he was the only undertaker alive around these parts. Had there been someone to burry him, Dex would have shot him right on the spot. Connors dug deep into his pocket. He pulled out sixty dollars. He gave to Marble's undertaker. "Help me load 'em in the wagon," he said.

~*~

"That look odd to you?" Libby Tilden asked her friend Abigail McCain as the passed by the funeral home and watched two men hauling bodies out instead of in.

"Not more strange than the two of us, Sunday-go-to-meetin' duds on, both of us on this worn out old horse, I don't suppose," Abigail answered. "You got a plan where we're going to find this Newt of yours?"

Newton Blake's got a gal? Dexter Connors asked himself silently, hearing the two girls as their horse passed his wagon. *Right pretty one too.* He would let them pass. He would wait until they were out of sight. He wished he could be polite and give them directions, but that would lead to questions such as 'How did he know where to fine him', or 'Are you with him?', or 'What's with the bodies?'— questions he should not answer, not here in front of the sixty-dollar undertaker. After all, a greedy man could find value in such information, couldn't he?

~*~

Otis Johnson pitched a fit when Alexander Penovich told him his store was gone. Penovich wanted to wake him last evening when it happened, but hadn't. Newt had convinced him that poor Otis would only lose sleep along with his place of business, and that it would keep until morning. "Blake," Johnson began. "Nothing has gone as planned since the day I sent out that telegram to get you here."

"Looks like it's goin' like planned fer them Klan boys," Ira Shanks threw in.

"Ira!" Newt warned. And Ira quieted. "Look, Otis," Newt went on, "maybe a better way to look at this is to count your lucky stars. You're not thinking right. Those men were coming for you. They'd have just as soon burned you alive as look at you. You know that's true. Not me, not you, not anybody else here could have stopped that burning. At least we got some of them that done it." And Otis Johnson began to simmer.

~*~

Tully Backus paced in front of the men he still had left after the last evening's raid. His anger ran so deep that words would not surface. He stroked his hair, spat in the red dirt, kicked a clod sending it into the Crowed where men dodged it. Who was this fellow at the constable's office? How did anyone dare to lock him up? Was there a leak within his own organization? Obviously there was. Who? Why? He knew the people he had come with. And the only one other than them was Crowe and Crowe might be a fool, but he was a loyal fool. What about the dozen Isaac Burris sent? Could one of them be a turncoat? Unlikely. They had been handpicked by Isaac himself. And who is this Newton Blake whose name comes into play in every fourth or fifth sentence lately. He mulled these questions over in his mind for a time, then came up with three names, locals, a miner named Ira Shank, one named Rex Hartley, and another named Ransome Feltus. Why had those three men so suddenly failed to show for work? They had to be spies.

"I want six riders," Backus finally ordered. "I want those fellows found. Crowe, you pick 'em and you lead 'em. Comb the woods and any neighboring towns and find 'em. This ends today. We vote tomorrow, so this ends today. Understand? And Crowe, if there're more of 'em than six men can handle, get more men. Don't take chances. That fellow who put me in a cell was no dummy. This band, whoever they are, they're well organized."

Kaleb Pruitt approached Tully Backus as soon as his speech to the men, Crowe particularily it seemed, was over and the Crowed began to break up. "Are you sure you want to send Crowe?" he asked.

"Crowe's a warior. He's exactly who we want to send."

"But what if he gets himself killed? He's also the candidate," Pruitt offered.

Backus thought about it for a moment. Pruitt was right. Crowe needed to be protected, not sent out in front of a raiding party. "CROWE," he shouted.

"What?" Crowe yelled back form amidst the small Crowed of men saddling horses. "More orders?" he asked and walked toward Backus and Pruitt.

"Kaleb Pruitt here will lead the raid. You hang back with me."

~*~

Young Gordon Pratt, a volunteer from the St. Paul union, one of Alexander Penovich's men, had dozed off while guarding the north trail into the camp. The horse was upon him before he heard it coming. His rifle flung into shooting position and an instant before he pulled the trigger his mind questioned the action. He blinked. A woman. No! Two women. What were they doing out here in the woods. They stared down the barrel of his rifle. "You gonna shoot, Mister?" one of the women asked. Pratt lowered his gun.

"Sorry, Ma'am," he said. "What are you ladies doing out here? I nearly shot you."

"I might ask you the same," Libby Tilden said.

"Were you sleeping?" Abigail McCain asked him.

"What do you ladies want?" Pratt asked.

"Are you guarding Newton Blake's camp?" Libby asked.

Pratt became flustered. He tensed. He did not answer.

"If you are," Libby went on, "I'd appreciate it if you'd tell him Libby Tilden is here to see him."

Chapter Twenty-nine

Shock filled all of the men's faces when Gordon Pratt rode into the camp, his shift at guard only half over, with two women on one horse in tow. Virgil Dare, suddenly awakened from his nap by the unanticipated intrusion, shoved his hat from his eyes, drew his pistol, and damn near shot the girls thinking they had been a rider of the opposition bringing Pratt back into the camp at gunpoint. Lucas Mann slapped a hand over Virg's gun just in time to stop him. "What the hell?" Alexander Penovich shouted. Newton Blake came running out of the makeshift tent.
"Libby?" he said.
"Aren't you about ready to come home, Mr. Blake?" she asked. Several men laughed.
"Libby?" Newt asked again. "What're you doing out here?"
"I thought I made that clear. I've come for you."

~*~

Doc Waters slept in his own bed last night alone — unusual since that first early morning when he found Molly lurking in the dark of his room wanting to join him. He had let her in then and he had never shut her out since. And now as he lay there long into the morning, alone and exhausted from an inability to sleep, he found that he had let her into much more than his bed. He missed her. He missed her like he would miss his arm. He would be glad when this is over and he would have her back.

He nearly failed to hear the knock on his door, too deep in thought, but whoever was there was persistent. He rose, finally, and went downstairs to see who it was. It was Tully Backus with an injured man. "He's been shot."

"How'd that happen?" Doc asked.

"I'm not certain. He just showed up like this, fell off his horse. That's all I know," Backus insisted.

"Showed up where?" Doc asked.

"He showed up where I was. That's all you need to know. Now… where's that girl of yours, your nurse, Molly, I believe is her name?"

"She's not here," Doc told him.

"She lives here, don't she?"

"Yes. But she's not here now," Doc said. "That's all you need to know."

The telephone operator, Backus thought. *Cold my ass. That wasn't the regular operator with a cold.* "Just fix him up, Doc. I'll come for him later." And he left.

Doc Waters sensed danger. He carried the injured man to a cot, then went for a gun. The wounded man was Klan; he could wait. Waters felt a need to check on Molly Carpenter.

As Doc reached the bottom of the stairs to the Telephone office above the bank he heard gunfire, three shots, two from a small caliber derringer Molly kept in her purse, one from a Colt. He rushed up the steps only to run into Tully Backus, gun held loosely in one hand, arm dangling, blood dripping from his fingertips, and he knew what had happened and he knew instantly that his Molly was dead. Grief, hate, anger, all filled him in a heartbeat. He pulled his gun and shot Tully Backus cleanly through the heart and watched his limp body tumble past him and into the dirt at the bottom of the stairs. He continued toward Molly and when he found her he would stay with her, holding her, loving her. She would die in his arms. There was nothing he could do to prevent it. He held her long into the afternoon while the Klansman on his cot bled to death.

~*~

Dexter Connors pulled the buckboard, stiff Klansmen and three stuffed gunnysacks on board, into camp from the south. The noise of the wagon masked the six approaching riders. They were on them in a flash, guns blazing, loggers and union men scrambling, horses trampling everything in sight, blood spurting from wounds and pooling around fallen men. Libby Tilden and Abigail McCain took for the woods screaming. Two riders followed. Virgil Dare and Newton Blake ran after them on foot. One attacker spotted Newt and Virgil Dare in pursuit and rode off deeper in the woods and out of sight, dodging bullets as he rode.

The other horseman held a gun on the two women. "Turn around," he ordered. And the women did. "Abigail?" he asked.

"Kaleb?" Abigail asked. Then she shot him with the same derringer she had used on his brother. He did not die instantly. He got off one round. It penetrated her heart. Libby Tilden caught her fall and sat with Abigail's head in her lap. "Why did you shoot him?" Libby asked.

"Kaleb… helped… his brother. He… could've stopped… Owen." She looked up into Libby's eyes.

"Thomas…" she said.

"Shush… just stay quiet. We'll get you to a doctor. Your gonna be just fine."

"No… no use… Thomas… he's not…" And she gave up.

Libby looked at Newton Blake through tear filled eyes. "What does that mean, Thomas…he's not?" she asked him.

"I don't know, Libby. I'm going to take you someplace safe." Newt said. "When this is finished I'll come for you, and together we'll do something about your friend. Come." And he held out a hand to help her to her feet. "Where's Clara?" he asked.

Libby told Newt all about her old friend, Clemma Clery, and Newt took her and Abigail's body to Marble, dropped Abigail at the undertaker's and her with Clara, then rushed back to camp. Men had gathered bodies. Two Klan and four of theirs, Lucas Mann, Steadway, Gordon Pratt, and Rex Hartley. Ira Shank was wounded. Otis Johnson had made it through the raid unscathed. "How many were there?" Newt asked.

"I counted six," Virgil Dare said.

"Then four of them got away."

"Three. That feller the woman killed, he's still in the woods."

Alexander Penovich knelt between two of his fallen comrades. "What'll we do now?"

"We go after them," Newt said.

"Sneak attack? Like these fellers done?" Penovich asked gesturing at the Klansmen on the ground.

"Nope! We ride through town. An army. Far as we know, we outnumber them about two to one." Newt looked around and shook his head. He thought back to his first day in Calumet. "Crowe's mine," he said.

"This is all his doing."

"What if those who got away headed for reinforcements?" Ira Shank asked.

"They didn't," Newt said. "They'll go back home to warn the others."

"I'm still favor a sneak attack," Penovich said.

"No!" Newt said. "That's what they'll look for. We go head on at them. That's what they won't expect. That… they won't be looking for; it is the sneak attack."

Penovich looked at Virgil Dare. "How'd you ever escape this man?"

"It was close," Virgil Dare admitted as he put a forefinger to his half missing ear.

"C'mon. Let's mount up. Dex, dump those bodies. We're gonna need that wagon. Ira you ride with Dex. We'll drop you and Otis at Docs place on the way." And Newt went for his horse. "I don't know about the rest of you, but I want this ended. I don't want to see one live Klansman in Calumet when the polls open in the morning."

~*~

Three men rode up and hitched horses to the rail in front of the Iron Man Saloon. Inside, Emil Crowe sat smugly on a stool sipping at a glass of whisky. He did not turn to look at the new arrivals. "You win or lose," he asked.

"Hard to measure," Oscar Barlow admitted. "We lost three men." He took the stool next to Crowe and ordered himself a whisky. "They might have been surprised, but they sure come 'round fast. Near as I know, we got five of 'em in all.

"How many of 'em are there," Crowe asked and took another swallow of his drink, slapped the empty on the bar, and motioned for the barkeep to refill it.

"Think you ought to drink so much? They'll be along for us anytime." Crowe's head swung in Barlow's direction, his eyes wide open, unblinking, wild, angry. "Don't mind me," Barlow said and took up his own drink. Crowe turned back to his.

"They'll look for us at the camp. Now... how many men?" Crowe asked.

"Us or them?"

"Us!"

"We're seven now," Barlow said. "Maybe Tully Backus got through to Isaac Burris in Hibbing by now and more are on the way. If not, seven!"

"How about them?" Crowe asked.

"Ten, maybe nine."

Outnumbered. Crowe liked that. He liked being the underdog in a fight. Victory was so much sweeter and reputations so much larger, especially when rumor got done with things. History would not record a seven to nine victory; history would set it at seven to twenty. At least by the time word got to Duluth where Crowe's Klan leaders were.

Emil Crowe donned a broad smile. "Seven to nine, eh?"

"Any of the locals joinin' us?" Barlow asked.

"They'll vote on our side, some of 'em anyway, but none of 'em's gonna fight, not against there own," Crowe told him.

~*~

Doc Waters, his vest full of Molly Carpenter's

blood, sat in a chair on his porch, a somber — almost void of emotion look on his face. He even made the effort to raise a bloodied palm in a slight wave as the buckboard followed by rider after rider settled to the side of the road in front of his house. Tully Backus's body lay in the front yard. Doc had gone back for him as soon as he got Molly home and up to their bed.

Newton Blake walked onto the porch. "What's happened, Doc?" he asked.

"I had to kill him, Newt," Waters explained. "He shot Molly, you see."

Newt looked at Backus' corpse laying in the grass. Something was wrong. There was little blood on Backus' clothing and far too much on Doc's. "Is Molly alright?"

"Sure… she'll be just fine. I'll see to that."

"Where is she, Doc?"

"She's up in our bed… resting."

"Mind if I look in on her?" New asked softly.

"She'd like that, Newt. You know she's always thought good of you. She'll be glad to see you." Doc Waters got up to join Newt. Half-way up the stairs he said, "If she's asleep, let's not wake her, okay?"

"You bet, Doc," Newt said.

When Newton Blake felt Molly Carpenter's neck, he found no pulse. Her skin was cool to the touch. He saw no blood on the bed sheets. She must have bled out on Doc's vest as he carried her home. He looked at Doc sitting in a chair in the corner of the room holding his face in his palms, dried blood mixing with his tears and flowing red again. Newt went to him and placed a hand on his shoulder. "I'm so sorry, Doc. I'm so sorry." He pulled up a second chair and sat with Doc for a time. He had to ask. He knew that Tully Backus found

Molly at the telephone office. Did it mean that more Klan were coming? "Did Backus get off a call to Hibbing?"

"No," Doc said. "There wasn't time."

Chapter Thirty

"Ira Shank needs tending, Doc," Newt said. "He took a bullet. Best we get downstairs."

Otis Johnson got up from the soft cushion of whatever was in the gunnysacks he and Ira had used as a seat in the back of the wagon. "Ira's blood is all over these," he said. "Hope they aren't something that'll ruin."

"Just feathers, Otis. And there'll be plenty of blood on 'em sooner or later," Dexter Connors insisted with a devilish smile.

Newt approached Ira shank. He ripped Ira's sleeve open at the wound on his arm. "Bullet went right through," he said. The bleeding had stopped. "How does it feel?"

"Good enough to fight," Ira insisted.

"Well, you might just get to after all. We don't find them all and kill them, and this'll be the first place they'll head. I want you to let Doc have a look at that, then I want you to guard this place. They'll figure we'll be hiding Otis out here."

"Won't we?"

"Yep! In the cellar," Newt said.

"Not that smelly cellar again," Otis Johnson objected.

"In the cellar," Newt said.

~*~

Dexter Connors pulled the buckboard to a stop in the middle of the street directly in front of the Iron Man Saloon. He could feel eyes on him. He did not need to look. Newton Blake was right. This was a bold move that would send shivers of fear down the backbones of all inside. No one with small power would dare such a move. And now as he slowly climbed down from the wagon seat and made his way nonchalantly around the other side he hoped Newt was correct about one other thing, that he (Dex) was perfectly safe in doing so because those inside would think this was some kind of trap. Newt guessed they'd think that if they fired a shot, the result might be some sort of Armageddon. Maybe the wagon was filled with dynamite, they'd suspect, or nitro — a load large enough to level the Iron Man and all who were in it.

The cloud of dust the horses' hoofs raised shielded the riders from the Iron Man's occupants. No one could tell how many were coming for them, but it looked to Emil Crowe and Oscar Barlow as they watched the cloud approach, that it was considerably more than they expected. Had some of the locals joined the fight? Had there been more men who were not at the camp when the raid took place? "Nine or ten my ass," Crowe said. But as they came closer he began to see. This Newton Blake was smart. He new how to use things, things like the fact that it hadn't rained in days and the roadbed in front of the Iron Man turned to a base of powder when it lacked moisture. And that on a powder like this, spreading out the riders and running the horses would kick sand high into the air, nasty for riders and animals, but excellent cover. *Not so many,* Crowe thought. But it was too late to relay that information to his men. He became the only one to know — they weren't so outnumbered as they had all thought.

    Seconds before the first horse came in front of the saloon riders formed in a single file a dozen feet apart, the first rider getting several shots off at the place as he passed at a dead run, then the second, then the third, and so on until all of the riders had passed. One man popped out of the door just as the last rider passed, aimed his gun, then felt the sting of a bullet from Dexter Connors's rifle. Newt and his riders stopped a distance past and regrouped. "Ride low," Newt instructed his men. "They'll be expecting it this time." And they road past, same plan. One rider fell. One more man came from the saloon and aimed at the back of the final rider. He too felt the sting of Dexter Connors's rifle bullet. Three more passes, each of them with less and less returned fire, and the plan would change. Newton Blake's force, Dexter Connors included, would implement an all out frontal attack on the Iron Man, on foot, guns blazing. No heads would pop up, and no bullets would find their way to them. Inside — bloody bodies. They took inventory. Emil Crowe? Missing. "Son-of-a-bitch!" Newt said. He went back to the street and mounted the first horse he could catch.

    Newton Blake had stayed one step ahead of Crowe and his Klansmen throughout the battle. Now would be no different. He knew where Crowe would head. He would head to Doc Waters' to kill Otis Johnson. Crowe knew it was over for him. He knew he would not be Mayor. He decided neither would Johnson. When Newt walked through Doc's front door he found Doc pinned to a wall, Emil Crowe's knife to his throat. And Ira Shank laying on the floor, the back of his head having been opened up by the butt of Crowe's handgun. "Where the hell is that little weasel?" Crowe was insisting Doc tell him concerning the location of Otis Johnson.

"He doesn't know," Newt said. "This fight's between you and me, Crowe. It's the one you didn't finish the first day I came to this town. Remember that?"

Crowe looked over his shoulder, eyes as wild as Newton Blake had ever seen in all his years of fighting crime. "Alright then," Crowe said. "Knives or guns." He hoped for knives. He had seen Newt shoot. And he had seen him draw.

"Your choice," Newt said. He didn't care. He could take Crowe. He had to take Crowe. Crowe was responsible for all of this. All of the deaths, too many deaths, Molly's included, were Crowe's to claim. And those same deaths and the need for Newt to avenge them would drive him to victory over the evil that was Emil Crowe. "You choose, Crowe." And he turned and walked into Doc waters' front yard to ready himself for battle.

Men, Newt's men rode up as Crowe appeared. Dexter Connors drew his gun. "He's mine," Newt yelled out, and Dex holstered his Colt.

"Crowe wins, Dex, and you shoot him. Understand?" Virgil Dare said.

Dex looked at Dare. His face was pale, the back of his jacket was blood soaked. He wobbled a bit in his saddle. "You hurt bad?"

"A scratch," Virgil Dare said.

The first slash of a knife opened the sleeve of Newton Blake's jacket. Newt looked at the sleeve, grateful he had the jacket on. But the coat turned red. Crowe had done damage. A second slash came. Red appeared on Newt's belly. He jumped back out of Crowe's reach in time to avoid the next attempt which would have caught him in the neck. They danced. Newt laid Crowe's arm open at the shoulder, then a slash to his thigh. Blood spurted out. He had hit an artery. Crowe jumped back and grabbed a bandana from around his neck and tied off the leg. He stepped back in. He stabbed Newt in the side. Newt grabbed Crowe's knife hand just as he had on their first fight, and just as he had done then, he squeezed until he heard bones crack and watched Emil Crowe fall to his knees. Crowe's knife still in his side, Newt placed the blade of his under Crowe's chin and pulled his face up. "Look at me," he said softly. "Crowe… look at me!" And when Crowe did, Newton Blake reached down and pulled the bandana loose from his leg. He watched Crowe's eyes as the life drained from them there on Doc Waters' front lawn.

"Well… would you look at that, Virg?" Dexter Connors said. But Virgil Dare could not look. He could only fall. The bullet in his back had finally claimed him. As he landed in the dirt of the street his young friend and protégée recalled his wish coming into this fight, that he wanted to go out of this life in a blaze of glory — like Butch Cassidy. Dexter Connors would be happy for him, something no one would understand. For Dex was the only man who knew and the only one who would ever know. Virgil Dare was dying of cancer. This was the better death.

Doc Waters pulled the knife from Newton Blake's side. "I need to patch that up," he said.

"There's too much to do," Newt objected.

"They're going to have to do some of it without you. You'll bleed to death if I don't at least sew you up, and it'll get infected if I don't clean it out. That slice on your arm and belly too." Doc made a good case.

Newt complied, not for his sake, he felt invincible after taking Emil Crowe, but for Doc. Doc had lost Molly and his need to heal, to cure, to treat, might just save him from his grief for a time. And when Doc was done with him, Newt would help him deal with Molly's corpse laying up in his bed. That, after all, the dealing with all who were lost to the war in Calumet that day, was a big enough part of what needed doing anyway. Alexander Penovich could see to the rest.

See to the rest, Alexander Penovich did. His first order of business was to gather all of the fallen Klan. He and his crew would start right there at Doc's. There was Tully Backus lying on the lawn. There was one dead on a cot inside the house, and of course there was Emil Crowe. Once these had been loaded on the wagon, Dexter Connors steered for the Iron Man Saloon where all of the dead soldiers still filled the floor inside. They gathered bodies, loaded them in the wagon, and headed for camp where a few men had been sent on ahead to get the fire blazing. It would be a long day with work that would last them until the early hours of election day and leave them with a memory that would never fade so long as they lived. Trucks had to be rounded up. Two from the mine, one from the town. Someone had to go to Marble for rope since Otis Johnson's store no longer existed. And more feathers were needed, and more tar. Seventeen Klansmen had to be tarred and feathered, more than anyone had figured on, at least all at one time. And eighteen miles of bad road needed to be traveled with three not so dependable and already overworked and now overloaded trucks before daybreak.

But it did happen. Isaac Burris, illustrious mayor of Hibbing and Mesabi Range leader of the KKK, would wake up to the largest display of hanging tarred and feathered bodies, nearly one for every light pole, in the history of the Klan. All those feathers and none for in his cap.

At nine o'clock on election day morning, the three trucks pulled into the camp south of Calumet where it had been agreed they would meet. It was in the middle of goodbyes, Penovich and his remaining men along with the bodies of their fallen were to catch a train from Marble, that Alexander called out, "Ransom Feltus."

"Yes?" Rans said.

"You coming with us?"

"I think I'll stay around a bit — see what develops. Give my best and my thanks to Abe Curran for me." Otis Johnson and the council was still seeking a new constable. Rans thought he might give that a shot. He had a boyhood dream of someday being a lawman. This was his chance.

"I'll do that," Penovich said. "Anything else?"

"Yeah." He dug in a pocket and came up with an envelope. "Give this to Dolly Markus for me." Dolly was the secretary at the union headquarters in St. Paul and the girl of Ransom Feltus' dreams. In the envelope was an invitation for her to join him in Calumet, fifty dollars, and a train ticket.

Doc wished the union boys well, then began to mingle with the loggers. Newt thanked Alexander Penovich and the others, then joined Doc. And as the St. Paul boys rode off, Penovich stopped, pulled his hat from his head, ran a hand through his hair and said,

"Ya know, Newton Blake, this is the best organized and executed fight I ever been in." Newt smiled at him. "Just one thing, though."

"What's that?" Newt asked.

"Where's your Mayor?" And he rode off.

"Shit!" Newt said. "Otis. He's still in the cellar."

Chapter Thirty-one

Election day behind, Calumet gaining its first government led by Mayor Otis Johnson, Newton Blake longed for the prairie grass of Missouri. He did not, however, wish to return to his career in law enforcement and he did not want to go alone. He wanted to farm and he wanted to do so with Libby Tilden. She agreed, but her friend, Abigail, she considered unfinished business.

"There's a man, Abigail's husband, Newt. His name is Thomas and they have the farm just west of mine. Thomas sleeps during the day and works the paper mill at night."

"What's this Thomas look like?" Newt asked. He would go find him.

"I don't know," Libby told him.

"You don't know?"

"I've never seen him. He was always sleeping whenever Clara and I went to visit, either that or working."

Newt rode the twenty miles to have a look. He found no one at the farm. A man's clothing hung in the closet, boots on the floor near the door. Dishes were stacked on the counter near the sink, half of them clean, half of them soiled — odd. So Newt rode on. He went to Grand Rapids — to the paper mill where he was told they had never heard of a man named Thomas McCain. Newton Blake, lawman that he was, went to the telegraph office. He recalled Libby telling him that her friend, Abigail, had come from Michigan and that her husband had worked for the Ford Motor Car Company there. He telegraphed Ford and he telegraphed the local law and asked both of them for any information they might have on Thomas and Abigail McCain to be sent to him in Marble.

"Did you find Thomas?" Libby asked him.

"I'm afraid I did," Newt told her.

"You're afraid?"

"Libby, there is no Thomas McCain. There was, but he's dead. He was shot to death in his bed in Michigan. The marshal there has been hunting Abigail ever since. He claims he can prove it was Abigail who killed him." That was enough bad. He did not have the heart to tell her there had been a child lying dead with Thomas McCain.

~*~

The death of Emil Crowe and many of his men, their bodies having been returned to Isaac Burris in Hibbing — tarred and feathered — served as a deterrent for the Klan, preventing them from ever again setting sights on Calumet or any of the range west of Hibbing. The Klan's political stature in Hibbing and along the rest of the Mesabi Range dwindled after the war in Calumet, ending finally in their vacating the area forever. Their downfall was simple. They were on the wrong side, something Isaac Burris came to realize too late. Had Crowe and his men stood with labor instead of management, the stronghold they might have developed would have been immeasurable.

~*~

Newton Blake moved to western Missouri, near Jesse James' family homestead, with Libby Tilden and her daughter, Clara. They brought with them the body of Molly Carpenter who wanted to be buried anywhere in Missouri and a statement from the newly appointed constable of Calumet, Ransom Feltus, a document proving that Virgil Dare had indeed been killed and that his body had been buried in the Calumet cemetery, thereby giving ownership to any bounty claim still existing to Newton Blake.

~*~

Dolly Markus moved to Calumet and married Ransom Feltus. They would have two children, neither of whom would grow to maturity before their father was gunned down trying to stop a bank robbery. The holdup's chief bandit, a young man named Dexter Connors, was shot and killed by Ransom Feltus as he laid bleeding in the street, drawing in his last few breaths of Mesabi air.

~*~

Doc Waters trained in human medicine and set up an actual clinic. Abigail McCain's Ford Model T sat in the shed behind his house for many years, Doc having never taken the time to learn to drive. He passed away twenty years later while on a train ride to Missouri to visit Molly's grave. He knew he was dying when he set out on this journey. Newt and Libby buried him beside Molly in a tiny cemetery bordering Jesse James' childhood home.

~*~

The Calumet mine prospered, union manned, for many years. It eventually ceased operations, its richer ore having been harvested like so many mines along the Mesabi. The fourteen saloons that once lined the streets of Calumet in its hay-day, dwindled in number as mining decreased, and disappeared completely with the commencement of prohibition in 1919, leaving Calumet a shell of a town. Two such saloons returned later, but neither with 'The Red Rose' or 'The Iron Man' on the sign over its door.

END

Made in the USA
Charleston, SC
09 April 2010